QUEST FOR VENGEANCE

QUEST FOR VENGEANCE

DAVID TINDELL

To my father, James J. Tindell:
Soldier, educator, husband, father, grandfather,
man of faith.
He showed me the way.

Vengeance is in my heart,
death in my hand.

William Shakespeare

Before you embark on a journey of revenge,
dig two graves.

Confucius

JUNE 1999 – KOSOVO

Major Mark Hayes barely had enough time to attach the new oak-leaf tabs to his battle dress uniform before heading out into the field again. He knew he should've passed on the mission, delegated it to his new second-in-command, but because he'd soon be sitting behind a desk somewhere back in the States, he couldn't resist.

The new XO was a young second lieutenant, just a year out of West Point. Mark had been just like him once, a green and eager 2LT fresh from the Academy and anxious to prove himself. The kid had just arrived in Kosovo and seemed to have the right attitude about these things, which wasn't always the case. When his newly-promoted company commander told him he'd be sitting this one out, the rookie didn't pout, didn't bitch, he just nodded his head and said "Yes, sir."

The kid's turn would come soon enough. Mark's turn was now; he'd been in country for nearly a month as part of the American contribution to NATO's Kosovo Force, trying to enforce the shaky peace that NATO bombing had brought about between the Yugoslavs and the ethnic Albanians in the rebellious province. The deployment was supposed to last no more than six months, and Mark had been on enough of them since he'd been a rookie himself, thirteen years before, to understand that when your chance came, you took it.

But the hot summer day in northeastern Kosovo had gone to shit almost as soon as Mark and his men dismounted from their Humvees and began their patrol. The village should've been quiet, the Serbs should have been on their side of the border about ten klicks away. But they were here, opening up on the Americans from well-placed ambush positions. The only thing that saved the new major's men from immediate disaster was Mark's instinct, a carryover from his Desert Storm combat tour eight years earlier. You didn't see empty streets at eight in the morning, whether the village was in Kosovo or Kuwait, unless the people had been warned to stay inside. By the time the first shots rang out Mark already had his men scrambling for cover.

The gunners had stayed aboard the two lead Humvees, Mustang-1 and Mustang-2, and they began returning fire with their .50-caliber machine guns, raking the second stories of the two buildings where the initial Serb fire appeared to have come from. Two more concealed positions opened up in response. One of the gunners was hit in the arm by what might've been a ricochet, yelling in pain and dropping down inside the vehicle. His buddy in the next Humvee swiveled his weapon to one of the new targets and hammered away, but the incoming Serb fire didn't seem to slacken. The gunner in the rearmost Humvee, Mustang-3, had his weapon trained on their six o'clock and couldn't bring it to bear on the enemy without endangering the other gunners.

From his position beside a parked car Mark couldn't see much, but a flicker of movement on the roof of a building a block away caught his eye. There were men up there. He pulled his binoculars from their case, eased his way up enough to give him a clear field of view over the hood of the car, and sighted on the rooftop. Two seconds later he scrambled back down and clicked on his radio. "All Mustangs!" he shouted. "Antitank position at your eleven o'clock, two hundred meters! Get out of there!"

Mustang-3 responded immediately, leaping forward as the driver engaged the clutch, heading back down the road out of the village. 1 and 2 had to back up; the street was too narrow for them to turn around at the same time. Mark ordered the soldiers on the other side of the street to train their fire on the rooftop, well within range of their M16A4 rifles. Through the binocs Mark saw one of the three men on the rooftop take a round in the chest and fall back, arms splayed, but his two buddies kept working. They had guts, Mark had to give them that, but they also had what he recognized from his briefings as a Russian-made wire-guided antitank weapon, an AT-3 Sagger, and his Humvees were ducks on a pond at this range.

Across the street, a soldier ran forward from his cover and leaped up onto a small cement porch, then began climbing a circular staircase leading to a balcony on the second floor. Mark knew instantly that the soldier was trying to get to a better firing position to take out the remaining Serbs in the Sagger crew. The Serbs on the ground knew that, too, and began peppering the staircase and balcony. Sparks flew off the iron stairs and the stucco façade of the balcony began chipping away.

Behind Mark, his comm sergeant, Landers, shouted in his ear, the only way to make himself heard over the deafening roar of the

3

.50s and the chattering of the Serbs' AK-47s and the Americans' M4s. "Hemple's going for that balcony, Major! He's the best shot in the company!"

"I see that, dammit! Get on the horn to Brigade and report our position. Request tac air and QRF."

"Roger that, sir." Mark knew Landers would quickly carry out the order, but whether the brass back at Camp Bondsteel would approve air support and deployment of the Quick Reaction Force was the question. The QRF was at the base, forty kilometers away, and even if they got their helicopters in the air, by the time they got here it might be all over for Mark's unit. If they could get some NATO jets in here, that would be a lot quicker. It would depend on what was available on station over this part of Kosovo and how soon they could be designated for the mission. Mark knew from experience that wouldn't be a sure thing.

They were in a world of shit here, no doubt about it. Mark tried to peek over the car again but a Serb round slammed into the hood not a foot away, and another buzzed just over his head, forcing him to duck. "God dammit!" he muttered.

"No fast-movers in the area, sir!" Landers said. "Brigade is ordering you to withdraw!"

"Son of a…" Mark cursed his luck. His last patrol was going to be a failure, but the most important thing was to get his men out of there, now. "Everybody pull back," he said to Landers. "Tell the Mustangs to–"

"Incoming!" Landers yelled.

A projectile rocketed down from the Serbs on the rooftop. Mark could see it making course corrections, the commands racing

4

down the wire from the Serb controller. The lead Humvee driver saw it, too, and he cranked his wheel around as he hit the gas. It was just enough; the Sagger round clipped the right front of the vehicle without detonating and caromed into a building. The explosion blasted stone fragments into the street, one suitcase-sized chunk taking out the machine gun of Mustang-2 as if it were made of balsa wood. Mark thanked God the soldier manning the gun had dropped down inside as the Humvee began its retreat.

His soldiers were making a fighting retreat from their positions, moving quickly but with good discipline. Mark ordered Landers to get going and was about to follow him when he saw the balcony take another series of hits. Hemple went down, his rifle flying out of his hands and down to the street.

Without hesitation Mark dashed from behind the car and raced across the street. In five long steps he was there, Serb rounds whizzing past him all the way. He took the steps three at a time. Hemple was lying on the balcony floor, blood seeping from wounds in his left arm and side. His helmet was pulled back from the impact with the floor, and the young soldier's eyes were wide with fear. The stucco railing of the balcony gave them some cover, so Mark didn't have to move him immediately.

Mark pulled his med kit out of his thigh pocket and began first aid. The wound in Hemple's side had to be tended first. "Hemple! Can you hear me?" Mark had to shout it over the roar of gunfire.

"Yeah–yes, sir."

His breathing was rapid but that was from fear, maybe the first phase of shock. Or was it? Mark had to pause and take a deep breath, remembering his training from a refresher course in tactical combat casualty care a few weeks before. "Okay, hang in there with me, soldier. We're gonna get out of here." He unfastened Hemple's body armor and saw the dark spot on the lower right of the soldier's blouse. The round had entered just below the armor. When Mark pulled the blouse away, he saw that it was likely just a flesh wound, but flesh wounds could still cause a man to bleed out. He applied pressure bandages from the med kit to the entry and exit wounds.

He kept talking to Hemple, keeping him focused. The Serbs were still firing, but the chatter of their AKs and the Americans' return fire was diminishing. Mark heard the roar of the Humvees' engines as they pulled back. From the street directly below, a Serb AK loosed a short burst, but no rounds impacted the balcony. Mark allowed himself to think that maybe they hadn't seen them. He could get Hemple stabilized and then figure out a way to–

The door of the apartment burst open and three men rushed toward the balcony, their weapons pointed at the two Americans. "*Rukama! Rukama!*" one of them shouted.

Mark knew just enough Serbo-Croatian to understand, but he couldn't put his hands up now, he had to finish dressing the soldier's wound. "I have a wounded man here!" he yelled.

The man in the lead advanced to within three feet. "Hand up!" he barked in English.

Mark still had to secure the bandage with the tape. "For crissakes, I have to help–" He turned his head just enough to see the butt end of the rifle.

The truck was coming to a stop. He knew that much, and also knew he had a roaring headache. Was he blind, too? Everything was dark. No, it was something else. What–Christ, it hurt to just think. Blindfold. Now he could sense some light leaking in underneath it. How long had he been out? No way to tell. Rope bound his hands in front of him. Slowly, he tried turning one hand so he could touch his wrist…no, damn it, the watch was gone. Shit, his favorite, a Seiko he had bought when he graduated the Academy.

He forced himself to think of more important things. He heard men talking, the rear gate of the truck squeaking down, and then two pairs of hands grabbed him and pulled him over the gate. His feet hit the ground and he was able to stand, barely. He heard someone yell in pain. Who? The soldier? Yes, what was his name? Hemple. "Hemple, hang in there, buddy!" he shouted. Pain seared through his head from an impact. He staggered but the hands held him up, moved him forward.

Someone ahead of him said, *"Uzeti sa blindfold."* The rag was pulled off roughly. Mark had to blink several times, but then his eyes focused. The man before him was young, maybe mid-twenties, short but powerfully built. He wore a camouflage uniform, topped by an olive-green beret. From the patches and shoulder tabs, Mark knew he was facing a sergeant in the Yugoslav People's Army. Behind him, Mark could see a small single-storied house. A farm house, with a barn. So this was Serbia.

The sergeant looked at Mark and smiled. "American," he said, his English heavily accented, "you bomb our women and children, now we see how tough you are, here."

"Mark Hayes, major, United States Army, serial num–" The man slapped him with the back of his hand.

"Ordžati ga, ja ću je kapetan." The men beside Mark pulled him up straighter. The sergeant turned and began walking toward the farmhouse, ten meters away. The door opened and a man wearing a red beret stepped out. He resembled the sergeant, only older, and Mark sensed he was the captain.

"Aca, mi imamo Amerikanaca. Jedan oficir, jedan–" The sergeant's words were cut off as his head exploded in red mist. A split-second later Mark heard the snapping sound of the supersonic bullet.

He reacted instinctively, throwing an elbow into the gut of the Serb next to him, pulling away from the man on the right. The first man had been holding his AK and Mark tore it from him, brought it to bear on the second man only to see him rock backward as two bullets tore into his chest. The sounds of gunfire filled the air.

Mark dropped to the ground and rolled away from the path leading to the farmhouse. He was facing back toward two vehicles, a truck and an armored personnel carrier. Mark got a brief glimpse of two Serb soldiers dropping a stretcher to the ground and bringing their weapons up. The man on the stretcher bounced up from the impact and then back down with a moan.

The Serb Mark had elbowed fell on top of him, grabbing for the rifle. The men rolled over as rounds cracked overhead. Mark's training took hold instinctively. *Fight the man, not the weapon.* He ignored the shouts and screams coming from the farmhouse, focusing completely on the Serb who was doing his best to rip the rifle away. Releasing his own grip, Mark blasted the heels of his bound hands into the Serb's nose, which exploded in a cloud of blood and snot that splattered into Mark's eyes. With a roar of rage, the Serb pushed Mark away and rolled onto his side, reaching for the rifle. Mark reached instinctively for his combat knife, registering a moment of surprise as he slid it out of the scabbard. The idiots hadn't taken it from him. Now they would pay for that mistake. The Serb got one hand on the rifle before seizing up as Mark's blade plunged into his side.

The firefight had intensified. Mark pushed the dying Serb soldier away from him, then used the knife to cut the rope binding his wrists. He grabbed the AK off the ground and looked back toward the vehicles. One man lay still on the ground near the front of the APC, another took a round in the head and fell back. Three more Serbs were using the truck for cover. From beyond, Mark heard orders shouted in English with a British accent. To his right he saw four soldiers coming out of a hedgerow into the farmyard, firing at the house. One of the men waved toward the barn, and Mark heard an engine start up. The four Brits were trying to flank the farmhouse, but the Serbs inside must've gotten out through a back door and made it to a vehicle in the barn.

The rest of the British platoon had to be advancing on the Serb vehicles in front of Mark. Hemple lay on the stretcher, and he tried raising his good arm. Still alive, but maybe not for long. Mark scrambled to his feet and stayed in a crouch, running toward the wounded man. The nearest Serb saw him coming and turned to engage, taking three rounds in the chest from Mark's rifle for his trouble. Mark crawled forward to cover Hemple with his own body and brought the rifle around to the backs of the two remaining Serbs. He squeezed the trigger but the rifle jammed. Before he could clear it the Serbs were dropping their own weapons and raising their hands.

Soldiers appeared, some of the toughest-looking men Mark had ever seen, and right now they looked beautiful. Four of them manhandled the two surviving Serbs to the ground and began applying zip ties to their wrists. Another one, his hair streaked with gray beneath the beige beret, strode up to Mark and knelt down. "22 SAS," the officer said. "Are you injured, Major?"

"No, but my man here needs help."

The Brit waved to one of his men. "We have a wounded man here! Get Sergeant Dooley over here on the double!" Behind the farmhouse, the sound of the vehicle engine diminished. "Bugger," the officer said, "I think the rest of the lot got loose from us."

Mark had moved to a sitting position, his back against the side of the truck. Suddenly he was very tired and his headache was back with a vengeance. "Where are we?"

"Five kilometers inside Serbia," the Brit said. "We'd best hustle you gentlemen back into Kosovo and get you to hospital."

"I'm okay," Mark said, just as he started to tip over.

The last thing he heard was, "Bloody hell you are, Yank."

CHAPTER ONE
OCTOBER 2012 – ITALY

The man in the armor raised his sword and faced the crowd. "Caesar, we who are about die, salute you!" He bowed slightly and stepped back, slicing the air with his weapon. After three paces he stopped and banged the sword on his round shield. "Who among you is man enough to challenge me?"

Some of the women among the spectators tittered as a tall man walked onto the dirt floor. He was an American, spoke with a Texas drawl, and now was outfitted similarly to the man in the middle, with a metal helmet, a leather vest covering his torso above his blue jeans, and greaves covering his shins. His feet were shod in sandals. In his left hand he clutched a shield. The Texan's weapon, like his opponent's, was a wooden replica of the Roman *gladius,* a short sword that in the hands of a skilled first-century soldier would be formidable indeed.

But Jim Hayes could see this guy was far from skilled, despite the man's earlier boasts that he could handle anybody in the tour group. The Texan had his own cheering section, a man and two women. One of the women, a tall blonde, yelled, "Take his head off, Rick!" The other couple laughed.

Next to Jim, his wife, Gina, shook her head. Like Jim, she had devoted years to training in the martial arts back in the States, and she knew the difference between play-acting and serious personal combat. "He's the one who's going to get his head handed to him," Gina said. After spending a week here in the land of her birth, her Italian accent was more pronounced than usual. Today she wore her shoulder-length black hair up under a stylish hat, with her sleeveless top and jean shorts revealing arms and legs that were tanned and toned.

"No, he won't," Jim said. "The people running this place aren't taking our money to humiliate us. Carlo will put on a good show and let the guy win."

"He's been a *culo del cavallo* the whole tour," Gina said. "Carlo should make an example of him."

Jim glanced at his wife. Whenever she used profanity, which was rare, Jim knew she was seriously upset. Calling this loudmouth a horse's ass wasn't the worst thing he'd ever heard from her, but it was a cut above her usual polite language. He also knew that Gina was itching for a chance to take on the Texan herself, and that, Jim was sure, would be bad news for Rick.

Carlo was the *doctoré,* or chief trainer, of this *ludus* near the Italian city of Capua, south of Rome. With the popularity of the TV series *Spartacus* and movies like *Gladiator,* these mock training centers had sprung up in Italy, catering to tourists who wanted to know more about the lives of the Roman gladiators. This one had the best reputation of the several Jim had checked out prior to their trip. So far, the place had lived up to its billing. The buildings and grounds were carefully crafted to resemble the schools where ancient Rome trained men for its gladiatorial contests. Carlo and the other hosts had been very informative, and remarkably tolerant

12

of the tall American whose opinion of himself was undoubtedly high, based on the almost-insulting tenor of his questions. His girlfriend had tried to shush him at first but eventually gave up. Just before they had moved to the training area from indoors, Jim made a friendly attempt to get Rick to dial it down. The answer was just a contemptuous smirk.

To Jim's right, a slightly shorter man bearing a strong resemblance to him gestured toward the combatants. "I still say you should get in there with Carlo," Mark Hayes said. "You're probably the only one here who might really be able to take him." Next to Mark, his wife Sophie, proper and fashionable as always, shook her head, eyes rolling. Tall with sandy blonde hair, Sophie was often mistaken for a model, but more frequently was recognized as the BBC reporter she was.

"Hey, little brother," Jim said, "you put in twenty-five years in the Army, why don't you get in there?"

"Give me an M4 carbine and I'd have no problem," Mark said. "This stuff here is more your style."

"No thanks," Jim said. "I'll save mine for the *dojo* back home."

In the middle of the training yard, Carlo and Rick began to circle each other. "Don't mess him up too bad, Rick," the other Texan said. The buddy's girlfriend laughed and whispered something to the blonde.

Carlo bellowed and came at Rick, his wooden sword held high. He brought it down with a hard clacking sound on Rick's shield. The Texan countered and Carlo parried. Jim's years of experience told him that Carlo could've ended the fight right there with his own counterstrike, but the Italian, as Jim expected, held back, allowing Rick to gain more confidence. Just as he could see that Carlo was indeed skilled, Jim could tell that Rick's experience was almost certainly limited to a few bar brawls back home, and it wasn't very likely any of them had featured swordplay.

Rick swung his sword wildly and Carlo took the blow on his shield and staggered back, almost inviting the Texan to continue his attack. Rick obliged, and with three more whacks he knocked the shield from Carlo's arm, parried a weak thrust and brought his sword around to the Italian's throat.

"I yield!" Carlo shouted dramatically, dropping his sword and kneeling. He held up two fingers, the signal for surrender that Jim remembered from the TV show. The three other Texans whooped and applauded, but only a few other members of the tour group offered polite claps.

Rick raised his sword and shield, yelling a big Texas "Yee-hah!" On the ground, Carlo waited for a hand to help him back up. None came. Instead, Rick faced the crowd and said, "Now, who's next?"

Carlo stood and removed his helmet. His black hair was matted with sweat. It was a warm day, and Jim knew it had to have been hot under that helmet, which looked to be a pretty good reproduction of an original, with a metal crown, wide brim and a cage to cover the face. The Italian wiped his brow and asked, "Does anybody want to challenge our new champion?"

Rick pointed his gladius straight at Jim. "You there, Pops. Let's see if you fight as good as you talk."

"No thanks," Jim said. He could feel Gina digging an elbow into him.

"Go on, Jim," she said. "If you don't, I will."

Jim shook his head. "He's got twenty-five years on me, *bellisima,* and almost as many on you." Then he noticed that everybody else in the tour group was looking at him. Some were nodding. Evidently he hadn't been the only one who'd had quite enough of the young Texan's attitude. Carlo smiled at him with a hopeful look. The questions Jim had asked on the tour must have given the Italian some insight into his background.

"Come on, Pops," Rick said. "Show us what you got."

Jim could tell his brother was getting a little agitated. During Mark's time in the Army he'd never had much patience with show-offs. Jim had worked closely with his brother for the past year in Odin Security Services and he knew what was about to happen, but before he could say anything, Mark spoke in his old commanding officer's voice. "Cool off, buddy. You aren't good enough to make my brother work up a good sweat."

"Give it a try, *signor,*" Carlo said. He motioned to one of his assistants, who began pulling armor and weapons from a trunk.

Gina gave Jim a wicked smile and said, *"Insegnare quel'imbecile una lezione, il mio marito."* Teach that imbecile a lesson, my husband.

"No fair. You know I can't resist you when you talk dirty in Italian." He handed her his cell phone and straw fedora and stepped into the makeshift arena.

It took Carlo and his assistant only a couple minutes to get Jim geared up. As he was adjusting his helmet, Carlo said in a low voice, "I think you have the experience with the weapons, yes?"

"You might say that," Jim said. He hefted the wooden sword. He'd done a fair amount of training in *kenjutso,* the

15

Japanese art of the sword, although that had been with a *katana*, which was longer and heavier. He'd have to adjust his techniques on the fly with this one, especially since using the gladius required only one hand. He looked over at the young hotshot, imagining what Rick was seeing: a middle-aged man in a polo shirt, cargo shorts and scars on his right knee. If he was paying attention, he'd see that this guy looked to be in pretty good shape and moved easily, even wearing the armor and carrying the weapon and shield. But Rick almost certainly didn't have the experience of dozens of martial arts tournaments and countless hours in the dojo to guide him.

"Okay, gentlemen," Carlo said, "come to the center. Face the crowd and lift your swords in salute. Now, face each other. And...begin!"

Jim expected Rick to come at him aggressively and that's just what he got from the Texan. Rick yelled and charged, bringing the sword around in a wide arc from his right. Jim took the strike on his shield and felt the energy flow through the shield into his own arm. Calling on his training, Jim let the energy continue its course through him and into his sword arm, resulting in a solid strike that Rick took on his own shield. Jim moved away easily as his opponent staggered back, his eyes wide, but he recovered and came at Jim again.

Rick's attack was more measured now, but it was clear to Jim that the only thing his opponent knew about sword combat was what he'd seen in the movies. Jim took two strikes on his shield, parried a third and responded by using the sword the way Roman legionaries had, swinging low to cut at the enemy's legs. He struck hard against the leather greave covering Rick's right leg. The Texan yelped in pain and jumped back.

"Hey, man, what the hell!"

"You weren't listening to the tour guide, Junior," Jim said. "The next one would've come right up the groin." That was tempting, but instead he adjusted his feet and used a kenjutso technique, a series of strikes that drove Rick back. Jim could easily have killed him if he'd been armed with a real sword, but killing a man in combat was serious business, something both Jim and his brother knew about first-hand. This was just play time, and now it was time for it to end. Rick must have sensed he was in trouble. He lashed out wildly, parried Jim's sword strike with his own and charged, slamming his shield into Jim's left shoulder as he brought his sword back to stab.

Ignoring the pain in his shoulder, Jim kept his feet and reacted automatically, years of training coming into play. He brought the butt end of his sword down on Rick's hand, forcing him to drop his own weapon. The Texan's yell of pain was barely out of his mouth when he had to deal with another blow, this one to his side from the edge of Jim's sword. Jim used the shield for a sharp thrust to Rick's face guard, then finished by stepping around behind him, hooking his shoulder and employing a simple hip toss to lever the Texan down to the ground, hard. Jim brought the tip of his sword to Rick's throat. "Give it up before somebody gets hurt," he ordered.

"Okay, man. Jesus!"

Jim cracked him in the side of the helmet. "And that's for swearing."

The crowd applauded as Jim stepped back, flipped his sword

and handed it to Carlo, handle first. Mark came up behind him. "Let me help you out of your armor, Conan," his brother said.

Carlo's assistant came up to take the gear. The man was in his mid-thirties, Jim estimated, and he was looking at Mark with more than casual interest. He hefted the gear and walked back to the storage chest, giving them one last look over his shoulder.

Gina gave Jim a hug, and a few men from the crowd came over to shake his hand. Rick was helped up by his buddy and the four Texans kept to themselves. "That concludes our tour, ladies and gentlemen," Carlo said. "Thank you for coming and please make sure to visit our souvenir shop on your way out." The visitors began filing out, with one couple lagging back.

"Well done, Jim," Sophie said, hugging him. "My, you've worked up a sweat after all, Mark's boast notwithstanding."

Jim laughed at that. His sister-in-law was English and her manners tended to be a tad more proper than her American husband's. "Well, let's see what the store here has to offer before we head back to the hotel," Jim said.

Gina gave him a glare of warning. "Only one tee shirt."

Before Jim could offer up his usual protest, the man who had stayed behind came up to him. "So you do have some limits, then," he said, in English with a British accent. He was in his mid-sixties, about five-ten and based on his solid build, he knew a thing or two about staying in shape. His wife was nearly as tall with a trim figure and flowing gray hair. Jim thought she looked a lot like the actress Helen Mirren.

Jim took the man's offered hand. "Yes, a few," he said. "Jim Hayes. My wife Gina, brother Mark, sister-in-law Sophie."

"We've met," Mark said, a broad grin splitting his face. "Kosovo, '99. Colonel Cunningham, I presume?"

The Brit squinted at Mark, then returned the smile. "Well, hello again, Yank." He and Mark exchanged a vigorous handshake, and then the man turned to Jim. "Paul Cunningham, and this is my wife Evelyn." Jim shook the offered hand and it was like gripping a piece of iron. When Cunningham took Sophie's hand he said, "I believe I've seen you on the BBC, reporting from Afghanistan."

"That's right," Sophie said, smiling politely as she always did when someone recognized her. "That's where I met my husband."

Cunningham nodded at Mark. "When we saw you folks at the hotel this morning, I told Evelyn that you were familiar, Major. I wasn't able to place you till just now. I presume you are no longer a major?"

"Colonel, retired," Mark said, still smiling.

"Excellent. If you folks are heading back to the hotel, would you care to join us for dinner? We heard of a little *trattoria,* only a short walk away, said to be first-rate."

"We'd be delighted," Sophie said. They hadn't run into a lot of Brits on this trip and Jim knew she was probably anxious to talk to some fellow countrymen.

"Capital," Cunningham said. "Shall we meet you in the lobby around six? I doubt if we'll need a reservation."

They all agreed on the time and were starting to move toward the exit when Carlo's assistant came up to them. He was holding a battered old Nikon camera. "Excuse," he said, "but a photo, please? Can send it to you, special frame from gift shop." Jim couldn't place the man's accent, but it wasn't Italian.

"No, thanks," Mark said.

"Please, just one? You sign up in gift shop if you want the frame."

"Make it quick," Jim said.

"*Grazi*." He used his hands to motion the four of them together, then gestured for the Cunninghams to get into the shot. Three clicks and it was done.

Ten minutes later, Mark was at the wheel of their rented Fiat as they headed down the two-lane road from the ludus. Jim sat next to him in the front seat, with the women in the back. The plastic bag with Jim's fourth tee shirt of the trip–and according to Gina, his last one–was on the floor between his feet.

Sophie leaned forward to ask her husband a question. "Did you know that gentleman in the service?"

"I had a very memorable introduction to the colonel, yes."

Jim rummaged in his shopping bag. "Dang it," he said. "I forgot to check into getting that picture frame."

"There was no picture frame," Mark said. "The guy's story was bogus."

"What do you mean?" Sophie said from the back.

"I asked at the desk. They didn't know anything about it. I wasn't surprised."

Jim didn't like where this was leading. His brother was one of the most perceptive men he'd ever known, a talent that helped him achieve full bird colonel in the Army before retirement and then move on to a leadership position in one of the fastest-growing private security firms in the States. If Mark thought something smelled, it almost certainly did. "So what was the deal with that guy, then?" Jim asked him.

"I'm not sure," Mark said as he pulled out into traffic on the highway. "But I hadn't heard that kind of an accent since '99."

"So the guy isn't Italian?"

"Serbian. And the last time I heard someone talk like that he had a gun pointed at my head."

CHAPTER TWO
BELGRADE, SERBIA

"The email will be in your in box in a few minutes," the voice on the other end of the line said. The listener could tell that he was trying to control his excitement. Everyone in the organization knew what it would mean to the man who finally located The American. The bounty was now up to ten thousand euros.

"Thank you, Yuri." Darko Novak turned to his laptop computer, the telephone still tucked between his ear and shoulder. He really needed to invest in one of those hands-free headsets, but money was tight, and some corners had to be cut. Petty office supplies could wait. He accessed the internet and signed in to his Gmail account. Within seconds, the computer issued a soft chime and the message appeared.

Novak paused for a second, his hand on the mouse. So many times he had been disappointed. Thirteen years of frustration, of knowing who his quarry was, yet never being able to deal with him, came surging from his brain to his index finger on the mouse's left button.

"Are you there, Colonel?" the man on the end of the line asked.

"Yes, yes, I am still here, Yuri. It took a moment to get my computer powered up," Novak lied. "All right, I have the email."

He clicked on the message, and then the attachment. A photograph appeared, showing six people, three men, three women. He immediately recognized the man on the left. The one in the middle was possibly related to him, perhaps a little older. The older, shorter one on the right he did not know. As for the women, he knew the face of the one standing next to The American. The other two were unimportant, for now.

But, The American, he was very important to Novak. He composed himself for a moment, then said, "The photograph is very good, Yuri. Well done."

Relief flooded Yuri's voice. "Thank you, Colonel. Is it…?"

"I must do some further checking," Novak said. After all these years he had to make sure, although he knew in his gut that his long quest might finally be nearing its end. "I should know within twenty-four hours. In the meantime, I want you to maintain surveillance on this man. I will be sending some men down from Rome to assist you."

"Of course, sir. I know what hotel they are staying at, I heard them mention it. In fact, I am outside it right now."

"Excellent," Novak said, tearing his gaze away from the photograph. He had to concentrate on the conversation. "Tell me, what else have you learned?"

"I was able to approach the desk clerk at their hotel," Yuri said. "For a small consideration, he was willing to provide me with some information."

"How small?" Novak asked, instantly concerned. His budget was tight, and he didn't have much to spare for bribes.

"Fifty euros," Yuri said.

"That is fine," Novak said, having expected a number twice that size. "You did not include that information in your email, I see."

"Uh, no, sir, I—"

"That's all right, Yuri. Compose another message and send it to me. Take your time, I want everything you have at this point. Not just facts, I want to know what you felt from this man, and his companions. Do you understand me?"

"Perfectly, sir. I can have it to you in twenty minutes, probably less."

"That would be fine. If they leave the hotel, follow them. Send the email when you are able."

"I believe they will be leaving for dinner soon. I should have time right now. And Colonel, the clerk told me they are at the hotel only for this one night."

Novak knew immediately that he would have to make something happen very quickly, or his opportunity would likely be gone. They would be leaving Capua in the morning, then. Probably to Rome, less than two hundred kilometers away. "All right, Yuri. Stay with them, and keep me informed. I will be sending Dalibor and his team down. They should be there in two hours. And Yuri, do not do anything foolish. If this is the man we seek, he is a highly-trained, experienced warrior." Novak clicked the END CALL button and set the cell phone down on his desk, allowing himself, at last, to turn back to the photograph on the computer screen. His instincts told him time was of the essence, but before he acted, he would have to make sure.

Yes, it was The American, it had to be. But just to confirm, he brought up the news files he'd downloaded in the last few years. There weren't many. The American had lived a fairly quiet life, or as quiet as a decorated military officer could lead. There was one article, though, which contained a recent photograph. The largest newspaper in The American's home province had written a story on him some months earlier, noting his retirement from the U.S. Army and his acceptance of an executive position with a large security firm based near their major city of Chicago. Novak had to smile at the irony. He and his nemesis had both been military men, and now when their countries had no further use for them, they had moved into the most obvious section of the private sector, where men such as themselves could apply their skills and experience profitably.

Novak swiped a fingertip across the screen, dividing it in two with the emailed photograph from Italy on the left half and the newspaper article on the right. He sat back in his chair. It was The American, all right. There could be no doubt. The woman next to him was his fiancée, the BBC reporter. The story mentioned the couple was engaged to be married, and perhaps they were by now. As to the other men in the photo, Novak had no idea who the shorter one was, but the taller one had to be The American's older brother, also mentioned in the article. The one who had been in Somalia just a year ago, who had somehow fought his way out of a terrorist camp. Novak made a mental note to look up the brother again. So, they were traveling together. The dark-haired woman had to be the brother's companion. As to the older couple, he would tend to them later.

Novak allowed himself to experience the emotion of the

moment. He felt elation, yes, but that was quickly replaced by determination. Hatred, even. He had found his quarry at last.

A plan began to take shape in his highly-organized mind. To think logically, he had to cease referring to the man as The American, which was how Novak had thought of his nemesis for thirteen years. The American was now a target, and a target had to have a name. His own name would suffice. "Mark Hayes," Novak whispered. For so long, even after he'd discovered the name, he'd been almost afraid to say it aloud, as if giving voice to the words, however fleeting, would somehow cause the man to disappear forever. Of course that was foolish; the Serb could go to the rooftop of this very building and shout it to the sky right now, and The American—Mark Hayes—would not vanish, he would still be in Italy, just a few hundred kilometers away.

Just a few hundred kilometers. No longer protected by the awesome might of the United States Army, or the vast distance of the Atlantic Ocean and half a continent beyond that, out of Novak's reach, as he'd grudgingly admitted to himself years ago. As powerful as he was here in Serbia, indeed throughout the Balkans, Novak knew he had limits, like any other man. He knew that mounting an operation to bring Hayes to justice would never succeed as long as the target of the operation was in the mountains of Afghanistan, or especially in the United States itself. If he ever came to Europe, that would be another matter entirely.

And now, he was here. But for how long? Novak did not know if Hayes had been in Italy for a few days or a few weeks. If they were going to Rome in the morning, which seemed likely, they might be flying home that same day. Even if they stayed in the

Italian capital for two or three days, Novak knew that striking them there would be problematic. Too many people, too many police. No, something had to be done now, tonight.

He made a decision, then placed a call. It was answered after only one ring, which was not surprising. Dalibor was a good soldier. Fortunately, his team had just finished an assignment and were due to return to Belgrade in three days. Novak hated to cut their holiday short, but if they were successful he would pay them a sizable bonus. Novak's budget might be tight in most areas, but not this one. Their conversation lasted only two minutes. Dalibor would take charge of the operation when he arrived in Capua. Yuri would get his bonus and then would go back to being just a part-time, contract employee of Novak's firm. It was Yuri's great good fortune that Hayes had showed up at the place where he worked between assignments, and he had shown some initiative, to be sure, but the serious work that now had to be done would be entrusted to more experienced men.

After hanging up, Novak looked at the two photographs on the screen one more time, allowing himself to be carried back in time more than a decade, nearly two. Such times they were. There had been danger, yes, and blood was shed aplenty, some of it at the end of his very own blade. His own body bore more than a few scars, but he'd dished out far more than he'd taken.

Novak savored the memories of the missions. They'd gone into Croatia, Slovenia, and finally Bosnia and Kosovo. After the battle of Glina, he was the first man to be handed the coveted red beret by the outfit's legendary commander. By then they had come to be known as the Ninjas, and they were feared throughout the Balkans.

Then it had all gone to *govno.*

Novak stood and walked over to the cabinet, unlocked it and pulled open the double doors. The beret was there on the top shelf, with the insignia of the unit, highlighted by a howling wolf. To wear it now was a federal crime. What had once been a symbol of Serbia's most elite warriors was now banned from public view. The outfit's leadership was dead, imprisoned or living quietly in disgrace, with one notable exception.

Of all the officers of the Ninjas, only Darko Novak had survived the Serbian defeat and subsequent purges. He was arrested and charged with war crimes, yes, but his well-paid attorney got the charges dismissed on technicalities. Novak had managed to safeguard enough of his wartime booty to not only pay his legal fees, but set up his own private security firm in the Serbian capital. After careful consideration, he'd named it Red Dragon Limited, bringing one of the Ninjas' traditions together with ancient South Slavic lore. Even with such a name for his business, Novak had kept a low profile, but that was all right. Men in his line of work could not afford to be flashy. His clientele demanded discretion, and he provided it, along with ruthlessly efficient services. Novak had run the company with equally ruthless efficiency. It was tough going, but in the last few years they had finally generated some real profits. His new clients in the Middle East had proven particularly lucrative, and just this week he'd received a serious inquiry from a Hong Kong businessman, a man Novak suspected was a highly-placed agent of the Chinese intelligence service. The Chinese were expanding their influence in Europe and Africa, and they would need people to do the messy work they couldn't bring themselves to do. Things were looking up indeed.

He stepped to the window and looked down upon the streets of Belgrade. Night was falling and the street lights were coming on. In the distance he could see the imposing Belgrade Fortress at the confluence of the Danube and Sava rivers. Between his office building and the fortress, he could see some buildings that would stay dark on this night, as they had on every night since NATO bombs fell on them. The people had insisted the hulks remain standing as memorials to the dead. For Novak, they were bitter reminders of his nation's humiliation.

He knew that Mark Hayes had not flown any of the planes that dropped those bombs, but American pilots were among those who did. The entire point of the ambush in that Kosovar village back in '99 had been to demonstrate to the Americans that the Serbs, at least those on the ground, could not be intimidated. The Yugoslav Air Force might have been swept from the sky, but Serbia's fighting men at arms would not go down that easily. They would make the Americans pay a heavy price.

The last Ninja warrior picked up his phone. There was much work to do, and not much time in which to do it.

He did not intend to let his brother's killer escape again.

CHAPTER THREE
CAPUA, ITALY

The lobby of the Capys Capua was bright and modern, with a touch of Mediterranean elegance that appealed to Jim. He had enjoyed himself tremendously on his first trip to Europe and was already beginning to regret their imminent return to the States.

He'd come down to the lobby a few minutes early; Gina had shooed him out of their room while she finished preparing for their dinner with the Cunninghams. All he'd done upon returning from the ludus was take a shower, brush his hair and teeth, select a change of clothes and that was it. Why did women have to take so much longer to do essentially the same thing? His first wife had been the same way.

Shaking his head, Jim sat down in one of the plush chairs to watch the people come and go. He could still hardly believe that he was touring Italy with his new bride. His life had changed so much in just the past fifteen months, he had to restrain himself from the urge to pinch his arm. No, he wasn't dreaming.

Was it really only fifteen months? He thought back to the summer of 2011. Yes, it was the middle of July when he drove up to northwest Wisconsin, from his home in the southeast corner of the state, to compete in a martial arts tournament. Gina Cremona Dawson was there with a group from her Ashland dojo, and they struck up a conversation after Jim won his weapons event. He'd actually met her a few months before at another tournament in Green Bay. Like Jim, she'd been widowed a few years earlier, and they hit it off rather well.

That, he remembered fondly, was an understatement. He smiled at the memory. They'd gone back to her hotel, and after a dip in the Jacuzzi they went back up to her room. But instead of flaming out, as a lot of relationships with such torrid beginnings are wont to do, things grew from there. On New Year's Eve, just before they went out to attend a party, he'd presented her with a ring.

The wedding in April was a small affair at her church in Ashland. Mark stood up as his best man, of course, and Gina's best friend and fellow nurse was her maid of honor. Among the attendees were Gina's twin sons. Their father, her first husband, was an Air National Guard pilot who had perished in a training accident over Lake Superior in 2004.

It had been a busy spring and summer. After the wedding, Gina moved into Jim's house down in Cedar Lake while her boys went back to college in Duluth to finish out their senior year. In June, Jim quit his job at the local telecom and took an executive vice president's position in Odin Security Services' new Midwest office, headed by Mark, who had just retired from the Army on the twenty-fifth anniversary of his graduation from West Point.

Across the lobby, a statuesque blonde caught his eye and smiled. He grinned and nodded at her as he shifted his weight in the chair and flexed his right leg. The knee hadn't given him much trouble recently, but it was only a matter of time until he'd have to get it replaced. The college basketball injury had just been the start of it. Add the stress from another ten years of rec league ball, and then all the years of martial arts training. How many of those? He had to count. Had it been ten already?

"Excuse me?"

Breaking his reverie, Jim looked up to find the blonde standing there. "Hi there," he said. She was young, maybe mid-twenties, stylishly dressed in a long-sleeved electric blue silk shirt and black capris that emphasized her shapely hips and legs. Blue pumps completed the ensemble.

"I'm sorry, but I just have to ask you a question," she said, with a strong Australian accent.

Jim stood up, feeling somewhat self-conscious. "Certainly," he said.

"Are you the writer, the guy who wrote the book about fighting the terrorists?"

Even with everything that had happened to him in the past fifteen months, he still wasn't used to this. "If you're talking about *The Challenge,* that would be me. Jim Hayes." He extended his hand.

"Corker!" With a dazzling smile, she put her hand in his, but it was more of a caress than a shake. "My boyfriend loved your book. He read it on the flight over here. Wait'll I tell him."

"Where is he?"

She wasn't pulling her hand back. "He's in the bar. We're going out to dinner, and I was just coming back to–"

"Who's your new friend?" Gina asked

Christ, he hadn't even seen her walk up to them. So much for his situational awareness. "Uh, just a fan, honey." He withdrew his hand. "My wife, Gina," he said to the Aussie. "I didn't catch your name."

"Rebecca," the woman said. She was at least three inches taller than Gina, but suddenly she seemed smaller. Even though Gina was smiling, Jim could almost see the daggers shooting from her eyes into the blonde's.

"Nice to meet you," Gina said. To Jim, "Mark and Sophie will be right down. We should be ready to go. The Cunninghams will be holding a table for us."

"Well, perhaps we'll see you later," Rebecca said, not nearly as confident as she had been moments earlier. "My boyfriend will surely want to meet you."

"It'll be a pleasure," Jim said. He had to tear his eyes away from her as she sashayed away. To Gina, he said, "You look great, bellisima." And she did, in a sleeveless red top that displayed her toned arms and enough cleavage to be interesting without being blatant. Her black skirt with a slit in the left side showed off her equally-toned legs, down to the tops of her short black boots.

She gave him that look that he still couldn't figure out. Was it one of anger, or playfulness? Gina was a passionate woman, which he'd discovered on that first night way back at the tournament, but despite her training she still had an occasional problem keeping that passion properly channeled. At least, that was his opinion, which Jim had pretty much kept to himself.

"What is it with you and blondes?" she asked. The look changed a bit, and now Jim thought it was edging toward the dark side.

He laughed, but without much confidence. "I don't have a

thing with blondes. If that was true, why did I marry a brunette? Twice, in fact. I really think you're the one who has a thing about blondes."

She shook her head and sighed. "Sorry. I just..."

Jim knew what was troubling her: a painful memory from her first marriage. He lifted her chin. "Gina, remember that night in Marshfield, just about a year ago? The night we pledged our fidelity to each other?" They'd been meeting twice a month in the central Wisconsin city, about halfway between their two homes, since his return from Somalia. That particular October night had been very special.

"Of course," she said. "It was when I told you I was in love with you."

"And I said I felt the same way, and we promised to stay faithful to each other, to see where it would go. Well, I'm a guy who keeps his promises." Jim knew that was important to her because of what she'd gone through with her first husband. He held up her left hand and touched her wedding ring. "And here we are."

"Yes," she said, her eyes misting. "Here we are."

Jim caught movement over her shoulder. "And here come the other newlyweds. Let's go eat."

Dalibor Lukic had seen much in his thirty-nine years, but rarely anything as magnificent as the body of the Italian woman in his hotel room just two and a half hours ago. Women sometimes complained that he wanted to rush things. They wanted romance, tenderness, and to spend time together. Fortunately, this woman had not been like that. She was a smoldering sex machine, and the moment he shut the door behind them, she was removing her clothes. Fortunately, his phone hadn't chimed until after he rolled off her. When he saw the company logo on the screen he knew that his Roman holiday was about to be cut short. It was a good thing he'd taken care of his personal business first.

Now, there was real business to take care of, perhaps not quite as pleasurable, at least not in the same way. He sat at the table alone, only five or six meters from their target. The trattoria was taking advantage of the mild autumn evening by having its outdoor seating area open, and most of the tables were filled, including the two that had been pulled together to accommodate the American and his dinner companions. The owner of the restaurant was undoubtedly happy that he had so much business on a weeknight, and so was Lukic, for the many patrons gave him additional cover. To keep up appearances, he had just ordered a beer and was giving some feigned attention to his menu, although he had no intention of ordering a meal. The Americans were enjoying their dessert and would be leaving soon. Lukic and his men would be moving then as well.

"It sounds like you've had a wonderful time here in Italy," Evelyn Cunningham said as she dipped her spoon into her *gelato.*

"We certainly have," Sophie Hayes said. "I've been here before, but that was for work, and I didn't have a chance to see many of the sights. So it's been wonderful, yes."

Mark squeezed his wife's thigh, and she responded with a quick glance and a smile. He looked across the table at Paul Cunningham, still not quite ready to believe that this senior citizen was the SAS colonel who'd led the unit that rescued him from the Serbs thirteen years earlier. The concussion he suffered during the firefight in the village had caused some memory loss, just enough to forget about Cunningham's visit in the base hospital. But he had no reason to doubt the man's story now. His recall of the assault on the farmhouse was right on the money. That much Mark remembered with relative clarity.

"Where are you off to next?" Cunningham asked.

"Rome tomorrow," Jim said. "A couple days there and then we fly home. Gina will be our tour guide. She went to college there."

Gina gave her spoon a final lick and dropped it back into the bowl. "At the American University," she said. "I majored in nursing, but I got my master's in the States."

"It'll be a busy day," Jim said. "The Vatican museum, then the Forum and the Colosseum. I'm really looking forward to that one."

"He's wanted to see it since we were kids," Mark said. "He watched every cheesy old gladiator movie there was."

"It must have rubbed off on him, considering how well he did earlier today," Paul said. That brought a grin from Jim. Even though Mark had seen the ancient stadium before, it would be fun to share the experience with his brother. He just hoped Jim would be able to keep things in the proper perspective. A lot of gladiators had fought at the Colosseum, and a lot of them died. Combat wasn't nearly as glorious as those old movies made it out to be. Jim had gotten a taste of the real thing last year. Mark had seen a lot more of it, and if he never saw any again that would be fine with him.

Mark had enjoyed himself on the trip, too, but still didn't feel right to have taken vacation so soon after starting his new job. His retirement from the Army in May was tough enough to handle, but he'd dealt with that by heading to England for his wedding and then jumping right into the new job at OSS, executive director of the company's new Chicago-area office. His old West Point roommate had started the company five years earlier on the East Coast and wanted to expand. His offer made Mark's decision to leave the military a lot easier, especially since it contained salary and perks that put his Army paycheck to shame.

The job was good and would get better, but not a day went by that Mark didn't think about his time wearing the uniform. Had it really been twenty-five years? Yes, and add four from his days at West Point. From teenaged football star to decorated combat veteran, it had been a long road that had not been without its bumps, including a broken marriage, but he'd made it. Between his military pension and his new six-figure salary, he was more comfortable financially than he'd ever been in his life. But somehow, he didn't feel comfortable, and that bothered him. Maybe it had been too much change, too quickly.

Mark glanced at his brother. Jim seemed to be having a good time on the trip, his first to continental Europe, but sometimes Mark sensed tension between his brother and his new bride. A certain amount of that was understandable. Hell, he and Sophie weren't exactly love birds 24/7, but something seemed a little off between Jim and Gina.

Whatever it was, it hadn't affected Jim's performance on the job. He'd really taken the marketing division by the horns, and in the training division they were ahead of schedule in getting their employees ramped up. Jim was smart enough to understand that in areas like firearms training, he needed help, so he'd brought in some quality instructors. But in the use of other weapons and especially hand-to-hand, he was top-notch. Mark had really been pleased, but hadn't really said so, had he?

Why had he been so hard on Jim at the office? Was it because they were brothers? In many ways they were still adjusting to this new normal, this everyday closeness. Sometimes it was good, like today at the ludus. On other days they hardly spoke. Despite that, they were planning on building houses on the same small lake in southern Kenosha County, just north of the Wisconsin-Illinois line and only a thirty-minute drive to their new office building near Waukegan. Mark was in charge of finding the right spot.

It had not been a terribly smooth adjustment for either of them. Well, what did he expect? They'd been virtually estranged for years. With Mark on overseas deployments or at some stateside post, and Jim living up in Wisconsin, there weren't exactly too many opportunities to get together. But really, in the twelve years before Jim's little adventure in Somalia, they'd seen each other only at the funerals for their parents and then for Jim's first wife.

There was something between them still, and Mark couldn't quite put his finger on it, but he knew he'd have to do it pretty damn fast. They weren't getting any younger, and they were both heavily invested in the future of their new employer. Their wives were good friends. There was the possibility that Mark's sixteen-year-old son, Eddie, would be coming to live with them, perhaps as early as the upcoming holidays. Much to Mark's surprise, the boy's last email had asked if that might be possible. If it happened, the boy would need an uncle, just as much as he surely needed his father in his life again. Something had to be done to get whatever it was out into the open and deal with it.

Mark had always been able to do that in the Army, from being captain of the Academy football team through every command he'd had in the field. Now it was time to get it together on the home front. That was easier said than done, he knew. Unlike the military, he couldn't just give an order and make things happen. Real leadership was more than knowing how to give orders.

Sophie was talking to him. "Earth to Mark."

"Oh, sorry. What?"

She shook her head. "I was saying that we ladies would like to check out those shops down that street over there. Perhaps you gentlemen might find a pub where you can swap your war stories?"

"They've been remarkably restrained up to now," Evelyn said, getting a laugh from her husband.

"I'll get the check," Mark said.

"Nonsense, your money's no good," Paul said. He signaled the waiter.

"All right, but the first round's on me."

Lukic downed the last of his beer as he watched the Americans rise from their table. He pulled out his cell phone and Yuri answered on the first ring. "They're moving," Lukic said.

"I see them." Yuri was sitting at another trattoria down the block. "What do you want us to do?"

"Call Jakov and tell him to get the vehicle ready. If they separate, we will take the American."

"What if he stays with his wife?"

"Then the colonel will get two for the price of one."

CHAPTER FOUR
CAPUA, ITALY

The street was lined with shops and the occasional tavern for about three blocks. Gina saw Sophie's eyes brighten with anticipation. "Do you want me to hold your credit card for you?" she asked.

Her sister-in-law smiled back. "I think I can maintain self-control," Sophie said, "but please feel free to intervene if things get out of hand."

Mark just rolled his eyes. Gina presumed he'd known Sophie was a serial shopper. But, to her credit, his new wife was discerning. Gina had known some women who shopped simply for the sake of shopping, and their homes were constantly cluttered with useless junk, their closets overflowing with shoes and outfits. Sophie, on the other hand, was always stylishly dressed and the town house she and Mark were renting was spotlessly clean and organized. Remarkable, really, for a woman who'd spent the better part of the last ten years living out of a suitcase.

Capua was nice, although Gina would've preferred staying in nearby Santa Maria Capua Vetere. But Jim had liked the Capys when their travel agent was discussing hotels in the area, and its location near the ludus sealed the deal. The city was just north of Naples, and after a strenuous day yesterday, climbing Mount

Vesuvius in the morning and then exploring ancient Pompeii in the afternoon, they'd decided to stay a night here after touring the ludus, rather than driving the remaining 200 kilometers to Rome.

Besides, if they'd headed straight to the capital they never would've met the Cunninghams here, and she'd taken to Evelyn right away. The older woman reminded Gina of her favorite aunt, who was a *contessa*. Evelyn had the same air of elegance and sophistication without being ostentatious.

This area of the city was bordered to the west by the River Volturno, which curved around a peninsula and back to the east. Gina had never visited Capua proper before, and she could see the city had its charms. She found herself eagerly anticipating the next hour or so, when she could spend time with the women while the men went somewhere else.

Jim pointed out a trattoria to their right. "How about that place?" he asked his brother.

"Looks good to me," Mark said. "Ladies, have a good time. Sophie, remember–"

"Yes, dear," his wife said, with a wink at Evelyn.

"Well, we're off, then," Paul said. He kissed his wife on the cheek. "Be good, dearest."

"Always."

Novak was still at his office. Although he sometimes worked out of his home, for an operation of this importance he wanted to stay at his desk. The drive to his villa outside Belgrade could take as long as an hour, depending on the traffic, and although he had Bluetooth capability in his Audi, he didn't want to be distracted by driving.

He really would've preferred to have been on the ground in Italy, directing his team firsthand, but there wasn't time to get there.

Lukic was a good man, though, one of his best. He'd served under Novak in the Ninjas and the recently concluded op in Rome had proven once again that the former staff sergeant first class hadn't lost a step in the intervening years. Novak had sent Lukic and his team to fulfill a contract with a certain Bulgarian businessman who had been unable to collect a debt from an Italian *mafioso*. The Bulgarian was under close watch by Interpol for his alleged connections to human trafficking, and could not afford to risk any more exposure by sending his own men, just in case something went wrong.

Nothing ever went wrong when Red Dragon Limited was on the job, though. Novak knew that while the Bulgarian's involvement in trafficking was anything but alleged, his euros were as good as anybody else's. Lukic had little trouble completing the assignment, and RDL was in line for a very nice bonus from their new friend in Sofia. The bonus made Novak feel better about sending his company jet to pick up Lukic and his team at an airfield near Capua. Normally his men flew commercial as a cost-saving measure, but this time they would have a special cargo, and more discretion, as well as speed, was required.

Novak checked his watch again. He was tempted to call, but his policy had always been to refrain from annoying his men in the field. Pick good men, give them adequate training and resources, then let them complete the mission. That was the key to success, in the military and in business. But that didn't mean he never became impatient.

A minute later his phone buzzed. Lukic's phone avatar, a snarling wolf, was on the screen. Novak touched the button and held the phone to his ear. "What is happening, Dalibor?"

"Colonel, the target has gone into a tavern with the two other men. The women are strolling along the sidewalk. They are shopping."

Novak knew that might take a while. He also knew that to take the American in the tavern would be problematic. "Are you and your men in position?" he asked.

"Yes, sir. Yuri and I are covering the street. I have three men in our vehicle, parked near the end of this block."

Novak did a quick calculation. "Three in the vehicle? I sent five men to Rome, including you. Where is the fifth?"

"I left Kopanja in Rome to monitor the last transaction. Mazzuoli's man is to wire the final deposit to our client at 1400 hours tomorrow, at Banca D'Italia."

Novak wasn't happy that his entire team would not be in Capua to take care of this most important task, but he understood the necessity to make sure the Italian gangster Mazzuoli followed through with his promise to pay his debt to the Bulgarian. If something went wrong, at least his man in Rome could keep an eye on things. Dalibor and his men could be sent back to take care of the problem if necessary. "Tell me about the street the women are on," he ordered. "I am looking at it on Google Maps right now."

"The shopping area is three blocks long. There is some vehicle traffic, but not much this evening. Pedestrian traffic is manageable, I would say."

Novak knew what Lukic was thinking. "And the lighting?"

"Dusk is falling. The street lights are on, but their effect will be negligible for the next twenty to thirty minutes."

Novak was silent for a few seconds, then asked, "If you were to take the woman, where would you do it?"

"At the end of the third block. I have directed my men and their vehicle there. I am at the intersection with the street where they dined."

Novak was tempted to order Lukic to send him photos from each end of the street, but he forced himself to trust his sergeant's tactical judgment. He made a decision. "If the women get to the end of the block and the men have not yet joined them, take the American's wife. You know the one from the photo I sent you?"

"Yes, sir. The taller one, light brown hair. She is the BBC reporter, yes?"

"That is her. She is not to be harmed unnecessarily, is that understood?"

"Perfectly. And her companions?"

"They should be no trouble, but if anyone interferes, deal with them."

Novak didn't have to be there to know Lukic was smiling as he replied, "Yes, Colonel."

Jim was still nursing his first beer, but Paul was already on his second and Mark wouldn't be far behind. The two ex-military men were hitting it off famously, and although they certainly hadn't excluded Jim from the conversation, he couldn't help but feel somewhat left out. Those two had a history of experiences that Jim would never have, and he felt the envy creeping up on him again.

Since his experience in Somalia, he'd gotten to know a lot of veterans back in the States, and they always welcomed him, but only to a point.

Well, that was only natural. It was the same way with him and fellow martial artists, after all. Unless you'd been in a dojo, had gone through the training and tied on the black belt, you could never know what it was really like, and you would never truly be a part of that fraternity. That bond was one of the things Jim enjoyed the most about the training, and Mark had told him on the flight to Europe that the one thing he missed the most about the Army was the camaraderie with his fellow soldiers. Now, he'd found one, here in Italy.

Jim had read about these Special Air Service guys, Britain's elite warriors, and he could easily see Paul Cunningham as one of them. Yes, he was pushing sixty and undoubtedly thicker around the middle than he'd been while in uniform, but the way he carried himself told Jim everything he needed to know. And then to hear the man's stories…

"So, the first time I take Evelyn to meet my mates, one of my squaddies is taking her around the dance floor like she was one of those hot-for-the-sheets Jenny Wrens we used to know when we trained with the bootnecks, so I had to step in before things got out of hand, you know."

Jim laughed. "What the hell are you talking about?"

Mark jumped in. "I'll take a stab at it. A 'squaddie' was one of your guys, right?"

"Right-o," Paul said, taking a sip from his beer.

"And I've heard 'bootneck,' that's a Royal Marine?"

"The same. And the Jenny Wren, they were the women's auxiliary for the Royal Navy, before they were incorporated into the regular ranks, but female sailors are still called that."

"I'll bet they love that," Jim said.

"Oh, I don't think so, but they give it right back to the men now. They aren't like the birds my dad knew when he was in SAS during the war. The gals these days, they can be real, what do you Yanks call them? 'Ball-busters'?"

Mark raised his bottle. "Right on the money, mate." He clinked his bottle with Paul's, then with Jim's.

Jim checked his watch. It had been nearly forty minutes since they'd left the women. "I hope they haven't burned through their credit cards," he said.

The shops, Gina thought, had turned out to be very nice indeed. They'd been through some pretty exotic shopping areas on this trip, like the jewelry stores on the Ponte Vecchio in Florence, and then there was the glassware and lace on the islands of Murano and Burano near Venice, but these shops were just fine. They had reached the final store on the block; after this, they'd cross the street and head back toward the pub where the guys were waiting. Gina hoped Jim was enjoying himself. She still felt a little badly about giving him a hard time back in the hotel lobby. The Australian woman had just been a fan, that's all. She knew that, but at the same time, old habits were hard to put aside.

Meeting Jim Hayes had been the best thing that ever happened to her, short of the birth of her twin sons. Her first marriage had been so stormy, sometimes she'd wondered if she would ever survive with her sanity intact. Falling for the dashing U.S. Air Force pilot was understandable; she was hardly the first Italian woman to marry an American officer. At first she'd dealt with his deployments stoically, like Air Force wives were supposed to do, but then his first affair came along, then the second. After the first one she'd started her martial arts training, primarily as a means to deal with stress, so when the next one happened, she stood her ground and demanded he choose between his marriage and his girlfriends. He had chosen the marriage and Gina thought he was really making an effort, that they might have a chance. Then came the day he flew into a storm over Lake Superior and didn't come out. Her boys had lost their father, and she'd lost a chance at getting back the man she'd once adored.

Sophie was showing Evelyn a pair of boots in the last store on the block. Gina stepped outside and breathed in the cool evening air. It felt good to be back in Italy again. She should really visit more often. Her parents and little sister missed her. Maybe now she could afford to bring them to America for a visit. Her new job at the clinic in Kenosha was going well, and with Jim's income in the picture she could start thinking of things she'd never been able to consider before. She—

The man looking at the next-door store window turned away just as she locked eyes with him. Where was the situational awareness Jim always told her to practice? She forced herself to consider her surroundings. There were few pedestrians out tonight, and only three other customers in the store besides Sophie and Evelyn, all women. In fact there were very few men on the narrow sidewalks, and all of them were with women. Except for this one. Gina forced herself to take in the whole scene and not stare at him. She checked her phone, then her purse, all the while shooting glances at the man, who was about five meters away.

He was still looking into the window, and Gina realized he was trying to observe her by using her reflection. She took a casual step closer to the shoe store doorway, reducing the angle. She saw him reach up to scratch his ear and that's when she noticed his hands. They were rough, the knuckles calloused, the ring and little fingers at odd angles, as if they'd once been broken.

Fighter's hands. Just a month ago she'd attended a weekend self-defense seminar Jim had scheduled at his office building. A retired Navy SEAL and his wife had come in from Minnesota to talk to Jim's people and their spouses, and put them through the paces with weapons as varied as collapsible batons and tactical flashlights. She'd been so impressed that she'd bought one of the flashlights. She rummaged around in her purse again. There it was. She slipped the ring of the flashlight around the pointer finger of her left hand and brought it out, keeping it concealed.

She heard a vehicle pass by on the connecting street. An older Fiat, but as she saw it chug away she saw something else: a nondescript van, parked across the street, diagonally across the intersection, facing in their direction. The van's lights were off, but she thought she saw movement inside. She looked at the back of the vehicle and saw the telltale signs of exhaust. The engine was running.

Alarm bells started to go off in Gina's head. She automatically steadied her breathing as she'd been trained to do. She'd never been in a real combat situation before, but her training had always been pretty realistic even before she moved in with Jim, and he'd helped her take it to a new level. Controlling her breathing was the key. Jim had learned that from the Russian *Systema* guys he'd trained with and he'd taught it to her. It was working, tamping back the fear that had started to rise.

Gina turned back to the doorway of the shoe store. She had to go back inside and take Sophie and Evelyn out a back door. Something was going to happen here, and she remembered the first rule of self-defense: don't be there. But here they were, exiting the store, Sophie with a couple bags, Evelyn with one. The man at the next door window turned toward them and started walking, his right hand now in his coat pocket. His eyes were locked on Sophie.

"Run!" Gina yelled to the women, but they just stood there, mouths agape. Gina rushed passed them to the man and went for the gun.

CHAPTER FIVE
CAPUA, ITALY

Sophie Barton-Hayes had grown up in the Kilburn neighborhood of northwest London, a peaceful place, but her career had taken her to places that were anything but, filled with men who were just as inclined to pull a gun or a knife on you as to extend the hand of friendship. When she saw the man to her right, she knew immediately that he was one of the first kind.

She pushed Evelyn back into the store. "Get to a back room, lock the door!"

The older woman was the wife of a soldier. She knew an emergency when she saw one and didn't protest. Sophie reached into her purse for the pepper spray she carried with her everywhere, and as she pulled it out she saw Gina launch her attack.

Her sister-in-law was a demon. She grabbed the man's hand and Sophie saw that it held a gun. Gina seemed to flow, moving the gun hand around and up. The man's face, eyes already pinched from Gina's light, opened up with a yell as she stomped on his instep. The gun hand continued its rotation, pulling his entire body back and down.

The second she heard the thud of heavy footsteps, Sophie knew she'd been paying too much attention to Gina and none at all to anyone else. She turned and brought her pepper spray up as three men closed in on her from the left. The closest one took the blast of spray on his shoulder, slapped her hand aside and shoved something toward her chest. Sophie saw the black device and heard the crackling and her brain screamed STUN GUN before it was shut down by half a million volts.

Gina had the man down on the cobblestoned street, covering the gun with one hand to prevent the hammer from engaging the firing pin. He was starting to recover now, his vision still impaired by her flashlight, but he was a trained man and she knew she had to finish him now or–

From behind her she heard a crackling sound and then Sophie's gasp of pain. Gina turned, her hand still covering the man's gun, and there were three more of them. One was holding Sophie up and leading her toward the intersection, her legs wobbly, head lolling to one side. The other two men were coming in Gina's direction, fast. One had a pistol, the other what had to be another stun gun.

She had one guy down, but even so it was still three against one. She had to even the odds somehow. With a two-handed twist she yanked the pistol from the man on the ground and brought it around to face the two new assailants. She'd only had one session on the firing range, had done well, but when she squeezed the trigger nothing happened. The safety was still engaged. No time to find it, the two men were on top of her. She threw the gun toward the face of the man with the pistol, then heard the crackle and in an instant her entire left arm went numb. The pain was like nothing she'd ever felt. A wave of dizziness swept over her, and she barely saw the fist coming at her, couldn't bring her other hand up to redirect it. The impact unleashed a volcano of white heat inside her head.

Jim checked his watch. "Hey, it's been about an hour, we should probably find the girls, don't you think?"

"They said they'll be working their way back up here," Mark said. That second beer had given him a bit of a buzz. He hadn't remembered Italian beer having quite that kind of kick. Paul was on his third and looked as sober as a priest, albeit a pretty jolly one. Well, those SAS guys always had known how to hold their alcohol.

"I think I'll just step outside, see if they're close," Jim said.

Paul laughed. "If Evelyn finds a shoe store, we may not see them for days."

"Well, tell them to come on in," Mark said. His brother looked worried. What did he have to worry about, anyway? They were in Italy, for crying out loud. Jim was like an old woman sometimes.

"I'll be right back," Jim said. He left the table and headed for the door.

Looking past him to the front window of the pub, Mark saw a man running past it outside, heading down the street. Was he wearing a peaked cap?

Jim opened the door of the pub just as another man ran past. This one was definitely a cop. Jim looked down the street and his eyes went wide. "Mark! Come on!" he yelled, and took off in pursuit of the policemen.

His bad knee was throbbing and his lungs were searing, but

Jim knew, somehow he knew, that his wife was in trouble down there and, by God, he was going to help her. By the time he was midway down the street he was close to panic and he had to control his breathing, as much as possible while running full tilt, to hold his emotions in check. But she was down there. His first wife had bled to death in his arms seven years before and he was not going to let it happen again.

But what if he was too late, again? The terrifying thought spurred him on. In front of the last shop on the block he shoved his way through the gawking bystanders. A policeman was out in the intersection, looking down the street, holding a radio microphone to his mouth as he strained to see something in the distance.

"Gina!"

She was lying on the cobblestones, a trickle of blood coming from her lips. The side of her face was starting to swell, but he saw her eyes flicker. Thank God, she was alive! A cop was kneeling next to her, checking her injuries. She looked up and her eyes focused as she recognized Jim. She tried to say something, but could only choke out a guttural sound as her jaw moved and she closed her eyes in pain.

"I'm here, bellisima, I'm here," Jim said as he touched her face. To the cop he said, "I'm her husband. What happened?"

"There was a fight," the man said. "An ambulance is on the way. Do not move the head, sir, may be neck injury."

"Jim, I–" Gina winced in pain again, then reached for Jim's hand. He clutched it with both of his. She held on, and nothing had ever felt so good to him. She moved her head, trying to look around. "Sophie," she said.

"What? What about Sophie?" It was Mark, joining Jim on one knee. "Where's Sophie?"

Evelyn was there. Tears were streaming down her face. "They took her, Mark."

Paul was there, taking his wife into his arms. "What do you mean? Who took her?"

"Four men," Evelyn said. She struggled to control her emotions, failed. A sob broke free, but she rallied. "Gina fought them. She fought them, Mark. She had one of them down, had his gun, then another one struck her with something, on her arm, and then he…he punched her."

Paul gathered her close. "It's all right, dear," he said, stroking her hair. "You're safe now."

"They took Sophie," Evelyn said. "Took her, in a van, down that way." She pointed across the intersection, in the direction the cop was looking. "I should have done something!" she wailed.

Mark stood, his face a confused mask of fear and confusion. Jim could hardly grasp it himself. Sophie was kidnaped? Who were they? Where had they taken her? To the policeman near Gina, he said, "Did you get a description of the vehicle?"

"We have more help on the way, sir," the cop said. He was young, but he was keeping it together, staying professional. "Please, your wife, you must let the ambulance people help her."

Gina was struggling to sit up. "Stay down," Jim told her. He was starting to calm down. His wife was hurt, but she would live. He said a prayer of thanks, and one for his sister-in-law. She would need all the help she could get now.

CHAPTER SIX
OVER ITALY

It was dark. The smell was like rope, and when Sophie breathed in, something rough collapsed around her nostrils and mouth. She coughed once, twice, and breathed slowly. That was better, no obstructions. But, something warned her to stay still.

She heard a man's voice say something in a Slavic-sounding language. She was fluent in German and French, conversational in Spanish, and had picked up some Arabic and Pashto during her travels to war zones, but this one she didn't know. Another voice, also a man's, spoke in the same language. Definitely Slavic.

She couldn't breathe too deeply, not just because of what she now concluded was a burlap bag over her head, but because her chest hurt. Trying to ignore the pain, she took stock of her immediate position. She was lying down on some sort of bed. No, a couch; she shifted slightly and felt the back of it on her left arm. She had to be careful, she didn't want to let her captors know she was conscious. Her hands were in front of her, wrists bound. Very slowly she moved her feet, just to get some feeling back in them, but also to find out if her ankles were bound. They were.

She was in an aircraft, of that she was certain. A jet, judging from the sound of the engines. Certainly not a commercial airliner.

The realization that she was in the air made her heart sink even more. They were on their way out of Italy. With a shock she realized that Libya was only a short flight away. One hour, maybe two. The pain in her chest intensified for a few harrowing moments, until she remembered that the men were not speaking Arabic. She had to force herself to think logically. Although they could still be heading south over the Mediterranean, it wouldn't be logical for Russians to be flying her there. No, they would be heading northeast.

But why? She struggled with the question, fought to control her breathing, to maintain the guise that she was still unconscious. They couldn't want her to squeeze a ransom out of someone. Her parents weren't wealthy, and she and Mark certainly were not. The BBC might pay a ransom, but….Sophie came to another conclusion. It wasn't about money. It was a political act. To make a statement? To draw attention? Maybe to force a prisoner exchange.

The voices were several feet away. She heard three distinct ones, all male. No, four. The fourth one sounded angry. The angry guy got into a heated exchange with another one, who sounded as if he was trying to be the voice of reason. Eventually the angry guy calmed down.

A door opened, a cabinet of some sort. There was some rummaging around and then she heard the beeping of a microwave oven, followed in seconds by the aroma of cooking food. Something spicy. Suddenly she was ravenously hungry. There was a crinkling sound, then someone gulping a drink, and she was thirsty. But still she did not move. It took every ounce of discipline she had.

Time went by. How much, she had no way of knowing. The

57

men were eating something, drinking, moving around the cabin. Most of the time they weren't very close to her. How big were the cabins of private jets? It had been a couple years since she'd been on one. Her employer, notoriously cheap, insisted that its people fly commercial. But she was sure she was in the back end of the cabin.

The men began settling down. Sophie heard snoring, then someone, the guy who'd calmed the angry one down before, gave an order. In a few seconds she sensed someone close to her, heard the sound of someone settling into a chair only a couple feet away. She hardly dared breathe.

Suddenly she realized she was no longer wearing the light leather jacket she'd had on in Capua, the jacket Mark had bought her in Istanbul. What else was she wearing? She struggled to remember what she'd changed into after the gladiator tour. Yes, she had on a light silk blouse, slacks, pumps. Nothing out of the ordinary. A small, logical part of her brain told her that it made no difference. Even if she were wearing a parka and three layers of wool shirts, she was still at their mercy.

She felt fingers tug at the top button of her blouse, and she couldn't suppress a shudder. The man's hand hesitated, then moved to the next button, and the next. She felt the hand slide underneath the fabric, over the skin between her breasts. The fingertips were rough, slightly calloused, making their way to the edge of her bra. It was white lace, demi cup, with the front clasp. Mark loved her in it, loved to flip that clasp–

The fingers found the clasp, stopped, examined it. She heard the man's breathing deepen. The voices behind him seemed to be paying no attention to him. The fingers tugged at the clasp, couldn't figure it out, hesitated, and then gave up. They worked their way up her left breast and found her nipple through the lace.

CAPUA, ITALY

The detective put down the phone and walked over to where Mark and Jim waited. The *carabinieri* station was small, smelling of smoke and sweat, with phones ringing and men and women bustling about. Jim thought it was pretty much like the precinct station houses he'd seen on American TV shows, only here everybody spoke Italian and they wore uniforms that would've been considered almost comic-opera elaborate back in the States.

It was a few minutes before ten o'clock, nearly four hours since Sophie had been taken. They'd been waiting here at the station, and Jim was sure Mark would consider them to be four of the longest hours of his life. At least Jim had spent some of them away from here. He'd followed Gina to the hospital in a police car, stayed at her side while they treated her cuts and bruises, and took her back to the hotel. He put her to bed and left her in the care of the Cunninghams, who insisted they would be fine while Jim went to help his brother.

"*Signor* Hayes," the detective said, "there has been a new development, and I am afraid it is not a good one."

"What do you mean?" Mark asked.

"A van matching the description of the one used in your wife's abduction was found at the airport thirty minutes ago. Nobody in the passenger terminals recognized her from the photographs we showed, but two service crewmen reported seeing someone being escorted by several men into a private jet."

"Oh, God," Jim said. It kept getting worse.

Mark swallowed, took a deep breath, and asked, "Were they sure it was her?"

"No, they did not see any faces and were several meters away. The light was not good, but they were fairly certain that one of the members of the party was not in command of his—or her—faculties. They assumed at first that the person may have been intoxicated, and his friends were taking him back to his aircraft."

"They didn't report it?" Jim asked.

"They had no reason to at first, signor," the cop said. "There had not been any sort of security alert. Only when airport security came around and found the van, did the workers tell what they saw."

"All right," Mark said, "where did the plane go?"

The detective sighed and shook his head. "I am afraid that we do not know. For sure, anyway."

Mark's hands balled into fists. "And what exactly does that mean?"

"The aircraft may have filed a false flight plan. We have reason to believe that the information the pilot gave us was, how you say it, bogus? The registration number he reported corresponds to an aircraft registered to a company from Napoli…Naples. But when we contacted the company, they assured us their aircraft never left its hangar this evening."

Mark clutched his head and took a couple steps away from them. Jim turned back to the detective. "I assume you're checking that out?"

"Of course. Our office in Naples is doing so even as we speak. But the company, it is of good reputation. I do not think they were involved."

Mark came back, barely holding in his anger. "So what did the airport radar show?"

"After the take-off, the plane turned to the east. The radar tracked them to the mountains, the Apennines, and then, gone."

"When did they take off?"

The detective checked his watch. "According to the control tower, nearly three hours ago."

Mark put his fingertips to his temple, as if he had a splitting headache. "A corporate jet can do five hundred miles an hour. They could be anywhere by now. Christ, they could be in North Africa!"

Jim placed a hand on his brother's shoulder. "Take it easy, Mark. Gina said the guy she fought didn't look Arabic."

The detective nodded. "Your brother is right, signor. The witnesses did not report anything indicating the assailants were terrorists."

Mark took a deep breath. "Sorry. I know you're doing your best," he said to the detective. "What about air traffic control? I know that flights here in Europe are passed off from one control center to another like back in the States."

"That is correct," the detective said, but to Jim he looked a little less confident than he sounded. "We have been in touch with Eurocontrol. The control center for Italy is Rome. They are searching through their data and I expect a report from them soon."

"Mark, why don't we go back to the hotel?" Jim looked at the detective. "I'm sure this gentleman will contact us as soon as he has any news."

"I most certainly will."

The lobby of Capys Capua was empty as they came through the entrance. Jim headed for the elevator, but Mark held back. "I'll be up in a few minutes," he said. He nodded toward the bar. "I've just gotta…"

"I know," Jim said. He knew his brother had been dealing with a tumultuous cascade of emotions over the past several hours. Hell, Jim had, too. He was very fond of Sophie, and the pain of her abduction was cutting into him.

He felt anger, too, at the men who had done this, whoever they were. And he had no doubt Mark's level of anger was several magnitudes higher than his. That could be dangerous, could drive a man to do something he shouldn't do.

"Will you be all right?" Jim asked. Even as he asked the question, Jim knew the answer. He'd seen that look in his brother's eyes before. Not the look of the confused, frightened husband from a few hours ago. No, this was the look Mark had displayed once or twice at work, when faced with a serious challenge. The look of a commander.

"I'll be fine," Mark said. "Go upstairs and check on your wife, Jim." He reached into his jacket pocket and pulled out his phone. "I'm going to be tending to mine."

The siren awakened Mark, ripping him from a nightmare. He had been back in Afghanistan, on patrol with his troops, and the village they entered was populated entirely by headless children. They walked silently as the horrified Americans dismounted from their vehicles and tried to help them. Mark followed one into a house, hoping to find the child's head, and indeed there was one on a table. It was Sophie's head, and as he watched, she began to cry, mouthing the words *Why didn't you save me?*

He staggered from the bed and pulled the curtains aside, looking down onto the street from his third-floor window. A police car was already three blocks away, receding into the distance, its blue lights flashing, the distinctive oscillating wail diminishing. He'd heard it countless times during his deployments, but tonight–this morning, really, his watch said 4:11 a.m.–it had a special meaning for him.

There were no messages on his phone, no light blinking on the hotel phone that sat silently on the desk. Mark tossed the cell phone back onto the desk and sat on the bed. He reached for the nearby lamp, then pulled his hand back. He really didn't want to see the empty bed. He could feel it, smell it.

The sheets still carried her scent, the special rose-and-lavender perfume he'd gotten her from a shop in Istanbul deep inside the Grand Bazaar. When was that, during their first trip together? No, that was to Mumbai, spring of '11, shortly after they'd met. Was that really a year and a half ago? He was visiting a British unit in Helmand Province, during what would be his final tour in Afghanistan, and she was embedded with the regiment, filing reports for BBC. He was in the mess hall and saw her sitting alone, poking at her shepherd's pie. She wore no makeup, had her brown hair put up in a tight bun, but she was still beautiful, wearing a long-sleeved olive drab tee shirt that looked like it was made for her, accentuating certain parts of a very nice figure. A British lieutenant had noticed the same thing and was moving in for the empty seat across from her, but Mark gave him a look that was universal among soldiers and the lieutenant reluctantly chose another chair.

She'd busted him right away. After he introduced himself, she said, "Sophie Barton, BBC, and these, as you have undoubtedly noticed because I saw you staring at them, are my girls, as you Americans say. But I prefer the French, *la tétine.* More elegant, wouldn't you agree?" He had no idea what to say to that, and began to rise, face reddening, before she laughed and asked him to stay.

Their romance moved quickly after that, as quickly as it reasonably could considering they were in a war zone. They saw each other when they could and discovered they had much in common, including previous marriages that had foundered on the shoals of their careers. Unlike Mark, she was childless; his son Eddie lived with his mother back in the States. Their lovemaking was alternately tender and ferocious, driven by the knowledge that the next day, perhaps even the next hour, could find one or both of them gone, blown apart by an IED or drilled by a Taliban bullet. But they'd survived, and when she brought him home to London to meet her parents in the fall, he proposed and she accepted.

That particular campaign had been one of the most arduous of Mark's life. First he had to find a ring, then ask her mother discreetly about Sophie's favorite places. Finally there was the maneuvering that brought them to the Carlton Tavern. They were at a cozy table, and she was telling him how it was the only building on the street to survive the Blitz when he motioned to the window. When she looked back there was the ring, sitting in its opened box in front of her.

Now he might never see her again. Mark lowered his face to her pillow, drinking in the scent. The memory of their sleepy sex, just twenty-some hours before, came washing back over him. He saw her hair splayed over the pillow as she smiled up at him, felt her legs around him, heard her cry of joy. For the first time since this horrible nightmare started, he let the tears come.

CHAPTER SEVEN
ROME, ITALY

J im reached forward from the back seat and tapped his brother
on the shoulder. "At a time like this," Jim said, "it's nice to have
friends."

Mark nodded. "It's nice anytime."

The gates of the British Embassy opened up after Paul
Cunningham had a word with the guards and passports were
examined and returned. The SAS veteran slipped back behind the
wheel of the rented Alfa Romeo and drove them into the compound, leaving the traffic of Via Palestro behind them. On any
other day, Jim would have paid close attention to the hundreds of
cars, some of them so small they seemed like toys. Fleets of
motorcycles weaved their way through the traffic in flagrant
contradiction of every traffic law known to man, or at least to
Americans. But, he noted the riders were all wearing helmets.

Jim had dreamed all his life of visiting Rome, and here he was,
but right now he wished he was home, back in his tidy house in
small town Wisconsin, with his wife puttering in the kitchen,
putting the finishing touches on yet another excellent meal. If this
was a Sunday—and why not, it was his daydream, he could make
it any day he wanted—he'd be parked in front of the TV, trying not
to openly question the play-calling of the Packers' coach. After the

game, win or lose, he and Gina would enjoy their meal, then maybe go for a walk. Later they'd snuggle in front of the tube again, watching a movie, before heading to bed.

Gina wasn't here, though, not in this car. She was back at the hotel they'd checked into a couple hours ago, with Evelyn Cunningham keeping her company. Jim's wife was in better shape than she had a right to be after getting her first taste of street combat the night before, but even though she protested loudly and threw in a few colorful Italian phrases, Jim had put his foot down and insisted she stay at the hotel. He'd almost said something to the effect that the men would take care of this one, but fortunately he'd held that back. Gina had acquitted herself in Capua as well as any man could've done and better than most. Were it not for her injuries, Jim wouldn't have been opposed to bringing her along.

But the military men were running this operation now, and even though they were technically ex-military, Jim was seeing another side of Paul Cunningham this morning, with his brother matching him step for step. Over the past few hours this crisis had shifted, at least as far as the Hayes and Cunningham men were concerned. It was no longer a street crime to be investigated and resolved by the police. This was an army operation now, and the soldiers were in charge. In that respect, Jim knew he was lucky to be along.

Another security guard directed them to a parking space. Jim was happy to get out of the cramped car, even though it meant hearing the cracking of his knees as he stood and stretched his legs.

A man in British Army utilities emerged from a doorway, offering a smile when he saw Paul. Hand extended, he came forward. "Colonel, it's nice to see you again, although I wish it were under better circumstances."

Paul took the hand and gave it a firm shake. "I can't thank you enough for your assistance, old man." He turned to the Americans to make the introductions. "Gentlemen, this is Lieutenant Colonel Simon Westlake. Simon, my friends Colonel Mark Hayes, U.S. Army, retired, and his brother Jim Hayes."

"A pleasure," Westlake said. Handshakes were exchanged. "We have a briefing room prepared in our secure section. Colonel Hayes, I think you might know our other guest today."

"Who would that be?" Mark asked.

Westlake just smiled. "He asked that his name not be mentioned, as he is here unofficially, but he did authorize me to say that you should recognize him from your last deployment."

In a trip that was full of firsts, this was another one for Jim. He'd never been inside an embassy before. Mark, on the other hand, looked right at home as the brothers followed the two Brits through a warren of elegantly decorated hallways and offices. The Union Jack was on display, although not as obviously as Jim suspected Old Glory would be in an American embassy, and he saw at least three portraits of Queen Elizabeth.

The number of personnel in uniform increased as they entered an area marked by a sign as the military attaché section. In addition to British flag patches on shoulders, Jim saw those from other countries, including a few Americans. Many of the people they passed nodded at Westlake, and a few recognized Cunningham with smiles and waves.

They came to a heavy door marked only as CONFERENCE 2—SECURE, and Westlake slid a card through a wall-mounted reader. A light above the device changed from red to green and the door swung inward with a slight hiss. Inside was a rectangular table surrounded by eight chairs. A red-haired woman in civilian clothes sat at the far end, tapping on a laptop computer, and standing next to her was a man with short-cropped blonde hair, wearing utilities in an unfamiliar camouflage pattern, a maroon beret tucked under an epaulet on his left shoulder. He was leaning on the table, studying the computer screen, and when he stood up Jim knew this was a highly trained man. Such men carried themselves a certain way, exuding what was almost an aura. Jim had seen it before when he'd trained with top martial artists back in the States, and among the CIA personnel he'd worked with a year ago. This guy was someone not to be trifled with, and Jim was glad to see the man's eyes sparkle with recognition as he saw Mark. Thank God he's on our side, Jim thought.

For the first time in what seemed like days, but was really only a dozen hours or so, Mark felt a tinge of hope. The man in front of him was one of the most impressive people he'd ever worked with. If Captain John Krieger was here, powerful people with a lot of resources had heard about Sophie's kidnaping and were standing ready to help.

But it wasn't "Captain" anymore, as Mark recognized the insignia on the uniform. He extended a hand. "I see it's Major Krieger now," he said. "Congratulations."

Krieger's grip was strong and his tight grin betrayed as much emotion as Mark was likely to see. "Colonel Hayes, it is good to see you again, although I would have preferred if it were for a more enjoyable reason." The slight German accent was still there, and so was the impressive physique that was hardly hidden by the man's uniform. He looked like something right off a recruiting poster.

"Damn glad to see you, Major." Mark made introductions, identifying Krieger only as being with NATO. Paul Cunningham had almost certainly heard of Krieger's outfit, the special operations force known as Unit 7, but as far as Mark knew it was still a clandestine branch of the NATO military, something Jim wasn't authorized to know. As the visitors took seats on one side of the table, Mark added, "I'm glad my calls last night were productive."

"It is not every day that our headquarters gets a call from the director of the CIA," Krieger said. "Fortunately, I was on a training exercise in the Alps when I got word from Brussels to conduct your briefing. Colonel Westlake and his staff have been of great assistance."

Westlake had taken one of the three empty seats on the other side of the table. Behind him, a flat-screen TV mounted on the wall came alive with a map of southern Europe. "Your situation has a high degree of political sensitivity," he said.

"How so?" Jim asked.

"Colonel Hayes' wife is a citizen of the U.K., so of course our embassy here stands ready to provide whatever assistance we can. Complicating matters is her position as a BBC journalist, and a rather well-known one at that, adding a strong possibility that her abduction has political overtones." He nodded at Mark. "I understand that the CIA director is your former commanding officer, Colonel?"

"That's right," Mark said. The General, as Mark would forever know him, had given Mark command of Camp Roosevelt, in the mountains of eastern Afghanistan, about eighteen months ago. The command was a fine cap to Mark's career in the Army, and his close relationship with the General also had allowed Mark to participate in some important covert missions during his tour, including the one with Krieger and his unit into Iran. Mark suspected that little adventure, productive as it was, would be classified for a long time to come.

Westlake continued. "We were authorized by London to tap into NATO's air defense network in an effort to track the aircraft used by your wife's abductors. It is, as you might surmise, somewhat more thorough than the civilian system maintained by Eurocontrol. We were fortunate that one of your Navy's Aegis cruisers, USS *Shiloh*, was in the Adriatic, heading south after a courtesy call at the Italian naval base in Brindisi. Between the air defense net and *Shiloh*'s radar, we were successful in locating the aircraft."

Mark's eyes narrowed. "Where did it go?"

Krieger was holding a remote control and pressed a button. On the screen, a pulsing red dot appeared over a spot in Italy between Rome and Naples. "The jet had turned off its transponder," he said. "That is illegal, of course, even for a military aircraft operating in this airspace, but our methods of detection take that possibility into account. It is something our Russian friends sometimes do when they decide to test our defenses in the Baltic area. The target aircraft's flight path was recorded."

A red line began moving eastward from the dot, turned to the north when it was over the Adriatic, made landfall at the coast of Croatia and came to a stop in another country Mark recognized immediately, causing the hair on the back of his neck to stand up. "Serbia," he said.

"That is correct," Krieger confirmed. "To be more precise, a small airfield outside Belgrade. The jet landed there at 8:12 p.m. Zulu, or 9:12 local time."

"The director has ordered his people to liase with MI6 on this matter," Westlake said. "In my posting here, you might say I work rather closely with that office."

"Simon, you always wanted to be another Ian Fleming," Paul said.

"I have enough of that work to suit me, and I still get to go out into the field with the lads every now and then," Westlake said. "Between the two agencies, we were able to come up with this." He nodded to Krieger, who pressed the button on the remote.

The screen shifted to an image like ones Mark had seen many times before. Infrared satellite imagery, taken from what he assumed was one of CIA's KH-11 "Keyhole" birds. He knew from his work on the General's staff, before going to Roosevelt, that the outfit sometimes known sarcastically in the military as Christians In Action routinely surveilled Eastern Europe and the Balkans, even though all of those nations, outside of Russia's borders anyway, were now either NATO members or leaning in that direction. Every now and then the surveillance got a little too personal with certain parties, but the birds were always up there, well above the political fray.

"Is that the airport where they landed?" Jim asked.

"Yes," Krieger said. The orange shape was clearly that of a small jet, in front of a hangar. "This image was taken approximately thirty minutes after the aircraft landed. Unfortunately, we were not able to track any vehicles that might have been used to transport the subject into the city. However, when we compared this imagery to daylight shots from previous dates, we were able to identify the hangar and the aircraft itself." The screen changed to a crystal-clear view of the airport from virtually the same angle as the nighttime shot, and the jet on the tarmac had the same look as the orange silhouette.

Another shot appeared, from a slightly different angle, and the camera zoomed in on the aircraft, enlarging it to the point where it almost filled the screen. Mark saw three men, one coming down the short steps from the cabin to the runway, another pushing a cart, a third fueling the aircraft with a hose leading from a truck. The jet's registration number was clearly visible.

"I'm betting that number's not the same one the Italians saw on the jet last night," Mark said.

"Indeed it is not," Westlake said. "It is, we think, the authentic registration of the aircraft." He looked at Mark, then at Jim. "Colonel Hayes, the rest of the information we have for you is classified at a higher level of security clearance than we would normally allow for civilians to access. However, I was told that the director personally vouched for you, and for your brother. MI6 has cleared Colonel Cunningham, but I must tell you, gentlemen, that before we proceed I will require assurances that what we are about to discuss is not to be disclosed to anyone outside this room." He reached into a file and produced three documents, sliding one to each of the three visitors. "I shall need your signatures on these non-disclosure agreements."

"Understood," Mark said immediately. Paul and Jim added their agreement and each signed, passing a pen around between them. When Westlake had the documents back in his folder, he nodded to Krieger.

The NATO officer held his thumb over the button. "The aircraft is registered to a company owned and operated by this man, who I believe made your acquaintance some years ago, Colonel." He pressed the button and a photograph appeared on the screen.

The room was silent for two seconds, three, then Mark sat back in his chair as recognition flooded through him. "Oh, shit," he said.

CHAPTER EIGHT
GROCKA MUNICIPALITY, SERBIA

On any other occasion, Sophie would have said that the room was comfortable. In fact, the only thing keeping it from seeming like most other three-star hotel rooms she'd inhabited were the bars on the windows. Just one more part of this nightmare from which she couldn't seem to wake up.

The bars didn't inhibit her ability to observe her surroundings, and she had forced her fear back into a corner of her mind while her journalism training took over. She tried to observe and catalog everything. The smallest detail could prove important, even life-saving. As such, she had thoroughly explored the room and its adjacent bathroom, noting the surveillance camera built into the molding in one corner of the bedroom. She had no doubt it had a wide-angle lens that would capture everything that happened in the room. They had, however, overlooked one thing, and there would be a way for her to take advantage of that. She just had to figure out how.

Her captors had brought her here in the middle of the night, keeping the bag on her head until she was in the room. There was no clock to be found and they'd taken her wristwatch, but fortunately it was a relatively cheap knockoff she'd bought on a whim at an Egyptian bazaar. If these people thought they could get serious money for a fake Breitling at the local pawn shop, they might get a surprise. It would be one small victory for her.

She'd forced herself to get some sleep, awakening shortly after dawn. They were in the country, and it certainly didn't look like North Africa. This room was in a corner of the house, on the ground floor. She knew there was at least one other story because she'd heard footsteps above her. One window looked to the east, and she could see low mountains not too far away. The other window faced north, and there was a large river about a mile in the distance. She was able to judge the directions by observing the shadows of the trees on the grounds, which extended at least a hundred yards northward from the building. There were no roads to be seen, however, at least from this room.

Sophie sat on the double bed and stared at the bathroom. When she'd awakened, she answered nature's call, had no choice really. There was a bathtub with a shower, but as far as bathing, the only thing she'd done so far was to carefully wash her left breast. There was no mark from where the man on the plane had touched it, but it still felt unclean to her, even now. Who knows what else the man might've done if one of the others hadn't yelled at him?

She had to force herself to stay calm, stay away from thinking about all the hostage situations she'd heard about in recent years, even the handful of survivors she'd interviewed. Just about a year ago she'd had a conversation with Lara Logan, the CBS reporter who had been assaulted and nearly killed in Cairo. What had happened to Logan, and to other women she'd talked to, was unspeakable.

But Sophie didn't have to go there yet. Mark would come for her.

She knew she'd have to hold onto that. Her husband was the most disciplined, most honorable man she'd ever met. She'd fallen for him almost at first sight, loving how she felt with him: not just sexy and loved and desired, but safe, protected. It was horribly old-fashioned, she knew, but right now that feeling, that sure knowledge that her husband was hunting for her, was what she needed to sustain her, to endure what was to come.

And what would come? This place she was in, everything indicated she was dealing with civilized men. They could've raped her on the plane. They hadn't, and had stopped the one of their number who had touched her. But there were no guarantees. What had happened on the plane could happen again, could be a lot worse. Mark would get her out of here, she knew that with a certainty deep in her soul, but even when she was safe and alone with him, would his touch remove the last of the filth that was already there, and that which was to come? Could it?

Her next breath came in a great sob, and she buried her face in her hands.

ROME, ITALY

Jim had felt like the odd man out since they'd entered the embassy. It was a feeling he often had on the job these days, when he was working with so many people who'd accumulated years of military and police experience. He had never worn the uniform, and thus wasn't one of them, not a member of the tribe. Many of them knew his story, some had even read the book, but their respect had to be earned. Usually that meant earning it the old-fashioned way, on the mat. When they saw he could handle himself, even with men half his age, they started paying attention.

And now, here he was again, the outsider. The military men in the room all knew who the man in the photograph was. His brother's visceral reaction told Jim that sometime in the past Mark had encountered this man, and it hadn't gone well. He was a dangerous man, clearly, who was involved in Sophie's kidnapping. That meant he was also involved in the beating of Jim's wife, and so Jim had as much skin in this game as anybody else. It was time to make sure they all knew that.

He had to use just the right amount of forcefulness along with tact. "I'm assuming this guy has a name," he said, brushing aside the worry that his tone might have taken it one step too far. The Brit officer had been courteous to him, but Jim couldn't get a read on the German, although Mark clearly held him in high regard. Krieger's ice-blue eyes narrowed slightly, but Jim didn't flinch.

"As a matter of fact, he does," Krieger said. "Darko Novak, the head of a security firm known as Red Dragon Limited. The company is based in Belgrade." The screen split, with a logo appearing in the window next to the photo. Jim's marketing experience told him that whoever Novak had employed to create it knew their stuff. The dragon motif was subtle and yet carried a message of strength and confidence that could not be mis-understood.

"I ran into his outfit a couple times when I was with the regiment," Paul said. "A very tough lot, they were."

78

The company logo was replaced by another one, this one a shield-shaped emblem featuring a snarling wolf inside a wreath of oak leaves. Red, white and blue ribbons tied the wreath at the bottom. "Novak served in the Yugoslav Army in the 1980s," Krieger said. "In 1991 he transferred over to a new unit within their state security service. They became known as the Ninjas, and wore a distinctive red beret."

Westlake consulted a notepad in front of him. "Novak was decorated by the unit and promoted after his actions in the battle for Glina, a small town in Croatia, in the summer of '91. According to the transcript of his war crimes trial, Novak was responsible for the summary execution of at least eleven Croatian police officers."

"I did not have time to prepare any visuals about the Balkan War," Krieger said. "It was a chaotic time indeed. Many died."

"Historically, this particular version is known as the Third Balkan War," Westlake added. "It began with the breakup of the Yugoslav Federation in '91. The individual republics began to declare independence from the central government in Belgrade, which was dominated by ethnic Serbs. First Slovenia, which was able to separate after a short conflict. Croatia's was a much more difficult and costly endeavor. Eventually the fight over Bosnia and Kosovo escalated to the point where NATO became involved."

"And you were over there, Mark?" Jim said.

"Yes, I was," his brother said, staring at the photo of Novak. "I went in with my unit as part of KFOR, Kosovo Force. We arrived in country early in June of '99. The Serbs were starting their withdrawal from Kosovo. Our job was to make sure they left without killing anybody along the way."

"Britain actually had the majority of troops within KFOR, didn't they, Simon?" Paul asked.

"That's right," Westlake said. "Germany was second in terms of troops deployed, just ahead of the U.S. numbers." He looked at his notes again. "We are dealing with hard men indeed, gentlemen. In 1996, Novak's paramilitary unit was incorporated into a special operations force, supposedly under the control of SDB, the Yugoslav state security service. The acronym for the new outfit was JSO. It was disbanded in 2003 after some of its officers were implicated in the assassination of the Serbian prime minister."

"Was Novak involved in that?" Jim asked. "You said he'd been tried for war crimes."

"That was for his alleged actions at Glina," Westlake said. "The ICTY, the International Criminal Tribunal for the former Yugoslavia, was established by the UN in 1993. It has completed most of its work, although there are a handful of defendants whose cases are still on appeal, and one or two yet to be tried. Novak was arrested in 2000, tried at The Hague a year later, and acquitted. Insufficient evidence, apparently."

"He is not innocent," Krieger said. "He was responsible for more deaths after Glina. My unit's commanding officer asked NATO for permission to dispose of him at least twice. The requests were denied."

"Well, that's a shock," Mark said. "So, everything points to this guy having ordered Sophie's kidnaping. But why?"

Krieger's eyebrows raised. "You did not know, Colonel?" He glanced at Cunningham.

Paul took a deep breath, then said, "The action in '99, when my lads rescued you, Mark. The sergeant who was in charge of you was Novak's younger brother."

Mark sat back, looked away from the screen, and finally said, "He was killed in the firefight."

"Yes," Paul said. "If I recall, my sniper took him out. MacGregor, a Scot and the best marksman in the regiment."

Mark shook his head. "His brother had probably radioed ahead that they were bringing in an American officer as a prisoner. Novak got a good look at me just before the firefight started. No wonder he blames me."

Jim leaned forward, elbows on the table. "All right, so this guy hates your guts, Mark, because he holds you responsible for his brother's death. He's probably been laying for you all this time. He has Sophie somewhere in Serbia. We can notify the police there, they can—"

Paul barked a bitter laugh. "You don't know these people, Jim. Novak has probably bought off half the Belgrade police force."

"By the time we get the diplomats involved, she'll be dead," Mark said. "Novak just wants me. It's only a matter of time before I hear from him. All right, then, I'll accommodate him and we'll settle this. But not on his terms."

"You're not going in there alone," Jim said.

"Unfortunately, Colonel," Krieger said, "I am quite limited as to what assistance I can provide. There are some electronic assets I can tap into, now that we know where Novak's headquarters is, but as far as operators to assist you on the ground, I'm afraid—"

"I meant me."

Mark's head whipped around. "You're not going anywhere

near Serbia," he said to Jim.

"In case you forgot, my wife just got out of the hospital. His men put her there. They could've killed her. There's no way I'm not going in with you."

"We'll discuss this later," Mark said.

"Screw that, little brother," Jim said. "You're in charge back home at the office, but over here, we're partners."

Paul must have sensed what was coming. When they left the secure room, he said, "There are a couple gents I want to say hello to while we're here. I'll catch up with you lads at the car."

Mark was glad to hear that. Some things needed to be said and he wanted to keep this just between him and his brother. He led the way through the corridors, then suddenly stopped when they came to an empty sitting room. "In here," he said, jerking his head that way. Once inside, he faced Jim.

He took a breath to collect himself, then looked up at his big brother. Jim had always been the taller one, by a couple inches maybe, but Mark had always thought of himself as the tougher one. It was more than just all the football he'd played in high school and at the Academy, more than the near-constant physical training he'd undergone during his Army career. Yes, Jim was an accomplished martial artist and Mark respected him for that, but the operation Mark would soon be mounting would be dangerous and he had no time for amateurs.

"All right, I'll make this clear," he said. "You're not going to Serbia, Jim. It'll be me and a few men, experienced men. OSS has a team over here right now, a joint project we're doing with a firm in

Switzerland. I can have them here inside of twelve hours. I might also see if Paul can tap into his network for some ex-SAS guys who have experience in the Balkans."

"A hostage rescue operation, right?"

"Yes, of course. And–"

"Well, tell me," Jim interrupted, "in a hostage rescue op, is it standard procedure to have the husband of the principal in command? Or even along for the ride?"

Mark felt his anger rising and fought to suppress it. "This isn't open for debate. I'm in charge, it's my call."

But Jim wasn't backing down. "Suppose it had been Gina kidnapped and Sophie just beaten up. Would I be the one in charge then?"

"No, of course not." Seeing his brother about to erupt, Mark held up a hand. "Look, Jim, this is something that has to be done by people who know what they're doing. We're going into a potentially hostile country after a highly trained man who has a proven record of criminal activity. He'll be on his own turf, and he has plenty of resources to call on. And I won't be able to rely on getting help from anybody in Belgrade."

"For God's sake, Mark, you're talking about sending a squad of armed men into a foreign country after a guy who probably has half the government bought off. The more I think about it, the more it sounds like a kamikaze mission."

"Yet you want to come along on it."

"I've had some experience in tight spots overseas, Mark. Not in a hostage rescue operation, but I wasn't exactly playing gin rummy over in Somalia." Jim paused, then said, "We've been apart for too long. We...we missed out on so much together. Growing up, then later on. You in the Army, me doing my thing." He hesitated, took a breath, then said, "I only got my little brother back a year ago. If I lose you again, when I could've been there to help you, I'd never forgive myself." His eyes glistened.

In spite of himself, Mark felt himself tearing up, too. Before this last twenty-four hours, he hadn't cried since their father's funeral. He blinked, then said, "You know what Dad would say, if he was here right now?"

Jim smiled. Ed Hayes had been a Korean War vet, a no-nonsense guy who wasn't afraid to get his hands dirty, to take on responsibility. It was his juice, like it was for almost every other guy of that generation. "He would've said it was time to kick ass and take names, like he did before every Packer game."

"Yeah," Mark said, "but this isn't football." It certainly wasn't. Lives were at stake, but Mark had spent the better part of the past quarter century making decisions like this. He'd never given an order that he knew for sure would result in one of his own men losing his life, but there was always that possibility, even on training missions. And some of the men he'd given those orders to had indeed not come back.

Could he give an order like that to his only brother? Mark knew that Jim could handle himself. His CIA operation in Somalia had proven that Jim was far more skilled than the average civilian, and he hadn't folded under pressure, either. So what if he didn't have a uniform hanging in his closet back home, no medals, no citations? Mark had known more than a few men in uniform with plenty of those and they hadn't been worth a tinker's damn in combat.

What had been building up inside Mark since he'd left the conference room came to a head. He'd spent the past twenty-five years taking on responsibility, doing the tough jobs, defending the innocent against the bad guys. Now, one of them had his wife. Mark had to go in and get her. There was no choice about that. But he also knew, now, that he couldn't do it alone, not with so much at stake. Jim was right. Mark's emotional investment in this mission was like nothing he'd dealt with before. He would need more than just a few guys with guns. He would need someone to help him keep his eye on the ball.

He placed a hand on his brother's shoulder. "Okay. I guess I'll need an executive officer on this op. Are you up for it? Things are liable to get pretty ugly over there."

"We've both seen it before," Jim said. "Lead the way."

CHAPTER NINE
GROCKA MUNICIPALITY, SERBIA

Sophie had just finished dressing after her shower when there was a knock on the door. She heard a key move in the lock and the door swung open, revealing two well-built men, one with a drawn pistol.

The men were definitely not Middle Eastern, and a small wave of relief washed through her. Like most Western journalists, she dreaded being captured in a war zone by men who quite likely had little respect for Westerners and even less for Western women. But she also knew that while these men might be Europeans, that didn't guarantee anything. She knew from experience that Europeans, like people anywhere, were capable of atrocities just as much as those from other regions. Her own grandfather had served with Britain's 11th Armored Division and his tank was one of the first to roll through the gates of the Bergen-Belsen concentration camp in April 1945. Just before he died, he told his granddaughter about what he'd seen. As much horror as Sophie had witnessed on her assignments to the Middle East and Afghanistan, those people were still in League One compared to the Premier League-level Nazis, who'd been as European as people could be.

"Mrs. Hayes, please come with us," the unarmed man said, in English.

She chose this moment to make her first show of defiance. A small one, but enough, perhaps, to send a message. "It is Ms. Barton-Hayes, if you please."

The man blinked, sending a thrill down her spine, but the second one gestured with his gun.

She followed the first man down a hallway, the one with the gun behind her. She hadn't taken three steps from her room before the aroma hit her. Eggs, and...kippers? Yes. In spite of herself, she felt a hunger pang.

She forced herself to study the man leading the way. Mid-thirties, average height, dressed casually in slacks, sport jacket, open-collared shirt. He moved easily, with the athletic grace and confidence Sophie had seen so often in military men. Behind her, the man with the gun was similar, although perhaps a few years older. She'd also noticed that he was a good two steps behind, guarding against the possibility that she might try to attack him. Mark had taught her two different ways to disarm a man poking a handgun into her back, but that wouldn't work now. So, in just a few seconds she'd had a chance to evaluate the men, and therefore come to some early conclusions about the people in charge. They were professionals, probably not inclined to hurt their captive, unless she refused to cooperate.

The first man came to an open doorway and turned to face her, gesturing for her to go inside. She entered a dining room. An expensive mahogany table, surrounded by eight chairs, dominated the room. Table settings had been placed at one end and to its left. A man stood behind the chair at the head. Sophie stopped when she was still several feet away.

"Good morning, Mrs. Hayes," the man said.

"It's–"

He waved, as if brushing away a fly. "Please, I prefer that name. I'm aware of your professional name. It's cumbersome and needlessly, what is the word? Feminist."

His English was perfect, but with a distinct Balkan accent. She stood still, taking his measure. An inch or two over six feet, well-built, dressed in gray pants and jacket that looked well-tailored, over a black shirt. The top two buttons were unfastened, and a sprig of black and silver hair curled over the third button. His face was nondescript except for the neatly-trimmed salt-and-pepper beard and mustache, and his green eyes stared out below bushy eyebrows. He took a step over to the chair on the left, and as he pulled it back she could see a signet ring on his left pinky.

Sophie also knew, in a moment that threatened to cut through her brave front, that being allowed to see the man's face was not a good sign, not at all.

"Please, be seated," he said. "I know you must be hungry."

She rallied, determined not to show fear. "I shall pass on breakfast, thank you."

All that brought was an empty smile. "Really, Mrs. Hayes, let's be reasonable, shall we? There are certain matters we must discuss, and as it is this time of the day, and neither of us has eaten, I have had a breakfast prepared for us. There is no reason we cannot be civilized about this."

"Since when is kidnaping a civilized act?"

His eyes narrowed slightly, and she knew instinctively that this was a man who could not be intimidated. "You have one chance to leave this place alive, madam, and that is to cooperate with me. If you choose not to, then I will have Dalibor take you back to your room. You will stay there, and when I have concluded my business and you are of no further use to me, I will have him kill you. But he will take his time. He and his men might find other things to do with you first. I'm sure you would find that most unpleasant, to put it mildly."

Sophie knew what that meant, and it triggered a stab of fear that seemed to pierce to her very essence. Of course she had known that rape might be possible, had even expected it on the plane, but now it suddenly became much more real. She swallowed, but tried to maintain a brave front. "So much for being civilized," she said, unable to keep a tremor from her voice.

"The choice is yours," he said. He stepped away from the empty chair.

After a moment's hesitation, she walked around the table and took her seat. Her appetite, however, was gone.

ROME, ITALY

Jim gazed out the window of their hotel suite, trying to appreciate the architectural wonder that was St. Peter's Basilica, just a few blocks away. They'd deliberately chosen the Atlante Garden for its proximity to the Vatican, and right about now–his watch showed it was nearly one o'clock–they should've been in the midst of their tour of the Vatican Museum. He'd heard so much about the Sistine Chapel, but it would have to wait for another trip. In his suite next door, Mark was on his phone, setting up the mission to Belgrade. He hoped to leave no later than midnight.

Jim wasn't so lost in thought that he didn't sense movement behind him. The hand on his shoulder was gentle, and when he turned he saw his wife's bruised, swollen face. She'd never been more beautiful, as far as he was concerned, because she was here, and she was alive.

"We'll be back, *mi tesoro*," Gina said.

"I know," he said, circling his arm around her waist, pulling her close. She was so unlike his late first wife in so many ways; Gina was fiery and passionate, while Suzy had been more reserved and gentle. But he was a different man now than he was in college, when he'd met Suzy. So much had changed since that terrible day when she died in his arms. He was stronger now, physically, thanks to his endless training, and he was also harder emotionally. Sometimes that bothered him. When he was with Gina, though, he felt a passion that he had thought would never fill him again.

"Our next trip here, I will show you Rome," Gina said, leaning against him. "It will just be the two of us. We will explore the city, we will dine at fine restaurants, and when we are back in our room we will *fare l'amore appassionato*."

Jim's Italian was far from fluent, but he'd heard that phrase enough to know exactly what it meant. The heat it usually built up within him, though, was tamped back now. Making love was the last thing on his mind. He hugged her close. "That'll be great," he said. "But in the meantime–"

Mark came into their suite through the connecting door, and was looking at his phone. "We need to get moving," he said.

"Did you hear from Sophie?" Jim asked.

"Not yet," Mark said. "But I just got a call from Krieger. Remember he told us he could possibly hustle up some electronic surveillance on Novak?"

"He got something that quickly?" Jim was a little surprised, but far from astonished. Since joining OSS he'd been learning a lot about how companies, and governments, could intercept cell phone calls and data.

"It's actually from Westlake and MI6," Mark said. "He didn't tell me the particulars, but I'm sure it's from a program called BADASS. British and Canadian intelligence have been using it for years to gather smart phone voice and data. As a matter of course, they keep an eye on the Serbs. They got a hit from Novak's personal phone two hours ago."

"And?"

"One of his men is here in Rome, apparently finishing up a job that the guys in Capua last night had to drop when they got their new mission. He's at a bank right now."

Jim felt his heart start to speed up and he fought to stay calm. "Our team is en route from Switzerland?" he asked.

Mark checked his watch. "Their flight leaves Zurich in two hours, so they won't be here in time. It's up to us, Jim. We've got to get to that guy. He knows Novak's layout. Probably has a good idea where they'd take her, what we can expect there."

"What bank?" Gina asked.

Mark looked at his phone. "Banca D'Italia, on Via Nazionale."

"I know where it is," Gina said. "Right across from Teatro Eliseo, a theater. I saw some shows there when I was at university."

"How far away?" Mark asked.

"Twenty minutes perhaps, depending on traffic."

Mark looked at her, then said, "You know the route, and you know how to drive in Rome. You're at the wheel."

"Now, wait a minute," Jim said. "She's still–"

"We are wasting time," Gina said. She headed for the door.

CHAPTER TEN
ROME, ITALY

Gina hardly looked at the traffic as she gunned the engine. The Fiat almost leaped out of the hotel parking lot and into the street, swerved to avoid a motorcyclist and turned left onto Via Crescenzio. Mark was thankful they'd rented the 500X model, the biggest Fiat available, with seating for four and a strong engine. Not quite in the same league as his Ford Explorer back home, but it would do.

A block and a half from the hotel, they turned right, then left two blocks later onto Via Giovanni Vitelleschi. Ahead, Mark could see the imposing hulk of Castel Sant'Angelo, once the tomb of a Roman emperor. Mark couldn't recall which one, but he remembered reading somewhere that the tomb had been desecrated by the Visigoths during their sack of the city. And the Visigoths, he knew, had come from somewhere in what was now Bulgaria, not too far from Serbia. The invaders had undoubtedly taken a lot of Roman women as prisoners. Their descendants were still at it, although these days they were only taking one at a time.

He felt a tap on his shoulder. "What's the plan, Mark?" Jim asked.

Mark could hear the skepticism in his brother's voice. "The plan is to get this guy to someplace secure and have a conversation with him," Mark said.

"And we're just going to grab him off the street? Are you–"

"Relax, Jim." He held up his phone. "Westlake is sending a team from his embassy, but he needs time to cut through the red tape. Our job is to tail this character and make sure he doesn't get to the airport or train station."

"Who is this Westlake?" Gina asked, expertly swinging the Fiat around a slow-moving pickup truck.

Mark filled her in quickly, checked his phone again, and then added, "Since Sophie is a British subject, Westlake thought he could bend the rules a little and make an end run around the caribinieri. Fortunately, the guy we're after is a foreign national, so our Italian friends can usually be persuaded to look the other way for something like this."

"Well, that's good news," Jim said from the back seat. "The last thing we need is an international incident. Before the one we're liable to get into in Serbia, that is."

Mark shot a glance over his shoulder, but said nothing. His phone chirped with a text message. "The Brits have a team of four ready to move when we've spotted the Serb," Mark said. "When this is all over, I'm gonna owe Westlake more than a couple beers."

"This guy we're looking for, do we know what he looks like?" Jim asked.

"Not yet," Mark said, "but Westlake is working on that. MI6 has a pretty extensive database. I'd imagine that right now they're checking on Serbian nationals who entered Italy in the past few days."

"Let's hope they are quick," Gina said. "The bank is only about ten minutes away."

Pedja Kopanja kept a very close eye on the Italian gangster, which was not easy to do with so many beautiful women around to distract him. The bank's lobby was well-appointed and comfortable. In deference to the Italian, Kopanja did not accompany him to the desk of the functionary who would handle the wire transfer. All the Serb had to do was get the receipt from the gangster before leaving the bank. A piece of cake.

All in all, Kopanja thought, this operation had gone quite well. So well that Dalibor had no qualms about leaving him in Rome to complete the job while he and the rest of the team headed south to Capua. What were they doing down there anyway? Dalibor had been silent about that, telling the men who went with him that he would fill them in on the way. All he said was that it was an urgent order from Colonel Novak back in Belgrade. That was good enough for Kopanja. He'd worked for Red Dragon for three years now, ever since his discharge from the Army. This work wasn't quite as exciting as jumping out of airplanes, as he'd done in Special Brigade, but it paid a hell of a lot more.

He expected no trouble today. The Italians had been cooperative, although they'd required some persuasion. That had come in the form of a photograph showing the teenage son of Salvatore Bastianini, a *capo* in the Altieri family of *La Cosa Nostra*, bound and gagged with a gun pointed at his head. Kopanja had been the one holding the gun. Fortunately, the photo did not show him past his elbow. The Italians had long memories.

No worries, though. The Red Dragon men were experienced in this type of operation. A few days of surveillance was all it took to formulate an effective plan. Dealing with the boy's bodyguards had been child's play, and once the snatch was made, things moved quickly. Altieri's initial rebuff of their efforts to collect the debt owed to Red Dragon's Bulgarian client turned into grudging acquiescence. The photo had been enough to convince Bastianini that pleading with his don to pay the Bulgarian was a smart move. Of course, including the ring finger of one of the boy's bodyguards in the package might have sealed the deal. That had been Tomislav's idea. The bodyguard in question had made the mistake of wearing a rare Roman signet ring, one which had been given to the man by Altieri himself. Too bad for him.

At dawn yesterday the Italians had agreed to the deal: five million of the don's euros in exchange for his capo's son. Dalibor had said that the debt was really only four million, but when their client factored in his fee to Red Dragon, plus interest, five mil was what they'd been sent to Rome to get, and now Altieri's flunky was wiring the final million to the Bulgarian's bank in Andorra. Dalibor had suspected that the Italian's request to wait twenty-four hours to pay the final installment was merely a dodge as his men hunted for the boy. Well, if the old man had wanted to save some money, he had failed. Rome was a very large city, and the Red Dragon team had kept the boy well hidden. The flunky would get the address when he presented Kopanja with the receipt. Just to make sure, Kopanja would send a text to the Bulgarian's office to confirm the transfer.

The fat little Italian was waddling back to the lobby from the banker's desk, and he didn't look happy. Kopanja couldn't blame him. If he was ever forced to hand over a million of the Colonel's euros, Kopanja wouldn't be happy, either. But that would never happen. The Colonel was the smartest man he'd ever met. He'd never allow himself to be caught with his pants down, like these idiot garlic-eaters.

"The task is completed, signor?" Kopanja asked in English when the porker stopped in front of him.

"*Si,*" the man said, handing over a sheet of paper. Kopanja laid it on a table and took a photo of it with his phone. He attached the photo to a text and sent it off to the client in Sofia.

"Are we finished?" the Italian asked, his piggy eyes glaring at Kopanja.

"Be the patient one, my friend. Enjoy the scenery." He nodded at a gorgeous woman who was striding across the lobby toward the door. She looked like Monica Bellucci, the actress, which certainly sparked Kopanja's interest. Just a couple weeks ago he'd seen one of her movies, couldn't recall the title, but what difference did it make? She was naked and smoldering hot, and the memory reminded Kopanja that he'd been in Italy for a week now and hadn't bedded even one of its many beautiful women. Dalibor and one or two of the other guys had gotten lucky a couple nights ago, but Kopanja had struck out. Well, perhaps today his luck would change.

His phone dinged, and the text from Bulgaria confirmed the transfer. Kopanja smiled and tucked his phone into the inside pocket of his jacket. "Our business is complete, signor," he said with a smile. From another pocket he produced a slip of paper. "The location of the boy. But you must wait two hours."

"Two hours?" The Italian's face reddened. "If he is harmed–"

"It is a precaution, yes? For my colleagues and me to leave your fair city safely. Two hours. He is being watched, by a man on loan from an associate of ours. Your men get there even one minute early, the boy dies. *Ciao.*" Kopanja left the Italian fuming alone in the lobby and headed to the door, in pursuit of Monica.

Gina swung the Fiat around a small roundabout onto Via Nazionale and she angrily slapped the steering wheel. *"Merda!"*

Mark had never heard Gina use profanity, either in Italian or English. Jim must have been concerned, too, because he leaned close to the back seat to ask her, "What's the problem?"

"This street, it has no parking," she said. "I had forgotten."

"Where's the bank?" Mark asked.

She pointed through the windshield. "The next block, on the right."

"Can you park on a side street?"

"I don't know. Maybe." She muttered something in Italian that Jim didn't catch.

"Take it easy," Mark said. A park was on their right, and they were coming up fast on the next intersection. Beyond that loomed Palazzo Koch, the ornate 19th century palace that housed Banca D'Italia. He pointed at a street sign at an intersection. "Does that mean this next one's a one-way street?"

"Yes," Gina said, "and I can park on it." She turned left at the intersection onto Via Mazzarino. A hotel entrance was ahead and to the right, and she slid the car into an empty space. She jammed the gear shift into park and leaned her forehead against the wheel.

Jim reached from the back seat and put a hand on her back.

"You okay, honey?" She nodded, leaned back and reached back to touch his hand. Hers was shaking.

Mark's phone chirped with a new email notification. He called it up and scrolled through the attachment, which featured reproductions of six passports. He nodded in appreciation, but he wasn't surprised. He'd worked with MI6 a few times over the years in Afghanistan and Iraq, and they were always professional and thorough. "Take a look at these," he said, handing the phone to Gina.

Jim peered over the back seat. "Westlake must have some serious horsepower," he said.

"Get out and get to the corner," Mark ordered. "Keep your eyes on the bank entrance. When we have positive IDs, I'll send them to your phone."

"Got it," Jim said. He scrambled out of the car and hustled away.

"These two for sure," Gina said, pointing at one of the passports, then swiping to another, and then a third. "And I think this one as well." She handed the phone back to Mark.

Working quickly, Mark rearranged the three passports to the front of the line. "I'm sending this email to Jim," he said. "We need to cover the entrance from both ends of this block. Jim will be at this corner, I'll get down to the other. You have your phone?"

She pulled it out of her hip pocket and held it up. "What do you want me to do?"

"Stay with the car, but keep the motor running." He looked ahead, down the street. "I think this block to our left is a triangle. You can't turn around here because it's one way, but if you go up there and hang a tight left, you should be able to come back to that intersection with the roundabout."

"Yes, you're right," Gina said, still breathing hard.

Mark put a hand on her arm. "Relax," he said. "You're doing great." He reached for the door handle, but Gina reached over to stop him.

"Jim has no training in this," she said. "He is highly skilled in a lot of areas, but this spy stuff…"

"He'll be all right," Mark said. "He just has to avoid doing anything foolish. We have backup on the way." Mark looked at the photos again, then at the side mirror, trying to focus on the mission. He wasn't exactly on firm ground here himself, but he wasn't about to tell Gina that. He'd been on a few covert ops in his days in uniform, but it had been awhile. The Army didn't waste time training its infantry officers in the tradecraft of espionage.

But there had been plenty of times during his twenty-five years that a job needed to be done and he'd ordered the next man up to take the place of someone who'd gone down. When you were in a combat environment you didn't always have time to wait around for Battalion to send you some replacements. You might have to make do with what you had, and sometimes that was yourself. This wasn't a combat environment–not yet, anyway–but a job needed to be done, and he and Jim were the next men up.

He leaned over and kissed Gina on the cheek. "We'll be back soon," he said, and opened the door.

CHAPTER ELEVEN
GROCKA MUNICIPALITY, SERBIA

S ophie stood at the window, watching the men work their dogs. They'd been out there for nearly an hour, two men and two pit bulls, and the dogs reflected their masters: powerful, confident, and more than a little aggressive. But she also saw affection between them. An odd dichotomy, on the face of it, but Sophie had seen military dogs in action enough to know that the bond between canine and human could be very powerful.

She had never admitted it to anyone, not even Mark, but she was afraid of dogs. Her family had always been home to cats, usually two at a time, and she would never forget that day when she was eleven and a neighbor's dog, a large male of mixed breed, had slipped through the unlatched door into the back yard and killed her Siamese. Poor Maisy, engrossed in watching the birds splash in the bath that was the central feature of Mum's garden, hadn't made it back to the house in time. Her father, enraged, had called the police. The neighbor's dog was put down, but Sophie had never been able to shake the vivid memory of her pet's dying screams.

During her breakfast with her captor, she'd heard a dog barking, but it must've been a smaller animal, not these two behemoths out in the yard, with their large blocky heads and powerful shoulders. Objectively, she knew that pit bulls had been given a bad rap, as the Americans would say, and could be very sweet and loyal companions. But these two didn't look too sweet, chasing the...my God, they were fake human arms. The prosthetics were tossed by the men and the dogs assaulted them viciously, shaking them and growling. This wasn't playtime. These dogs were here to deal with intruders.

After breakfast she'd been brought back to the room and locked inside. It must've been past noon by now; the day was cloudy, so she couldn't tell by shadows, and without a watch or a clock she couldn't be sure. Removing any timepiece was part of the plan, of course: to keep the captive disoriented. There was not even a grandfather clock to chime on the hour, something one might expect in a home like this. But they hadn't bound her, hadn't put her in a windowless room. Why not?

She sat back down on the bed and held her head in her hands. They were playing mind games with her, offering her just enough sensory input to keep her hopes alive, yet not enough to give her anything remotely solid to latch onto. Occasionally she would hear other sounds from the house. Footsteps, muffled voices, and now there was the yapping again, followed by a very human laugh.

The man at breakfast, clearly the one in charge, had not offered his name or any other clue to his identity. He had asked several questions about her background, her work, and on any other occasion she would've enjoyed such a conversation, would've allowed herself to be charmed by this kind of man. He had an elegance about him, very continental. So unlike her husband in many respects. Mark was disciplined and confident, too, but he could be brash, like most Americans, and his sense of humor was surprisingly adept. He could make wry comments about TV shows that would make her smile, and occasionally would tell jokes he'd overheard while in service, so ribald they would send her into hysterics.

But the only thing the European had told her was that he had a specific piece of business to transact with someone, and her services were required. When the time was right, he would summon her. "I have every confidence that the transaction will be completed without difficulty," he told her. "Your release will come shortly thereafter."

Sophie had forced herself to look into his eyes when he said that. They were a vivid shade of green, and despite his charming smile she could see the truth behind those eyes. He had no intention of letting her leave this place alive.

ROME, ITALY

Jim stood near a newsstand across the street from the bank building, pretending to glance through a magazine while keeping an eye on the bank's entrance. He'd been there only a minute or two when Mark walked past, heading down the block. His brother didn't look his way but said, "Check your messages." Jim waited until Mark was several yards away before reaching into his pocket to pull out his phone.

The attachment to the text message showed six passport photos, Caucasian men who could've been from any country from Greece to Norway. His gut twisted as Jim realized that one of these could be the guy who had beaten his wife. One of them also could be the guy in the bank, so he turned his attention across the street.

After a few more minutes Jim started to think he should be moving on. Nobody else was hanging around the newsstand. Down the street, he could see that Mark had taken a seat in front of a restaurant. There was another restaurant right behind Jim on this corner–a Burger King, of all things–but there was no outdoor seating. Jim was about to call Mark when a woman exited the bank and began walking down Via Nazionale to the southwest, to Jim's right. She was incredibly striking, dressed to the nines, looking like an actress he couldn't place. As she reached the corner, he saw a man come out of the same bank entrance she'd just exited. Jim checked his phone, and got a hit on the fourth picture. The passport said he was a Serb named Pedja Kopanja.

Jim stepped toward the newsstand and punched in Mark's speed-dial number. "Got something?" Mark asked.

"Kopanja, and he's heading toward my corner, still on the bank's side of the street."

"Don't lose him. I'm on my way." The line went dead.

The woman turned left around the corner onto Via Mazzanino. Jim could see cars angle-parked on the one-way street, facing in his direction. There didn't seem to be much else down there, so she was probably heading for one of the cars. Kopanja turned the corner. He was definitely following the woman, ten yards behind her and closing.

If the Serb had a car down there, he'd be gone by the time the Brit team could get here. Jim had no idea how far away they were, but this guy was their best lead to find Sophie and he couldn't be allowed to get away. Jim checked the traffic and trotted across the street. He stepped up onto the sidewalk at the corner and was a dozen yards behind the target.

Where was she going? Kopanja had thought she might have her car parked down here, but she passed them all by. There were no other pedestrians. A sedan was chugging up the street, the man at the wheel jabbering into his phone. He glanced at the woman, did a double-take and nearly drove into the curb, right in front of Kopanja. The right front wheel came within centimeters of the curb before the driver jerked the car back. The Serb glared at him, and the driver looked away, eyes wide as he hit the gas.

These Italians, they were nothing but a bunch of *pičke*. The men, anyway. No wonder they had gotten their asses kicked in every war since…well, a long time. The women, though, they were different here. Kopanja watched Monica sashay her way down the sidewalk. Serbian women were earthy, not as elegant as these Italian babes. Kopanja's groin started to ache.

His orders were to report back to the Colonel as soon as the final installment was paid, and then fly to Belgrade. He knew he should make that call pretty soon, but there was time. And the flight home, that didn't have to happen immediately, did it? He still had a few hundred euros from their expense money. Monica would appreciate a fine meal, some wine, and then she would find out how a Serb could please a woman.

Without looking back, the woman turned left into a building. Kopanja didn't slow his pace, but he didn't hurry. The trick was to appear like he wasn't anxious. He paused at the entrance and, remembering his tradecraft at last, glanced back up the street. There was a man coming down the sidewalk, a big guy, and he didn't look too friendly. Maybe he'd had eyes on Monica too. Well, *poduvas mi karu, šupak!* Kopanja followed the babe inside.

Jim saw the Serb look back, then disappear into the building. Whatever stealth Jim might've had in play was now gone, so there was no time to waste. Four more loping steps took him to the entrance. Above was a stone fresco, showing a sad-looking woman holding something on a plate. Jim took a step inside and found himself looking down into a small but elegant courtyard one story below street level, with staircases leading down on either side of the entrance. Straight ahead on a stone column was a plaque bearing a name: *Chiesa Sant'Agata dei Goti*. Church of St. Agatha of the Goths. Why would the Serb be going into a church? But there he was, walking past an ivy-covered stone arch in the middle of the courtyard.

Jim took the stairs to his left, hit the bottom and quickly crossed the stone floor. Ahead of him were the large wooden double doors that served as the entrance to the nave of the church. Kopanja had just gone inside, closing the left door behind him.

Jim came to the doors and knew he had to make a decision. Kopanja could be waiting for him in there, or he could have continued on through the church, looking for a rear exit. Jim took a moment to calm his breathing, feeling himself slip into *haragei*, the sensation of calm and focus that would allow him almost literally to sense everything around him. He reached for the right-side door and pulled it open.

The beauty of the basilica was almost overpowering. The walls were gilded in golds and burgundies, with so many paintings in the classic style that his senses were almost overwhelmed. Large columns flanked the sides of the nave, with wooden pews crowding the large mosaic in the center of the aisle. Above the altar at the far end was a spectacular painted fresco. The pews were completely empty except for the woman, who sat in the third pew from the front on the right. Jim saw her bow her head, then raise it and look slightly above and to her left, and in the sunlight streaming through the rectangular windows he thought he saw a tear on her cheek.

But where was the Serb? Jim tore his gaze away from the beauty of the church, and of its sole inhabitant, and took a step inside, looking to his right. The shadows yielded nothing. But there was something to his left. He sensed a flicker of movement and the whisper of air as something moved swiftly toward his kidney.

CHAPTER TWELVE
ROME, ITALY

Kopanja didn't think the big guy looked Italian, but he could've been muscle hired by Altieri to tail him. Brit, German, French or Italian, they all bled the same. He moved out of the shadows, drawing the Russian-made NR-40 combat knife he'd used in his Special Brigade days. Yes, they'd taught him to kill the enemy by coming up from behind and slicing the throat, but this guy would go down with a simple thrust to–

The Serb's knife did not bite into flesh. It bit into nothing at all as his hand was moved up and around. The man moved with a swiftness and ease Kopanja could barely register. His eyes followed the knife but his brain only got to *Koji kur–* before being overwhelmed with sudden, searing pain flaring from his nose. His eyes teared up as the heat roared through his head, blotting out almost everything, but not enough to overwrite another feeling: the blade of his knife at his own throat.

A voice whispered into his ear. "No more trouble, Pedja, or else this goes a little deeper." The knife blade pressed inward only a millimeter or two, but Kopanja felt its sting. He ceased any thought of resistance and allowed himself to be led away.

Mark made it to the top of the staircase at the entrance to the courtyard in time to see Jim pushing the Serb out into the sunlight. The man's face was bloodied, his right arm pinned behind him. The man's left hand moved toward his waist and then his entire body seized up as if jolted by an electric current. Behind him, Mark saw Jim whisper something into his ear.

Mark hustled down the stairs and met them at the ivy-covered stone trellis in the middle of the courtyard. He almost called out his brother by name, but remembered operational security just as the word was forming. Instead, he asked, "What the hell is going on?"

"He pulled a knife on me inside," Jim said, nodding back at the entrance to the nave of the church. "I convinced him it was not a wise choice."

"Anybody else in there? Anybody see you?"

"A woman, I think she–"

There was movement at the doors. A beautiful woman stood there, one hand on the door, the other held to her lips in astonishment. Mark gestured toward her, and Jim turned slightly, keeping his captive in the chicken wing hold. Mark knew from experience that it could be extremely painful and Jim was making sure of that, as evidenced by the beads of sweat on Kopanja's forehead.

To the woman, Jim said, *"Va tutto bene, signorina."* He paused, then added, *"Polizia. Mi dispiace...disturbala."*

Mark took the Serb by his other elbow and the brothers led him past the trellis toward the stairs to the street-level entrance. "What did you tell her?" Mark asked.

"I said it was okay, we're cops, sorry to disturb you. Or at least that's what I hope I said."

Mark saw Kopanja's eyes shift from Jim to Mark and back again as they reached the foot of the stairs. Mark leaned close to his ear and said, "No, we're not cops, asshole, so we don't care about your rights. You're going to cooperate with us or we'll slice your balls off and make you eat them. Do you understand?"

Eyes wide with fear, the Serb nodded.

They reached the street level, but Mark told Jim to keep Kopanja out of sight while he called Gina to bring the car around. He had just signed off on the call when the screen of his phone lit up with Sophie's picture. His heart almost seized up. He hit the RECEIVE button. "Hello? Sophie, are you okay? Where are you?"

There was a brief silence, and then a man's voice. "Colonel Hayes, I get to speak to you at last."

The man sat behind an old, ornate desk in the library of the house. On his lap was a Yorkshire terrier, the source of the yapping Sophie had heard earlier. The dog, sitting quietly now as its master scratched its ears, stared across the desk at the newcomer.

Sophie sat in one of the two chairs facing the desk, an armed guard standing on each side of her. Her phone was pressed to the man's left ear, and from it she could hear her husband's voice. "Is that you, Novak? What have you done with my wife?"

The man's eyebrows rose and he looked at Sophie. "I am impressed, Colonel. Truly, you are every bit the resourceful man I imagined you to be."

"If you have harmed one hair on her head, you'll find out how resourceful I can really be." Sophie heard Mark's words through the tinny speaker and her heart leaped. She had to fight to keep from crying.

"There is no need for belligerence, Colonel. Your wife is here with me right now. I will let you speak to her." Novak tapped the speaker button and set the phone on the desk, leaning it against a cup holding several pens and pencils.

Mark's voice was clearer now. "Sophie, are you there? Are you all right?"

She had known this moment might come and had thought hard about what to say. "Yes, I'm here, Mark. All things considered, I'd rather be at home with you in front of the fireplace right now."

Across the desk, Novak's eyes bored into her. He made a move to reach for the phone, but hesitated as Mark's voice came through again. "Have they fed you? Don't let your sugar count get too high."

She had prepared for this one, too, and was ready with her answer. "I believe it's probably around one hundred," she said. "I'm all right, for now."

Novak snatched the phone and took it off speaker. "Are you satisfied that she is unharmed, Colonel?" A pause, and then Novak smiled. "Very well. We shall now discuss my terms."

Jim could overhear Mark's end of the conversation and knew it was Novak on the other end. And Sophie was alive, thank God. Gina was on her way with the car. All they had to do was get this joker to a safe place and let the Brits work him over. Jim had sat in on interrogation training at OSS, but the MI6 guys would be a few levels above that. It would be something to–

Kopanja suddenly twisted to his right, bringing his left hand around in a swooping arc. The punch didn't have much on it, but it was enough to cause Jim to rotate his shoulders to take his head out of the line of fire. He felt his grip on Kopanja's right wrist slipping even more, but before he could compensate, the Serb had broken free and was running down the street.

Mark saw what was happening and pointed at the fleeing man, mouthing *Get him!* Cursing himself for his carelessness, Jim took off in pursuit. But Kopanja was younger, maybe stronger, and had a head start. Jim knew he'd have to catch him before he got to the corner and onto the next street, where there was more traffic, more people, probably cops.

Kopanja was thirty feet from the intersection when the Fiat came around the corner and headed right at him. Jim saw Gina at the wheel, her eyes going wide briefly as she recognized the man running toward her. Kopanja angled to his right but Gina hit the gas and swung the car left to cut him off. The left front quarter grazed the Serb's thigh and sent him pinwheeling into a parked sedan. The back of his head caromed off the hood of the car and he went down in a heap.

The Fiat's brakes screeched as Gina brought the car to a halt. Jim vaulted around the front end and headed for Kopanja, who tried to regain his feet and failed, slumping back against the sedan. Jim glanced over his shoulder at Gina, who was getting out of the car. "Open the back door!" he ordered.

He was shoving the semi-conscious Serb roughly into the back as Mark ran up. In the distance was the distinctive oscillating wail of a police siren. "Everybody get in," Mark said. "We've got to get out of here."

Gina slid back behind the wheel as Mark came around the

front to get in the passenger side. In back, Jim sat on top of Kopanja, who was lying on his stomach, his head shoved into the far door.

"Where to?" Gina asked, throwing the shift lever into gear.

"Just go," Mark said. "I'll call Westlake, see where his team wants us to meet them." He looked back at Jim and his eyes were hard. "Do you think you can keep that clown under control now?"

"Yeah," Jim said. Mark held his stare for another two seconds, then turned to punch a number into his phone.

The Brits directed them to a warehouse in the Ostiense quarter. On the way, Jim frisked the Serb and relieved him of a folding knife, but he wasn't carrying a gun. Keeping Kopanja under control wasn't difficult; another chicken wing hold on the left arm did the job. This time, Jim made sure to keep his grip on the Serb's wrist locked in.

To their north was the Colosseum and the Forum, out of sight now. Jim had long dreamed of exploring the ancient stadium, imagining what it was like when the gladiators dueled on its sandy floor. They should've been there right now, Jim and Mark and their wives, enjoying the day and each other's company. Gina had always indulged Jim when it came to his "warrior stuff," as she called it. Yes, she was a martial artist too, and a damn good one, but for her it was about fitness and self-defense. While Jim was certainly in favor of that, for him, it was equally about the philosophy.

In their time, those ancient gladiators were its embodiment. To a certain point, anyway, Jim reminded himself now. Many if not most of those gladiators were slaves, forced to fight and often die at the behest of their masters. Men and women today had choices those men had never been allowed to have. Now, a person chose what to stand for, and when to fight for it. Seven years earlier, Jim had failed when he tried to defend his wife Suzy against attack. Since her death, he'd dedicated himself to training and study, determined to never let that happen again. He'd been put to the test the year before, when he confronted four men on the sands of a terrorist camp in Somalia. He'd met that test, but now here was another, even more serious. Then, his own life and the lives of two friends were at stake. Now, it was his sister-in-law, and probably soon his brother, not to mention himself. The stakes had been raised yet again.

He knew Mark didn't really trust him to be an asset on this mission, and Jim hadn't helped his cause by allowing the Serb to make a break for it. If Gina hadn't shown up with the car when she did, Kopanja would be in the wind right now, taking with him their best chance to find Sophie and turn the tables on Novak. There wasn't much margin for error anymore and Jim swore to himself he would not fail again.

Kopanja stirred underneath him and Jim tightened the hold enough to keep him quiet. Anything tighter might separate the man's shoulder, and that would be too bad, wouldn't it?

Gina turned the Fiat off the street and into a dirt parking area next to a corrugated sheet metal building. The only other car in the lot was a nondescript Opel, with a well-built man in casual clothes standing next to it. Two other men emerged from the building as Gina pulled in next to the Opel.

Mark was out first, and the man next to the Opel came over. "Colonel Hayes?"

"That's me. Our friend is in the back."

"Right." The Brit nodded to the two other men, who came over to the Fiat and opened the rear passenger door. Kopanja twisted his head to see them, started to say something and stopped with a grunt when Jim applied one last twist to the arm.

The man who opened the door was sandy-haired and built like a rugby player. He nodded to Jim approvingly when he saw the twist. "We'll take it from here, Yank," he said.

CHAPTER THIRTEEN
GROCKA MUNICIPALITY, SERBIA

Novak looked out the window of his study, idly scratching Vuk behind his ears. The dog would have to be taken outside soon to do his afternoon duty, but the men were outside again training their pit bulls, so little Vuk would have to wait. Novak trusted his men, to a point, but not their dogs. All it would take would be for one to break away from its handler, and Novak's beloved Yorkshire terrier would not stand a chance. Novak's temper was legendary, rarely seen but explosive when it did break free of his exceptional self-discipline, as it surely would if something happened to his beloved pet. He would prefer to avoid that, especially now.

Novak had assumed Hayes would not stand a chance, either, not with his wife in the Serb's hands. Hayes would do what he was told, and Novak would have his revenge at last. But something about the way the American had handled himself on the phone was unsettling. There was anger, of course, that was to be expected, and threats, naturally. Americans were the world champions at making angry threats. Following through on those threats, well, that was often something entirely different. But Hayes was not a bellicose politician whipping up a crowd of mindless supporters, nor was he a smooth-talking diplomat like those the Americans sent overseas to persuade Europeans and others to see things their way, always dangling the carrot with one hand while holding the stick behind their back with the other.

No, Mark Hayes was someone different. A military man, although not officially so any longer, but Novak knew exactly how that worked. A military man would eventually take off the uniform for good, but he would never cease the wearing of it. Especially not someone who had been an honors graduate of the American military academy. That stayed with a man forever. It was part of his character, his very essence.

Such things often inhibited these men in civilian life, where they could not simply give an order and expect it to be carried out without question, where the people they had to deal with often had little or no sense of honor or self-discipline. That could be frustrating, could cause serious problems in adapting to the new and chaotic world that existed outside the service. The smart ones adapted, finding ways to make their well-honed skills work to their advantage. Novak had done it, and now he suspected Mark Hayes had done it, too.

Novak put the problem into a side room of his mind, where it would be worked, and a solution would be found. He turned his attention to the dog in his lap. Vuk was seven years old now but still energetic, and Novak had to admit the dog was one of the few joys of his life. Yes, there was the pleasure of running Red Dragon, of accumulating the wealth and influence that had made him one of the most powerful men in Serbia, but that wasn't the same.

Years ago he had once read something, probably spoken by an American businessman, of all people, but true nonetheless. "You can love your wife, love your kids, love your dog, love your country, but never love a company, because unlike those other things, a company will never love you back." That was certainly true in Europe, and Novak suspected it was true everywhere. But the truth of it bothered him sometimes, for Red Dragon was his life now, and he had to admit that he loved it. He had built it from scratch into one of the most respected security firms on the continent. With daring, intelligence and ruthless efficiency, he had created a company that provided him with everything: power, money, this villa, a fleet of cars in his Belgrade warehouse, even his own helicopter sitting on the pad outside right now.

But as impressive as it was, Red Dragon had not provided him with love. He had never married, never had children. There had been women, of course, and still were, whenever he wanted, but as he neared his fiftieth birthday he found that even the company of women in his bed no longer had the thrill it once had, regardless of their youth and vigor. He had his work, his company, and the men and women who worked for him, but he could not truly be one of them. He was the boss, the Colonel, and could not allow himself to get too close to any of them. Not even to Milinka, his executive assistant back in Belgrade. She was ex-military, like Novak himself and most of his employees, and although she was divorced and quite attractive, he could not allow himself to compromise the business by engaging her romantically, or even just physically. The most intimacy he would allow with her was when she joined him on the judo mat, where he trained thrice weekly without fail, keeping him fit and ready to take matters into his own hands if necessary. Milinka was good, probably one of Europe's best senior female *judoka*, but she was not his equal there and he would never allow her to be. And although he suspected she was in love with him, he could not allow himself to reciprocate.

The dog, though, was another matter entirely. A gift from Milinka for his birthday six years ago, Vuk had become a part of his life very quickly. The terrier was the main reason why Novak chose to spend more time out here at the villa than he did at his lavish apartment in Belgrade. Out here they could wander through the woods and along the Danube without worrying about the dog running into traffic. Having the dog around him was calming, and from Vuk he got the unconditional love that, Novak admitted in his quietest moments, he had from nothing else.

Occasionally he would bring Vuk back into the city with him, where they would stroll through the parks of the Vracar district, near his penthouse, and contemplate the statue of George Petrovich, the Karađorđe, the founder of modern Serbia some two centuries ago. Even though he was still known as the *Veliki Vožd*, the Great Leader had ruled Serbia for only nine years before being ousted by the Ottoman Turks and eventually assassinated by his ostensible comrades in arms.

But Novak had learned the lessons of the Karađorđe well. Petrovich had been a warrior, leading his people in battle, and also a visionary. He saw within Serbia the seeds of greatness, a people who could and should dominate the Balkans. Petrovich's only weakness was that he was too trusting, and that had been his undoing. Novak trusted no one, at least not completely. While serving in the Army he had trusted his country's leaders, Milošević and his cronies, to quell the uprisings in the other Yugoslav republics, and they had failed, spectacularly so, bringing death and destruction, and bitter humiliation, to his people. But there would be another day, and when the dawn rose on that day, Darko Novak would be there. It was only a matter of time.

First things first, though. The Hayes question would be resolved soon, likely within the next twenty-four hours. Then he could resume his planning for the future. It might take him five years, ten, but eventually he would be taking up residence in the New Palace in Belgrade. The Presidency of Serbia was a largely ceremonial post these days.

But a new day was coming.

He scratched Vuk behind his ears, and the little dog looked up at his master. "Soon," Novak said. "Soon, my little friend."

ROME, ITALY

The three British security agents hustled Kopanja into the warehouse, handling him as effortlessly as they would a bag of dirty laundry. Mark was right behind them, but before he could get through the doorway it was blocked by the familiar stocky form of Paul Cunningham.

The retired SAS officer shut the door behind him and held up a hand as Mark tried to move past him. "I can't let you go in there, Mark. Sorry."

"What the hell is this, Paul? And what are you doing here anyway?"

"What 'this' is, my friend, is something you can't get involved with, any more than you already are. We'll take care of our Serbian friend. Don't worry, we'll find out where his boss is keeping your wife."

"And who's 'we'? Don't tell me you're conducting the interrogation."

"Another layer of deniability, as far as Westlake and his office are concerned. I have had some experience in these things." The look in Paul's eyes left no doubt about that. Mark knew that SAS troops were superb, and a man with Cunningham's background surely knew how to conduct a field interrogation and conduct it efficiently.

Mark forced himself to think. Things were moving fast, almost too fast. He was desperately tired and hadn't eaten anything all day. He looked toward the closed door. He wanted to hear something, anything, from inside. Shouts, screams, Kopanja begging for mercy, but there was nothing. Just his newfound Brit friend, a guy who looked like someone's uncle or grandpa, telling him to stay out of the room where his wife's fate might very well be decided.

He looked back to the car, where Jim and Gina were waiting. They weren't coming any closer, leaving it in Mark's hands. That was good. They were civilians. Highly trained ones, to be sure, but not in what was going to take place inside the warehouse any minute now. For that matter, Mark had to admit that he wasn't much better trained at interrogations than his brother and sister-in-law were. In his quarter-century in uniform he had questioned maybe half a dozen enemy prisoners in the field, and only because time was of the essence and he couldn't afford to wait for someone from Kabul or Baghdad to show up. He had read Field Manual 2-22.3 cover to cover more than once, but he wasn't in the Army anymore and didn't have to follow it, did he? The Brits had their own version, and the guys inside probably hadn't read it in a while.

Finally, Mark looked back at his British friend. "Look, Paul, I understand what you're trying to do, and I appreciate it, I'm sure you know that. You didn't have to become involved in this."

"My wife was endangered last night as well, you know."

"I do. But you know that what's going to happen in there is illegal, in Italy and everywhere else in the civilized world. I can't let you guys take the fall for that alone if this goes tits-up. If I'm in there, then I'm involved in it, and if I have to, I'll take responsibility."

Paul looked up at him for a long five seconds, then said, "All right, Mark. But your brother and his wife aren't getting anywhere close to this door. Are we clear on that?"

Mark nodded. "What did you have in mind for our Serb friend?"

"Have you ever heard of the 'mother-in-law's clothesline'?"

Mark had to think about it, but then something floated to the surface from long ago. What was it? Then he remembered: a bull session he'd sat in on with some coalition officers in Afghanistan, during his first tour, '02. An Australian major had said he'd seen it used on an insurgent in Borneo. The Aussie's description, he recalled now, was quite graphic. Mark looked back at Jim and his wife. No, there was no way in hell they could be allowed to see what was going to happen inside.

CHAPTER FOURTEEN
ROME, ITALY

Jim saw Cunningham go back inside the warehouse as Mark turned and began walking toward them.

"What are they going to do to him?" Gina asked Jim.

"What do you think?"

Jim heard a sharp intake of breath. "But–" She didn't have the chance to finish the sentence.

"I'm going in there," Mark said, "and I need you two to stay here. You have to promise me that you won't come inside."

The look on his brother's face was one Jim had never seen before. It was more than a game face, much more. Jim had seen those back in the days when Mark played football in high school and at the Academy. No, this was a whole new level of intensity. There was something distant in Mark's eyes. He seemed determined and yet resigned at the same time.

"You go through that door, Mark, you cross the Rubicon," Jim said.

"The Rubicon?" Gina asked. She looked at Jim, puzzled. "What does a river have to do with this?" Then her eyes widened slightly. "Oh."

Jim remembered reading about Julius Caesar's fateful decision to march his troops south across the river that marked the border between Gaul and Italy in 49 B.C. It was an act of insurrection, from which there was no turning back. "Do you know what Caesar said back then, Mark?"

"Yes. *'Alea iacta est.'* 'The die is cast.'" He offered a small grin that carried not the slightest hint of mirth. "I read history too, you know."

"Don't do it," Jim said. "Whatever happens in there, when you go inside, you're a part of it. Forever."

"They have Sophie, Jim. I'm already a part of it."

"What's Paul going to do?" Gina asked.

Mark just looked at her, but before he could speak, Jim said, "He's going to conduct the interrogation, so Westlake and his people can keep their hands clean."

Mark just nodded. "Plausible deniability. It's the way these things work sometimes."

Jim reached out and put a hand on his brother's shoulder. "Please. Stay with us. Let Paul take care of it."

Gina's face was red under the bruises. "You can't be serious, Mark! That guy will just tell you whatever you want to hear, just to stop the...to stop it. Surely you must know that. This never works, it–"

Mark cut her off. "It has to. We're running out of time. Novak told me if I don't surrender myself to him within twenty-four hours, Sophie dies. And he won't make it quick for her." He looked at his watch. "Now we're down to twenty-three hours. I have to let Paul take his best shot, and I have to be in there. If things go south I won't let him take the fall. She's my wife. I'm the one Novak's after. It's my responsibility."

124

Jim pulled his hand back, looked away, then sighed. If it had been Gina in Novak's hands, he knew he would do exactly the same thing. How could he fault his brother? He looked back at Mark. "We'll stay here."

Mark nodded, then turned and walked briskly to the door of the warehouse. He hadn't gone ten feet when Gina took two steps toward him, then stopped and turned to face her husband. One eye was still almost swollen shut, but it was filled with as much ferocity as her good one. "You have to stop him, Jim! He's throwing everything away! He will be in prison for years! The company will fire him, he–" She stopped, then burst into tears.

Jim gathered her into his arms. "It'll be okay, bellisima. We just have to trust Mark, trust that he knows what he's doing."

"Isn't there anything we can do?"

"Yes. We can pray for him. And pray for Kopanja, too."

Gina looked at him, fierce once again despite the tears on her face. "For that bastard? Why?"

"Pray that he gives up Novak quickly."

Mark stopped at the door, took a deep breath and thought of Kandahar.

It was the first piece of ground claimed by the United States in Afghanistan, mere weeks after 9/11, and by the time Mark got there six months later, the routine was established. The cargo planes came in at night and the new arrivals were hustled off by shouting, cursing MPs, shining flashlights that penetrated the burlap bags covering the heads of the prisoners. They were led to a special enclosure on the base that was off-limits to all but a few allied personnel, and Mark happened to be one of them on that tour. He remembered the concertina wire, the shacks, the lights that blazed down all night long from high stanchions. The soldiers on guard duty were always heavily armed, and once or twice they'd had to use those weapons.

The prisoners stank of sweat and piss and shit and other things Mark would later become well acquainted with in that godforsaken country. They'd all thought of themselves as pretty hot stuff when they were knocking around civilians, but by the time they got here that attitude was long gone, and the wailing and crying was almost constant. One at a time, they were thrown into the "pin-down" area, walled on three sides by sandbags, where they were forced to lie on their stomachs while MPs in surgical gloves cut away their ragged clothing. He remembered watching the medics examine them, and then the MP shouting, *"Wa' all'an lill act el emptihan!"* and the prisoners being pushed down for the ass inspection, shrieking in fear of being raped by the godless infidels. After being doused with lice powder, they were photographed and fingerprinted, then dressed in orange jumpsuits with a number scrawled on the back with magic marker. Most of them needed another jumpsuit after wetting themselves.

The interrogations were almost tame after that. Mark had sat in on enough of them to know the drill, and how different it was from how such things were depicted in the movies. They almost always took a long time, and the intel they gave up had to be checked and cross-checked. After several days the prisoner was usually flown somewhere else, maybe Gitmo or a black site, and some of them, Mark knew, were never seen again. One time, he had asked his superior officer about that. "They've been playing for keeps for years, Hayes," the hard-eyed colonel had said, "and now we are, too."

And we still are, Mark thought. He'd made a lot of decisions over the years that had sent himself and his men into harm's way, and some of them hadn't come back. But the mission had to be accomplished. It was always about the mission. Get the job done and eventually we can all go home to be with our families, live a quiet life. He'd looked forward to that so much, and now here he was again. Another mission. More tough decisions. He made another one and opened the door.

"Ne znam ništa! Pusti me!"

Mark almost felt the sting of Paul's slap himself. "Oh, you know something all right, laddie," the ex-SAS officer said to Kopanja. "Let's not play games. You tell us what we want to know and everybody goes home happy. Well, you probably won't be very thrilled, but you'll be in one piece. So let's try again: where did they take the woman?"

"Ne znam ništa o ženi!"

Another slap, this time to the other cheek, back-handed. "We know you speak English, so don't play dumb." Paul pulled over a chair and sat facing the prisoner. Back in the shadows near the door, Mark took a step to his right to get a better view.

The Serb was naked except for his underwear, black and short, with his belly drooping over the front. His legs were secured to the chair by several zip ties, his hands bound behind him and tied to the chair's back. His cheeks were red from Paul's strikes, but his eyes were hard, not a good sign.

127

"Fuck you!" Kopanja barked, spitting onto the floor at Paul's feet.

"Now that's better," Paul said, leaning back with his elbows on the chair's arms. "I like a bloke who has a pair on him. I can respect a man like that. You know, it's too bad we didn't meet a few years ago. I might've been able to use a man like you in my unit." He brought his hands together, pressing a fist into his palm. "On second thought, probably not. I don't like men who beat up women, or men who hang around with men who beat up women." He leaned closer. "We know everything about you, Pedja. We know you were in Special Brigades, we know you work for Red Dragon. Three years, right? That's enough time to know your way around the company. To get to know the boss, right?"

Kopanja shifted his shoulders and couldn't hide the wince. He glared at Paul. "I don't know anything about Novak."

"Well, he must know enough about you to make sure you didn't go with your mates to Capua. Why was that, do you think? He couldn't even trust you to kidnap a woman and beat up another one?" Paul shook his head.

That one had struck home. Kopanja held his head a little higher. "I had to stay in Rome and finish the job."

"Ah yes, at the bank," Paul said. He leaned forward, elbows on knees. "We don't care about whatever it is that you and your mates were doing here in Rome, Pedja. We don't care how many men you might've strong-armed or women you might've fucked, although I suspect as far as the latter, you probably didn't do too well. You were stalking that woman, followed her right into the church, you did. You're still looking for a piece of Eye-tie arse before heading for home, right?"

Kopanja licked his lips, glancing away. Mark knew Paul had scored again.

"Look," Paul said, leaning closer. "We've got nothing against you, personally. We know you didn't have anything to do with what happened in Capua. That was your mates, we know that. They're the ones who took the woman. They're the ones who roughed up her friend. But the thing is, Pedja, those ladies are married to some very good friends of mine. As you might expect, they're not very happy fellows right now, and can you blame them? Suppose it was your wife, or your sister. Or your mum. You'd be pretty upset about it, I'd say."

The Serb looked past Paul toward Mark, and Paul picked up on it immediately. "Yes, that's one of the lads I mentioned. He's not very happy right now, Pedja. Not at all. But I persuaded him to let me have a go at finding out what we need to know from you, before he takes over. And believe me, you don't want him sitting in this chair, so I'm asking you again to tell me where they took the woman. And if you're not straight with me, I'll have to tell my friend back there that you're not cooperating. He'll be very unhappy. He'll want to have a go at you himself, and let's just say it will be better for all concerned if you tell us what we want to know, before it gets to that point. So, where did they take the woman?"

Kopanja held his head higher. "Go to hell."

Paul sat back and sighed. "Well, that's disappointing." He looked back over his shoulder toward Mark. "Should I bring out the clothesline?"

Mark didn't hesitate. "Go for it."

Paul turned and nodded to one of the security men, who withdrew a length of cord from a small gym bag. Paul got up and whispered something in the man's ear. The agent began wrapping the cord around Kopanja's right leg, starting at the ankle and working his way up. The Serb's eyes went wide as he watched, and when the agent got to the knee and kept going up the thigh, Kopanja swallowed and looked at Paul, who was sitting in front of him again.

"I see you have some experience with this," the SAS veteran said. "Probably did a little of this kind of work in Special Brigades, right? Well, maybe that was left to the engineers. You might've not been directly trained with this type of thing. In our special forces, we learn how to do all kinds of things, but from what I heard about you Serbs, most of you just learned how to shoot civilians. Yes, march into the village, shoot the men, rape the women. But then me and my friend back there and our mates showed up and spoiled all the fun." He pointed at the gray cord now snaked around Kopanja's leg. The agent had finished the thigh and begun to wind the cord around the Serb's abdomen. "This is detonating cord. It's filled with pentaerythritol nitrate. You might've heard the acronym, PETN. Very volatile stuff, really. Now, most of the time this is packed pretty tightly in the cord so it burns quick, you see. None of this long-running fuse stuff you see in the old movies. But the thing is, Pedja, we can change that, so it doesn't burn so fast."

The agent had reached Kopanja's shoulders. "Should I do the arms, sir?"

Paul appeared to think that over. "No, I think not. In fact, I'll take it from here, thank you." The agent nodded and stepped back.

The former commando walked around behind the prisoner and took up the length of cord that had yet to be wrapped. He appeared to think about it, then dropped the cord, put his left hand over Kopanja's ear and pressed the tip of his right index finger into the Serb's head, just below the other ear. Kopanja screamed with pain.

Paul released the grip and picked up the cord. "Just wanted to make sure you weren't getting too comfy," he said. He contemplated the cord. "Let's see...I think we have enough to go back down to the other leg before we get to the good part."

Kopanja was panting now. He shook his head and swallowed again. "The...the good part?"

"Yes, of course. The naughty bits." Paul slid the cord down Kopanja's left side, keeping the cord outside the length that had been wrapped around his midsection, and started going down the left leg. "Now, where was I? Oh, yes. Timing. Det cord normally is used at a pretty reliable rate, you know. That is to say, a burn rate. 'Explosive mass per unit length,' I think the manual says. Expressed in grams per meter. The standard rate is ten grams per meter. This will produce a very quick burn. When you're in the field, you know, you don't want it to take too long. When you're blowing up a bridge, you're in somewhat of a hurry, as I'm sure you remember from your service days. But we can go down to only a gram or two per meter, which produces a nice slow burn. Should take, oh, fifteen or twenty seconds for that first leg."

The cord was now completely wound around Kopanja's left leg to the ankle. Paul snaked it back up along the leg to the Serb's crotch. "Time for the knickers to come off," Paul said. He pulled a folding knife from his pants pocket and flicked the blade open. Kopanja began to struggle against the ropes binding him to the chair. "I wouldn't do that if I were you, Pedja. You wouldn't want my knife to slip right now, would you?"

The Serb froze. He was breathing heavily, and Mark could see the sweat beading on his forehead and chest. Paul expertly sliced the front of Kopanja's underwear away and peered at what it revealed. "My goodness. You were going to try to impress that Italian woman with that little John Thomas, were you? Well, it's probably the chill in here. In any event, here we go." He began winding the cord around Kopanja's genitals.

In a moment Paul was done. He stepped back and surveyed his work. "All right, then. Anything you'd like to say, Pedja?"

The Serb was panting now, his eyes wide. He nodded his head.

"I didn't hear you," Paul said. He gestured to the agent. "Bring me the detonator, please."

"Wait!" Kopanja yelled. Tears began to run down his face. "Please, I don't know anything about–"

Paul leaned forward. "We've been through this, Pedja. We don't have time to waste. We're going to get the woman back, and we're going to take Novak down while we're at it. You lads don't know who you're dealing with. Now, we're done pissing around with you. One last chance, laddie." He sprang from the chair and clamped a hand around Kopanja's throat. "Where. Did. They. Take. The. Woman?"

Kopanja began to sob. "I...I will tell you what I know."

CHAPTER FIFTEEN
ROME, ITALY

Jim had lost track of the time, and that was unusual for him. He flopped down on the hotel room bed and saw the alarm clock glowing 5:37. Was it that late in the day? His Suunto Core wristwatch confirmed it.

He couldn't believe how tired he was. The physical exertion hadn't really been much; his workouts at the gym or the dojo back home were a lot more rigorous than anything he'd been through today. But he hadn't slept well the night before, of course, and they'd gotten an early start from Capua. No wonder he was running on fumes right now.

He wondered how Mark could keep going. Every man had his limits, even Mark, who was in outstanding shape, a habit he'd carried over from his Army days. In the past few months Jim had gone up against his brother more than a few times on the mat back at their OSS training facility and Mark had held his own. His close-quarters combat technique was a lot like Israeli *krav maga*, a discipline that made up for its lack of elegance with its lethality. And his mental discipline, which was just as important as physical training, was outstanding, on a level Jim had never seen among civilians. Sometimes, though, that was too much. Mark tended to keep things inside more than Jim thought was necessary. On the ride back to the hotel, Mark hadn't said a word about what had gone on inside the warehouse. Jim had asked about the interrogation, but Mark ignored the question as he sent text messages and checked his email. At one point, he said, "Where the hell are they?" When Jim asked who, Mark only said, "The team's not at the hotel."

Jim wondered if his brother might be approaching the peak of his own endurance. They now had twenty-one hours before Novak carried out his threat. The decisions Mark made in that time would be crucial, but the more fatigued he became, the less reliable his decision-making process would be. Yes, he'd worked under great stress in the Army, Jim knew, but this was different. It was...

The metallic squeak jerked him awake. For a brief, scary moment, he was caught in that zone between slumber and full consciousness. Where was he? Who was here? Then he realized it was the shower curtain being slid aside, followed by the footfalls of someone stepping out of the tub, then pulling a towel from the rack.

His watch told him he'd slept for nearly forty minutes. With a groan, he sat up and swung his legs over the side of the bed, and when his bare feet hit the floor he had another moment. He couldn't remember taking off his shoes.

Gina appeared in the bathroom doorway, toweling herself dry. "Have a good nap?" she asked.

Jim stood and stretched, and it felt good to get some of the kinks out. What he really needed, he knew, was a good workout, preferably in the gym back home. He felt a sudden pang of homesickness. No, what he needed was to get back home. They all needed to get back home. He turned back to face his wife.

Even with her face still bruised, Gina looked great, her body magnificently toned. How old was she now? Forty-six as of next month, he remembered. He'd never met an Italian woman before her, and during this trip he'd been somewhat surprised at Italy's diversity. There were women, and men, of all shapes, sizes and skin tones. Jim had wondered who she might resemble, then had seen a mid-60s movie poster featuring Gina Lollobrigida, and it all clicked. Raven hair framed a face that featured sensuous lips, with hazel eyes that could give him a look that weakened his knees. Below them was a delicate nose that flared when she was worked up, and he'd discovered that she had a relatively short fuse.

Nobody would ever guess Gina had once carried twins. Her figure was full but not overly so, a testament to her dedication to good nutrition and rigorous training, which in recent months had included archery. During their two days in Venice he'd found her a birthday gift, a bronze figurine of Diana, the Roman goddess of the hunt. He'd arranged for it to be shipped home, tolerating the extra cost because he wanted to surprise her. Right now that birthday party was just about the furthest thing from his mind, and so was sex, even though the sight of her in the nude had never before failed to arouse him, even a little. He considered that now and couldn't suppress a small grin. There was a first time for everything.

"What's so funny?" she asked as she stepped into her panties.

"Nothing. Well...not nothing. I was just thinking that this is the first time I've seen you like this and didn't want to throw you down on the bed."

"You could try to throw me down, but it might not work."

"It has before."

"That's because I let you." She fastened her bra and looked at herself in the mirror behind the head of the bed. "God, I look terrible." She fussed with her hair, then said, "When will this be over?"

"When we get Sophie back. By this time tomorrow we'll be heading to the airport for the flight home."

"I hope so." She sighed, then said, "Are you hungry? I could order room service. I could eat–"

The adjoining door to Mark's room swung open and Jim's brother stepped inside, his phone in his hand. "You're not going to believe this," he said, "but–" He stopped as he caught sight of his sister-in-law. "Oh, I'm sorry. I should've knocked."

"Don't sweat it, Mark," Gina said. "We've got more important things to worry about." She walked past him to the bathroom and pulled a robe from the hook on the inside of the door, then slipped it on.

"What's going on now?" Jim asked.

Mark held up his phone and looked like he was about to crush it in his hand. "I got an email from Randy," he said.

Randall Bannack was Mark's old West Point roommate and the president of OSS, the security firm he'd founded six years before. Now he was Mark and Jim's boss, and Jim suddenly knew the message wasn't exactly of the "good luck and good hunting" variety.

"He pulled the plug on the team," Mark said. "They're at the airport right now, but they're heading home tonight."

Jim was thunderstruck. "What the hell? Did you call him?"

Mark shook his head. "Not yet. He should be at the office, it's early afternoon there." Bannack had deliberately located the OSS headquarters in Fairfax County, Virginia, not too far from the George Bush Center for Intelligence, home of the CIA. The idea was to foster a close working relationship with that particular agency, and so far it was paying off. Thanks to the contacts Bannack had cultivated in the past few years, OSS had been picking up steady contracting work from the government.

"Get him on the horn," Jim said.

"Just hold on," Mark said. "It's not like Randy to just send an email about something important, especially involving a team on deployment. He's a hands-on guy, not a paper-pusher. Even if the paper's electronic."

"Then what–"

Mark's phone chirped with a soft trumpet fanfare. "That's the notification I have for a personal email from him," Mark said. "The stand-down order was from his corporate address." He touched a button, scanned the message, then said, "He wants me to call him on his red line."

"What's that?" Gina asked. She was sitting on the chair in front of the vanity. Her robe had fallen open and she snugged it back in place.

"The secure cell phone he only uses for Level One comms," Mark said. "Sorry, I have to do this in private." He went back to his room, shutting the door behind him.

"Level One?" Gina asked.

"It's a secure line Randy only uses to talk to his top people. There are six on the list, including Mark. I'm not on it."

Mark set the phone down on the desk and slid the glass door open, stepping out onto the balcony. He needed to get some fresh air and clear his head before making the call. Leaning on the railing, he gazed out over the city. The dome of St. Peter's was only a few blocks away. Sophie had wanted to visit there. She thought that maybe with her press credential she could get them into the tombs. Mark had thought there was very little chance of that happening, but he would've been happy to indulge her.

He looked at his watch. Just past six-thirty, so it was the lunch hour in Virginia. Mark knew Randy would still be in his office, sitting in his chair behind the antique desk, maybe looking out the window at the countryside as he wolfed down his usual meatball sub. Bannack had found an old building that had once been a technical college, bought it for a song and put a lot of work into the building and the five-acre campus. But hard work was something Bannack had never shied away from. Within three years he'd added two more buildings and carefully landscaped the campus. That had cost a pretty piece of money, but that was never a problem. Bannack's family had made a fortune in the shipping industry, and from his father and grandfather Randy had learned how to run a business. Within three years Odin Security Services was in the black, and three years later he'd opened a branch office in Chicago and hired Mark to run it, with another Academy classmate in charge of the Dallas branch. Business was good, and getting better. The world might be going to hell in a rocket, but there was money to be made out of the chaos.

Why had Randy ordered the team home? Why had he sent it

in an email, then asked for a call on the secure line? Bannack was a straight-shooter, it wasn't like him to pussyfoot around, even a little. When he led his battalion in Iraq, he always led from the front, right up until the day a mortar round took his right leg.

There was only one way to find out. Mark went back into the room, grabbed the phone and punched the speed-dial button. He paced the room while the connection was made, ending with the slight burring sound that indicated the line was secure. Bannack answered on the first ring.

"Randy, it's Mark. What the hell's going on?"

The voice came through from more than seven thousand miles away with a clarity that sounded like it came from across the street. OSS did not skimp on anything, especially commo gear. The only thing distinguishing it from a standard call was the slight echo. "Listen, Mark, I'm sorry about pulling the team out, but I had no choice. Two hours ago I got a call from Langley. The director."

Mark sat down on the edge of the bed. "The General?"

"That's right," Bannack said. The Director of Central Intelligence was Mark's former commanding officer during his last tour in Afghanistan, and Mark had always considered him a friend and mentor. He'd received a warm, hand-written note from the General upon his retirement from the Army this past spring. By then, Mark's old C.O. was several months into what Mark and everybody else assumed would be a long and successful tenure at the head of CIA, unless he stepped down early to run for president.

"Was it about this?" Mark asked. "About what's going on over here?"

"He knew the particulars. If I were a betting man, I'd lay odds that he got it from MI6. You told me you'd been liaising with one of their people in Rome, right?"

"Yes, but my contact here said he could keep it all close-hold, at least until we got Sophie back."

"Well, he wasn't able to, is my guess," Bannack said. "I'd say your man probably has his nuts in a vise right about now. The director knew about the kidnaping, knew about your tailing of the Serb suspect. You did get the guy, didn't you?"

"Yes," Mark said, "my brother took him down, actually."

There was a moment of silence on the other end, and then Bannack said, "How much is Jim involved in this?"

Mark ran his hand through his hair. "All the frickin' way. His wife was damn near killed by the guys who took Sophie. I had to use him to run the surveillance on the target. I didn't have any other assets available. The team was still in the air from Zurich. Jim tailed him into a church and the guy came after him with a knife."

"Listen, Mark, I'm not real sure about Jim getting into this any deeper. He's highly skilled, yes, and he had that little dust-up in Somalia last year, but the people you're dealing with now are a couple orders of magnitude above the clowns he had to deal with before."

Mark stood up, suddenly angry. "Hey, Jim is doing great, and I trust him, and you know damn well what he went through in Somalia was more than a goddamn 'dust-up'!"

"Okay, calm down. I'm concerned, that's all, Jim is doing a good job for us and I don't want to lose him. I don't want to lose either one of you."

Mark walked over to the window and stared out over the city.

"He'll be fine. Now what about the General? How does that connect with you pulling the team away from me here?"

There was a pause, and when Bannack spoke, Mark could hear the tension in his voice. "The government doesn't want anything upsetting the apple cart in Serbia right now. The war crimes trials are winding down and they just want to put all this Balkans bullshit behind them. In fact, I'm not at all sure they aren't monitoring our comms. That's why I sent the email the way I did. They might very well have hacked into our email account, and I'm not too sure about the phones, either, which is why I wanted you to make the Level One call. It's the most secure system we've got."

"I don't..." Mark pulled the chair out from the desk and sat down heavily. The fatigue was starting to get to him. He had to get some sleep, and soon, or things might start going even further south than they already were. "I still don't get it."

"Look, Mark, I'm sure it's not just about keeping things quiet in the Balkans. The General and his people are getting heat over Benghazi. You and I both know things were really bad over there and a lot of important people over here dropped the ball. The White House is trying to keep that quiet, at least until after the election. And that's only about three weeks away, you know. The last thing they want right now is another international incident that involves the CIA. The General's under a lot of pressure to keep a lid on things, and I think something else is going on, too."

"For the love of...What else?"

"I've just heard some rumors lately. The FBI is looking into him for something."

Mark was thunderstruck. "What the hell are you talking about?"

141

"I'm not sure what's going on there, but the point is, if you lead a strike team to Belgrade and things go tits-up, it'll come out that you once worked for the General and the media will make hay out of that, say it was some sort of CIA black ops goat fuck. Pile that on top of the Benghazi mess and the White House will go ballistic. I don't think they know about this thing with Novak yet, but..."

Mark sat back. He could hardly believe this was happening. "So he leaned on you, made you pull the team."

"I didn't have a choice, Mark. He didn't know about the team but he's a smart guy, he would know you'd ask for backup and I'd give it to you, and I swear to God, Mark, I would do that in a heartbeat, but he implied that if I didn't play ball, CIA would re-examine their ties with us, and we can't afford to lose those contracts. That's the bottom line."

"So I'm being hung out to dry, is that it? My wife's life is on the line and you won't help me? We got some actionable intel from the guy we bagged, but I'll need backup going in."

"Listen, Mark, I didn't get the impression that he wanted to do anything but help you, at the very least to stand aside while I got the company involved, but he's under a lot of pressure."

Mark exploded. "He's not the only one, for God's sake! If his wife was being held by some two-bit Balkan jerk-off, he'd send the goddamn 101st Airborne after them!"

"I know, Mark, but I did what I could. Now, my advice to you is to—"

"I don't need advice, Randy, I need backup, and it's pretty damn clear I'm not going to get it. So it'll just be me and Jim, and by God we're getting my wife back, and when we get back to the States, I'm coming over to see you, and I might just have my resignation with me." He threw the phone against the wall.

CHAPTER SIXTEEN
GROCKA MUNICIPALITY, SERBIA

Novak decided he needed to get some air. Dinner with his guest had not gone well. She'd said barely a word, picked at her food and then, after only twenty minutes, had asked to be excused. Reluctantly, he had acceded, ordering one of his guards to escort her down the hall and make sure she was locked in for the night.

It was too bad, really. A part of him had been hoping that some form of Stockholm Syndrome would set in for her, and she would at least be civil. He knew that a hostage showing sympathy for her captors happened in only about eight percent of such situations, but he'd held out hope she would be in that minority. Then again, she'd heard him on the phone a few hours before, telling her husband that he had only twenty-four hours to surrender himself to Novak or "steps would be taken." Sophie Barton-Hayes was nobody's fool.

It was a cool night, but not so chilly that a drive in his Audi with the top down would be unpleasant. There was a pub a few miles down the road he'd visited once or twice, finding it a pleasant place in which to unwind and escape the never-ending responsibilities that seemed to escalate as time went on. The last time he'd been there, what was it, two months ago? Yes, and that night he'd been chatted up by a lovely young barmaid. What was her name? Senca, or maybe Slavica. Perhaps she'd be there tonight.

He powered down his desktop computer and stood up, stretching. At the door, Viktor took a step inside, always alert to his boss's movements. "Can I get you anything, sir?"

"Yes," Novak said. "The keys to my Audi, plus my jacket and driving gloves. The brown leather jacket, the one I got in Prague last month."

"Right away, sir."

Two minutes later, Novak was at the front door, slipping into the jacket. "Who's on duty tonight?" he asked.

"Vladimir and Radovan," Viktor said.

"What about you?"

The young man gave him a tight grin. "My shift actually ended a half-hour ago, sir. I stayed on to see if I could help you with anything."

"Thank you, but you can retire," Novak said. The men stayed in a small barracks a few dozen meters from the main entrance to the estate. Novak had brought five men with him to help guard the woman. Two more were scheduled to arrive in the morning from Belgrade. That would give him eight men, including himself, to deal with the American when he arrived. More than enough.

Novak took the car keys from Viktor and hesitated. "Vladimir, you said?"

"Yes, sir." Viktor's expression changed ever so slightly.

Vladimir was a Russian who had been hired by Red Dragon two years earlier, after serving five years on the protective detail of some big shot oligarch in Moscow. The word Novak had gotten was that the man had been cashiered for being too friendly with his principal's wife, but Novak had taken him on after getting a solid recommendation from a colleague who operated a security service in the Russian capital. Besides, Vladimir was an expert handler of guard dogs, having learned much while in the Border Service branch of the Russian FSB, the successor to the notorious KGB. Still, there was something about the man that sometimes caused Novak to feel uneasy. Vladimir was cocky, although he was careful not to take that too far, at least when he was around the boss. He'd served one of the most powerful men in Russia and quite likely had bedded the man's wife. No doubt he considered serving a Serb, even one as powerful as Novak, to be a step down. Still, his work had been competent enough.

"Before you retire, do me a favor," Novak said.

"Certainly, sir."

"Have a word with Radovan, privately. Tell him that Vladimir is not to approach our guest, not to converse with her. I don't expect her to ask to come out of her room, but if she does, only Radovan is to deal with her. Is that clear?"

"Perfectly, sir. Have a nice drive."

The idea had seemed totally out of place at first, but then Sophie gave in and drew the bath. She could really use a change of clothes, at least undergarments, but the bath would allow her to relax, as much as a prisoner under sentence of death could do, anyway. And a nightly bath was part of her routine. She needed to hang onto something, and if this was the only part of her routine that could be used here, then she had to do it.

The tub was of the old free-standing, claw-foot variety, separate from the shower stall. After first checking to see if the door was locked–it was, from the outside as usual–she started running the water. A few simple toiletries had been provided, including a hair brush. Normally she washed her hair every other day and she was now overdue by a day. Perhaps tomorrow she would–

She stopped brushing and looked at herself in the mirror. Her face was gaunt and there were shadows under her eyes. There was no makeup to be had here and she wouldn't have used it anyway. What would be the point? She'd sensed that Novak was attracted to her, and that attraction might move him to keep her around longer. But she rejected that notion almost as quickly as she thought of it. In twenty-four hours either she would be dead or her husband would be, and she suspected the odds favored both of them being shot by Novak and his goons. She looked at the bathtub and considered shutting off the water and pulling the drain plug.

No. This bath might be her last one on this earth, but she would damn well take it.

The pub was ten kilometers from the estate. Novak had quickly discovered that the night air was chillier than he thought it would be, and the drive was not as comfortable as he'd hoped. Well, perhaps they had something inside that would take away the chill. A glass of *rakija* would feel good right about now, he decided. Just one, and then back home, unless of course the fair Slavica was there.

There were only two other vehicles in the small parking lot, a Peugeot sedan and a motorcycle. In his younger days, Novak had been a frequent visitor to the many clubs of Belgrade, until the non-stop dancing and drunkenness finally forced him to confine his visits to the *kafanas*, smaller places that one travel writer had described as a cross between an English pub and a Czech beer hall. The music, if there was any, was of the traditional Balkan folk variety and unplugged to boot. Much more Novak's style, and this place was like that. Novak put the Audi's top up and then went inside.

And she was there, her blonde hair cascading past her shoulders, her jeans loose enough to be comfortable and yet tight enough to enhance her figure. She smiled as she saw him. "Darko! It's been too long since you've visited us," she said as he sat at a table along the wall. "What can I get you this evening?"

"I have been thinking of rakija," he said. "What do you recommend?" There were hundreds of varieties of the fruit brandy produced in Serbia. He had his favorites, but he would let Slavica make the choice for him.

"We just got a new one in, a *dunjevača*, from the quince," she said. "It is splendid, but I have to tell you, it packs a punch." She cocked her head slightly and said, "Just two of them, and I'm helpless."

"Well, then, I'll have one, and perhaps you will join me?"

"Darko, I'm working! But," she added with a wink, "I'll see what I can do."

The bath had been exquisite, or about as exquisite as it could be under the circumstances. Sophie stepped out of the tub with real reluctance. The only thing she hadn't been able to do was shave her legs, as a razor was conspicuously absent from her meager toiletries. It was a nightly ritual for her, one Mark often liked to watch. At first she'd found that somewhat unnerving, but she'd come to enjoy his company, even subtly showing off for him. She knew her legs were her best feature, and she'd been pleasantly surprised to learn that her husband was a leg man. For now, though, the irksome stubble would have to stay.

Before getting into the tub she'd washed her panties thoroughly in the sink, then draped them over the heating radiator in the bedroom. Her blouse was getting very wrinkled, but they'd never allow her to iron it, and what was the point, really? She'd hung it over the edge of the door, hoping the steam from the bath would have an effect.

More than once, she halted her fussing and considered the ultimate futility of her actions, but then she would proceed. It was important to her, to hang onto something approaching dignity, even under these conditions. And they could be far worse, she knew. In her journalism career she'd seen some places where hostages had been held, hellholes primitive beyond belief. She supposed she could consider herself lucky, in that respect.

"Lucky," she said, as she toweled herself dry. "I wouldn't really call it that."

Constantly aware of the surveillance camera in a corner of the room at the ceiling, Sophie stayed in the bathroom as she pulled the blouse off the door and slipped it on. It hung low enough to provide her some cover below the waist, enabling her to maintain at least a modicum of modesty as she stepped out of the bathroom and reached for the panties on the nearby radiator. Turning her back to the camera, she stepped into the garment, realizing as she did so that her bum would be visible briefly to anyone watching the monitor. Well, she supposed she could tolerate that.

She'd left her bra in the bathroom and stepped inside to get it. The blouse wasn't sheer, but it was thin enough to leave little to the imagination if she wore no bra underneath, and that was where she drew the line. Before she could close the door behind her, she heard the sound of the key in the bedroom door.

A man stepped into the room, and she recognized him as one of the guards who had been training the dogs earlier in the day. He was of average height but broad across the shoulders, his dirty blonde hair closely cropped, and he was smiling at her as he removed his sport jacket. A pistol was holstered on his right hip.

Sophie stood with the bra in her hand and considered barricading herself in the bathroom, but knew that would be futile. "What do you want?" she asked with as much boldness as she could muster.

The man stepped into the bedroom and closed the door behind him. "Just came to check on you," he said with a thick Russian accent.

The moment he'd closed the door, Sophie knew what was coming. Even as the chilling realization gripped her, she knew she had to be strong. "Well, you've checked, and I'm fine, so get out."

"Yes, fine it is that you look. Very fine." He took two steps toward her.

"If you harm me in any way, your boss will not be pleased," Sophie said. She felt strangely calm. With everything that had happened, she had moved beyond fear. She remembered her self-defense lessons and quickly worked out the angles. If she could get past him and to the door, she could escape into the rest of the house, yell for help. On the other hand, if this was part of Novak's game, she had nothing to lose by resisting this oaf. She would go down fighting. Mark would want her to do that.

"Boss not here," the Russian said. He was now two steps away, maybe three. "Is best you not fight, *da*? Only make it worse for you."

She settled on a plan, a desperate one, but it was all she could come up with. She sighed deeply, looking downward. "All right, then," she said softly, inserting a tremble into her voice that was not entirely feigned. She took a step toward him, eyes still downcast, but she could still see him relaxing slightly as he brought his arms forward. He grasped her shoulders, gently but firmly.

"I have large gift for you," he said.

She looked up at him and smiled. "And I have one for you," she said. Reaching up quickly, she grabbed him behind the head and brought his face down as her right knee pistoned upward. The result was a crunching impact that snapped his head back up. Blood and mucous flew everywhere. She levered him aside onto the bed and made a break for the door.

Roaring with the pain, the Russian rolled off the bed and grabbed her by the hair, just as she was pulling the door open. He yanked back hard and she screamed. From the hallway came a flurry of scratches on the hardwood floor, followed immediately by a high-pitched yapping bark.

She tried to grab his arm to free herself, but only flailed her own arms in the air. Twisting her head, she saw his bloodied face, lips pulled back in a snarl, but he was looking out toward the dog in the hallway. Sophie could see it was Novak's Yorkie, barking furiously now.

Holding Sophie by the hair with his left hand, the Russian pulled his pistol with his right and aimed toward the dog. *"Zhal', chto ya khotel, chtoby moya sobaka ubit' vas,"* he muttered.

Sophie knew enough Russian to understand. He'd meant to feed the Yorkie to his own dog. "No!" she screamed, twisting herself around and shoving herself bodily into him. The gun went off, a thunderclap in the small confines of the room. In the hallway, the dog yelped. The Russian slammed against the baseboard of the bed and his grip on her hair loosened enough to allow her to pull herself free.

She glanced down the hallway and saw the dog scampering away, unharmed. Rage filled her, a fury she'd never before experienced. She saw the bra on the floor where she'd dropped it, picked it up and leaped onto the bed behind the Russian, who was trying to get to his feet. She wrapped the bra strap around his neck and pulled for all she was worth.

The Russian gagged and clawed at the cloth that was choking him. Sophie pulled harder and twisted. He clawed at the garment, trying desperately to dig his fingers underneath and relieve the pressure. A part of her brain told her that if she killed him it would go badly for her, for Mark, but she was done being humiliated, being threatened, being intimidated. It was time to show these bastards she wasn't as helpless as they thought.

She braced her feet against the baseboard, let out wild yell and yanked back as hard as she could.

CHAPTER SEVENTEEN
ROME, ITALY

"M ark, wake up." Jim shook his brother's shoulder. Mark stirred, then his eyes popped open and he sat up on the couch. He ran a hand over his face, feeling the bristle. He hadn't shaved since the previous morning. It seemed like a week had gone by since then. "How long was I asleep?"

"Nearly two hours," Jim said. "It's almost nine o'clock."

Mark stood up and tried to stretch out the kinks. The sleep had helped, but the fatigue had only been reduced, not eliminated. The weight of frustration and despair still draped his shoulders like a wooden yoke. Once again he told himself he had to put that aside. He had a mission, and he had to complete it. "Novak has a seat reserved for me on the noon flight to Belgrade," he said. "You might as well have let me sleep till morning."

"Mark, listen, I–"

"Forget it, Jim. It'll be just me on this one. I don't have any choice anymore, I have to play it Novak's way. Maybe, when I get there, I can work something out. I can…"

Jim shook his head. "Maybe for once you can listen to someone." He looked to the open connecting door as a man stepped into the room.

"Colonel Hayes," Krieger said, "I understand from your brother that you might need some help."

Gina had ordered room service for four, a salmon entrée with a side salad, light meals that would provide energy without filling them up. Mark ate mechanically as he and Krieger discussed their options. Jim was surprised at how hungry he was and had to force himself to eat slowly as he paid close attention to what the military men were talking about.

Krieger got right to the point. "The man from Red Dragon, the one Cunningham interrogated, what did he give you?"

"Three possible locations," Mark said. "There's corporate headquarters in Belgrade, a safe house in a residential section of the city, and Novak's private estate, about a two-hour drive from the airport."

"Could there be more? Do you think he was truthful?"

Mark chewed a piece of salmon as he thought, then said, "Sure, there could be any number of places where Novak is holding her, but we've got to start somewhere. As to whether he was telling us everything he knew, there's only one way to find out."

"Three targets, then," Krieger said. "Email them to me and I will plot out the coordinates."

"I hesitate to ask," Mark said, "but I have to. Can you give me any men?"

Krieger shook his head, and Jim could see the almost-hidden look of disappointment hit wash quickly over Mark's face. "Other than myself, I'm afraid not," Krieger said. "This is an off-the-books mission for me."

Mark looked away for a second, then back at Krieger. "If we were able to take an extra half-dozen men along, our odds would be a lot better," he said. "I certainly understand why you can't offer any. I know I can't get any help from my government, and my company has already been taken out of the picture by my boss. Soon to be my ex-boss, most likely. But under the circumstances, I really can't let you risk your own life." He looked straight at Jim. "And that goes for my brother, too."

Jim was about to object when Krieger jumped in. "You might have more friends than you realize," he said.

"What do you mean?" Jim asked.

Krieger sat back in his chair, appeared to consider something, then said, "Your brother may not have told you, but I am an American citizen by birth. My parents emigrated from Germany in the early fifties, after my father was released from a Russian POW camp. During his service in the *Wehrmacht,* one of his best friends was a young man by the name of Horst Kasner. And that gentleman was the father of a woman who currently holds a position of great importance in the Federal Republic."

Mark's eyes narrowed, then went wider, and his lips shaped into a sly grin. It was the first time Jim had seen anything resembling a smile from his brother since they were at the bar in Capua. "I'd heard that you had connections in Berlin," Mark said, "but I didn't know they went that high."

"My father and hers stayed in touch after the war," Krieger said. "So I have been acquainted with *Frau Bundeskanzler* since childhood. From time to time, she has called on me to perform what you might call special services for my parents' *Vaterland.* I was able to discuss the matter of your wife's kidnaping with her earlier today, and she persuaded my superiors to detach me for a few days of what officially is considered leave. I can also provide logistical support and weapons through my unit, but not manpower, unfortunately." He leaned forward, elbows on knees. "I'm sure you already know this, my friend, but I will say it anyway. Novak has no intention of letting Sophie live, even if you sacrifice yourself for her. It would be foolish of you to even think of giving him what he wants. That would not be the action of the man who fought beside me in Iran last year. That man was a true warrior, willing to defy great odds to complete the mission."

By the way his brother's eyes blinked, Jim could tell that one had hit home. "Your only chance of getting her out alive is to hit him before he is ready," Krieger said, "and you can only do that successfully if you have help. I offer my services and what resources I can bring with me." He nodded at Jim. "Your brother is an extremely capable man. His experience in Somalia speaks for itself. With us along, you have tripled your chances for success."

Mark nodded, and Jim could see he was deeply touched by his friend's gesture. "Jim, when this is over we'll need to make a detour through Berlin before we head home. I'll want to offer my thanks to the lady personally."

"You and me both," Jim said. He shook his head slightly. He'd always suspected that Mark had some friends in very high places, and that was becoming more apparent every day. And he hadn't missed what Krieger had said about his own abilities, either.

"All right," Mark said, back in mission mode again, "what about transport?"

"I called in a favor from a businessman I know here in Rome," Krieger said. "Two years ago, I led a team that rescued a hostage being held in Beirut. The hostage was one of his top people, and also had connections to some very important people in the Italian government. Thus, my unit was authorized to undertake the mission. We were successful. This businessman, he has agreed to provide us with one of his aircraft, a Lear that can get us to Serbia quickly."

"Novak will be thinking that I might come in ahead of schedule," Mark said. "He'll have people watching the airport in Belgrade."

"That is why we won't be flying to Belgrade," Krieger said. "We go past it, to the city of Vršac, near the Romanian border. From there, it is ninety minutes by car to downtown Belgrade. About two hours to Novak's estate, which is southeast of the city, close to the Danube." The German-American put his knife and fork down on the plate. Jim had noticed that he ate with great efficiency, and his utensils were placed just so, at four o'clock and eight o'clock on the plate. Somehow Jim wasn't surprised.

"Vehicles?"

"There is certainly a car rental agency or two at the airport," Krieger said. "One phone call should do it."

Mark nodded. "Weapons?"

"One light submachine gun and handgun per man. That's all I'm authorized to use right now, and all we should need, really. I have a certain amount of discretion when it comes to my unit's equipment, and if a few weapons, some ammunition and other gear are checked out for a few days, well, there are always training evolutions that require such things, aren't there?"

Mark grinned. "Yes, sometimes you have to get creative to keep the bean counters happy."

"What's the plan when we get to Belgrade?" Jim asked.

"With only three men, we cannot cover all three targets simultaneously," Krieger said. "Novak's corporate headquarters is, I think, the least likely place where he would be holding Sophie. His safe house in Belgrade should be our first priority. If she's not there, then I suggest the country estate."

Mark nodded. "If I were Novak, I'd keep her in the city. He has much quicker access to getting more men, and if he has to move her quickly it's a lot easier for him to get her to his headquarters." He glanced at his watch. "It's quarter to ten. If we can be wheels up by eleven o'clock, how soon can we be on the ground in Serbia?"

"The aircraft is a Learjet 70," Krieger said. "From wheels up to touchdown, I would say ninety minutes, perhaps less, depending on the wind."

"Mark's scheduled flight from Rome to Belgrade doesn't leave till noon from Leonardo da Vinci," Jim said. "Novak will have men at the airport to see that he checks in. If we're on the ground in Serbia by twelve-thirty, we can have eyes on all three targets by three, three-thirty. That will give us about seven hours before they would expect Mark to show up at the airport here in Rome."

Sitting next to Jim with her plate on her lap, Gina picked at her food, avoiding eye contact with the men. While Mark slept, Jim had used his brother's cell phone to call Krieger. That had led to a short but fierce argument, with Gina demanding to be brought along and Jim just as insistent that it would never happen. He'd ended it by putting his foot down: she would not be leaving Italy until they came back with Sophie, and they all flew back to the States together. It was the first time since their marriage began that Jim had so forcefully opposed her on anything, and he didn't feel good about it at all. Now, he put his hand on her back and gently massaged it. She blinked, but didn't look at him.

"If everyone's done, I'll take the plates," she said.

Jim offered to help her. Krieger motioned to Mark. "Colonel, a word in private, if I may?"

On the balcony, the night air was starting to cool. In the distance, the imposing dome of St. Peter's was bathed in light. "I will come to the point, Colonel," the NATO officer said. "We must have an understanding between us."

"And that is?"

"I am to be in command of the mission."

Mark felt his hackles start to rise. Krieger read the body language and held up a hand. "It goes without saying that your emotional involvement in this affair could conceivably cloud your judgment. It only makes sense for me to be in command."

Mark's shoulders sagged and he leaned on the balcony railing. "You're right, of course. It shouldn't even be up for discussion." He gazed out over the city, and once more thought of what he and Sophie could have been doing right now, should have been doing. Somewhere out there, having a glass of wine following an elegant dinner. He could only hope that wherever Novak had her now, she was being fed, allowed some privacy, that men weren't touching her, weren't–

He hung his head and fought to control his emotions. They

pushed right to the edge, ready to pull him over into a dark abyss that might not have a bottom. He was just about ready to go over when he felt a strong hand on his shoulder.

"Have courage, my friend," Krieger said. "We will find her. And when we do, Novak will face justice. *Your* justice."

Mark was pulling on a black tee shirt when there was a knock at the door of his room. If it was Krieger, he was about twenty minutes ahead of schedule. He stepped into the bathroom and ran a brush through his hair. He looked like hell. Worse, there was something tickling him in the back of his mind, and he couldn't get to it. He had the disturbing feeling that he was forgetting something, something vital to the mission. Shaking his head, he left the bathroom and went to the suite's main door. Looking through the peephole, he saw Paul Cunningham.

After returning from the interrogation, Paul had excused himself, saying he had to spend time with Evelyn. Now, the SAS veteran looked tired, but also upset. As soon as Mark opened the door, Paul hustled past him, then stopped and turned around. "You're going to Belgrade, aren't you?"

"Yes," Mark said. "I called your room and left a message about an hour ago."

"I got it, but I just now got free of Evelyn. She has absolutely forbidden me to go to Serbia with you."

Mark put a hand on the Brit's shoulder. "Hey, it's okay, Paul, I under–"

Cunningham walked away, shaking his head. "I told her, 'I've come with Mark and Jim this far, I have to go all the way,' but she was having none of it." He waved one hand angrily. "'You're sixty-three years old,' she says, 'time for you leave this to younger men.' I love her dearly, but sometimes she is just unreasonable. Completely unreasonable, I tell you."

In spite of everything, Mark had to smile. "I'll have to thank her," he said.

"Thank her for what?"

"First, for considering me to be a younger man," he said. "Second, for keeping you here. You've done your bit, Paul. Hell, man, we just met yesterday, and twenty-four hours later you're committing what are probably more than a few felonies, just to help us. I'm deeply grateful, but with Krieger, we've got this covered." Mark didn't feel nearly that confident, but he had to sound as if he was.

Cunningham had been around the block a few times, though, and by the look in his eyes he knew exactly what was going on. "He's helping you out, is he?"

"Yes." Mark said took a minute to fill in his British friend about the operation. As he talked, he realized how nebulous it must have sounded.

Paul sat down in the chair at the desk, his arms crossed, frowning. "I know what you're thinking," Mark said. "We're flying by the seat of our pants."

"That's putting it mildly. On the plus side, you have Krieger, and he's first-rate. But there are just three of you, and you have no diplomatic cover. You're counting on getting past the customs people in Vršac without trouble and hoping there is a suitable rental vehicle available. Those are just the first four problems I see, and at that point, you're not even on the road to Belgrade."

Mark sat on the edge of his bed, shaking his head. "It's a long shot, to be sure, but I don't see any other options. If I scrub the mission and just go there alone tomorrow like Novak wants, Sophie is as good as dead, and so am I." He stood up and started pacing. "I'm not kidding myself about our odds, Paul. If you have any suggestions, I'm all ears."

"Well, something did come to mind," Paul said. He pulled a cell phone out of his pocket.

CHAPTER EIGHTEEN
Grocka Municipality, Serbia

Novak was in a foul mood when he arrived back at the estate. The phone call from Viktor interrupted what had been a promising interlude with Slavica in his car, parked in a dark corner of the pub's lot. With great reluctance he had moved his hand away from her breast and picked up the phone. All Viktor said was that there was a problem and he requested that his boss return immediately.

Viktor was waiting in the foyer when Novak threw open the door. "What is it?"

"We had a problem with Vladimir, sir."

"What happened?"

The bodyguard looked rattled, which in itself was unsettling. Viktor was one of the steadiest men Novak had in his employ. But even though he was obviously uncomfortable, he looked his boss straight in the eye. "He attempted to force himself on the...on your guest."

"He did *what?*"

"I spoke to Radovan as you requested, just after you left. He swears he transmitted your order to Vladimir immediately. About a half-hour later...ah, perhaps you should let Radovan explain, sir."

"To hell with that. Where is Vladimir? I will have the *kurvin sin* drawn and quartered! He will feel pain as he has never felt!"

"I, uh, don't think that will be necessary, sir."

Novak's glare was a mixture of anger and bewilderment. He shoved past Viktor and walked quickly down the hallway. His captive's room was at the end of the hall, and two of his men flanked the partially-opened door. "Why is the door open?" he shouted back over his shoulder. "What the hell is going—"

He stopped outside the doorway when he saw the body. Vladimir lay next to the bed, arms splayed, his face an ugly dark red, eyes bugged, tongue lolling from his half-opened mouth. Above it, the nose was crushed and covered with blood. He was clearly dead, and Novak immediately recognized the signs of strangulation, something he had seen on three different men who had been on the receiving end of his own garrote. Novak pushed the door the rest of the way open and stepped inside the bedroom.

Sophie Barton-Hayes stood near the head of the bed. At first Novak thought she was wearing only her blouse, but then he saw the hem of her underwear on one hip, just below the shirt. She was calm, but her eyes no longer had the fear he'd seen before. Now there was something else, harder. Defiance.

Blood had spattered onto the floor and the multi-colored quilt covering the bed. A garment lay next to Vladimir, white with splotches of dark red. Novak reached down and picked it up. Her brassiere.

"You killed him?" he asked her, tossing the murder weapon onto the bed.

"Yes," she said.

"I am sorry," Novak said. "I had given strict orders–"

Her eyes flashed. "You can take your strict orders and shove them all right up your arse, you dirty bastard. If I were you, I'd have one of your goons drive me to the nearest airport, because if I'm still here when my husband arrives, he's going to kill every one of you. All I did was reduce the number by one. He will take care of the rest."

OVER THE ADRIATIC

Jim had never been in a Lear, and under other circumstances he would've enjoyed this ride immensely. The passenger cabin was plush and there was plenty of food and a full bar available, even though nobody wanted anything stronger than bottled water right now. The only thing missing was the well-built flight attendant who certainly would've been aboard if this were a James Bond film.

Thinking of a Bond girl was stupid, of course, and Jim chalked that one up to the fatigue factor. He felt himself sink back into the luxurious leather seat as the plane roared down the runway and lifted off. Mark was sitting across from him, next to Krieger. Nobody said anything until three minutes after takeoff, when Krieger excused himself and went forward to the flight deck.

The NATO operative had supplied them with tactical gear, including head-to-toe clothing that was a rush just to put on. Jim's pants were made of cotton canvas, with pull-tabs to adjust the waistband, reinforced seat and knees, and seven pockets. The long-sleeved shirt was another marvel of clothing engineering, with two breast pockets and special elbows and sleeves that made it seem as if he were hardly wearing anything over his tee shirt. Although he suspected the material was designed to keep him cool in hot environments and warm in the cold, he unzipped it down to his chest as he adjusted himself in the seat.

Across the small table between them, Mark frowned. "What's that symbol on your tee shirt?"

Jim automatically looked down, then zipped the top shirt up another two inches. "Nothing," he said. He wasn't about to admit to his brother that he was wearing the black tee with the Batman logo that he'd brought along for his workouts.

He could see a grin pulling unsuccessfully at Mark's lips. "Just keep it covered up," he said. "We'll be operating at night, so stay black."

"That won't be a problem with this stuff," Jim said. He stretched out his left leg and flexed his booted foot. "How the hell did Krieger come up with the correct sizes for these boots?"

"He told me after he met us this morning, he had a feeling we might be getting into something and he selected gear based on our photographs."

Jim cocked his head. "When did he take pictures of us?"

"He didn't," Mark said. "We were under constant surveillance when we entered the embassy compound. They knew all about us by the time we got to the conference room. With their software, coming up with clothing and shoe sizes was easy chips. Don't look so surprised, Jimbo. You're playing in the big leagues now." Mark leaned his head back against the headrest and closed his eyes.

DAVID TINDELL

Jim settled back and looked past his brother, toward the bulkhead separating the cabin from the flight deck. "The big leagues," he mumbled. The operators Jim worked with at OSS, almost all of them ex-military, used an occasional sports metaphor. But he'd started noticing how often people in sports and business used military metaphors. "Take the beach," "outflank them," "fire a warning shot." And the politicians were the worst. Every time he heard "war on women," he had to suppress an urge to gag. What did those business people, those politicians, know about war? Damn few of them had ever been in uniform, that was for sure. Mark had once talked to him about the disconnect between American civilians and the men and women who served the country in the armed forces. What was most disappointing to him about civilian life, he'd said, was how the civilians weren't being asked to make sacrifices at all; the military people, and their families, had to sacrifice all the time.

Jim knew he wasn't part of that disconnect himself. He had never been in uniform himself, thanks to his college knee injury, but his experience in Somalia last year had given him all the combat experience he ever wanted to have. "But here I am again," he said, shaking his head at the irony.

"Yes, here you are," Mark said.

"Sorry," Jim said. "Didn't mean to wake you."

"It's all right. I'm a little too wired to sleep right now anyway, though God knows I could use some shuteye." Mark gazed out the window into the dark. "Ship lights down there," he said. "We're over the Adriatic."

"What did Paul have to say?" Cunningham had stopped by

167

Jim's room to wish him luck, right after what had sounded like a heated conversation in Mark's adjacent room. "He sounded upset when he was in there with you."

"He was just pissed that he wasn't coming with us. But he did solve one problem for us. He got hold of an old SAS comrade in Romania who can supply us with a vehicle. Should be waiting for us at the airport in Vršac."

"Any extra manpower?"

Mark shook his head. "No, it'll be just the three of us." He took a deep breath and looked out the window again. "He also gave me some advice."

"A guy with his experience is always helpful."

Mark looked back at his brother. "Not tactical advice. Between me and Krieger we've pretty much got that covered. No, Paul talked to me about something else."

Jim was silent, waiting for Mark, who seemed to be gathering himself. "It was about what I'll have to do when we get to the target."

"You mean, what *we'll* have to do," Jim said.

"Nope. This one will be on me." He looked back out the window.

After signing off on the call to Romania, Paul had held his cell phone, contemplating something.

"Thanks for your help," Mark said. "Having a vehicle ready is one less problem we'll have to deal with."

"It's an important detail, but not the most important one," Paul said.

"The most important is finding Sophie and bringing her home. Alive."

Paul stood, and in his eyes Jim could see the steel that had carried his new friend through thirty years in one of the world's most elite combat outfits. "When you get there, it will be much more than a tactical problem in search of a solution," Paul said. "You're a soldier, the tactical solution will quickly become apparent. You and your men will prosecute the target efficiently, I'm sure. But there will be a point at which you will have to take an action, Mark, and it will likely be only you who can do it."

Mark knew what was coming. He nodded. "I know," he said.

"Do you?" The old commando took a step closer. "This will be like no other mission you've ever undertaken. There is nobody further up the chain of command to take responsibility. This time, you're the one at the top of the chain. Moreover, your adversary is not a Taliban fighter, not an Iraqi insurgent. Novak is a man unlike any you've ever encountered. You can expect no mercy from him. He blames you for the death of his brother and he's already decided he will take your life, and undoubtedly your wife's as well, in retribution. Whatever he has built for himself since the war, he has shown he is willing to risk it all in order to exact his revenge on you. Attempting to negotiate with him will be useless. That has already been proven."

"I–"

Paul pointed at him. "You must be prepared to kill this man. Turning him over to the authorities will be a mistake. He will be out of jail inside of twenty-four hours. Then he will hunt you again, and this time he will not stop just because you have left Europe. He will track you down at your home back in Wisconsin. You and your wife, and your brother and his wife, none of you will ever be able to rest easy, because Novak will be out there. Your only alternative is to kill him, and do it as soon as you can. You may not want to do it, but this is not a situation where you can take prisoners. The only question remaining is who will emerge from this confrontation, you or him."

Mark saw another ship below, sailing the calm waters of the Adriatic. From the lights, it looked like a cruise liner. Where was it headed? North to Venice, perhaps, or maybe south toward the Greek islands in the Aegean, or around the Italian boot and up toward southern France. He had thought about taking Sophie on a cruise like that. The next several hours would determine whether he would take her anywhere ever again.

He checked his watch. They were about an hour from Vršac. Pretty soon they would be feet-dry over Croatia and then quickly over Bosnia, and a few minutes later in Serbian airspace and starting their descent. When they got on the ground, things would get interesting.

Paul had been right, of course. As many missions as Mark had been on, and there had been a lot of them, this one was different. Would he be able to kill Novak? Mark had killed more than a few men, had given orders that had resulted in the deaths of many more. But as down and dirty as a lot of those operations were, they were more abstract than this. When he wore the uniform, his orders had always come down from above. Men sitting in a headquarters somewhere told him to fight and to kill the enemies of his country, to protect his own people and those who were at least nominal allies.

The idea always was to take care of the bad guys "over there," before they could come "over here" and attack his own people, and so for twenty-five years he had done his duty, and done it well.

Mark knew the challenge he now faced was the greatest of his life. This was entirely on him. He was taking his only brother, and one of his best friends, into combat. There was no guarantee any of them would come out of this alive. But they were standing with him, even though they knew the risks. They knew he would have done the same for either of them. He looked at his brother, dozing in his seat. Damn, he was proud of Jim. But he was afraid for him, too. His responsibility for Sophie, and for Jim and even for Krieger, suddenly pressed down on him.

He looked back out the window and took a deep breath. He recognized the fear inside him, but he would not let it defeat him. There was too much at stake. Someone had invaded his life and taken his wife. The woman he loved was down there in the darkness ahead of them. She was still alive, he knew that in his gut, and she was afraid, but she knew he'd be coming for her. She knew he would slay the man who had threatened her.

Her husband knew it, too.

Mark shook him awake. "We're starting our descent."

Jim yawned and sat up in his seat, shaking off the disorientation. Krieger was sitting next to his brother, and they were examining a map on the small table between the pairs of facing seats. "How long till we land?" Jim asked.

"Twenty minutes," Krieger said. He pointed to a spot on the map. "Then she's here, you think?"

Mark nodded. "Ever since we got back to the hotel from the interrogation, something was bothering me. I'd forgotten some bit of intel, something important."

"It happens," Krieger said.

"What was it?" Jim asked.

Mark looked over at him. "When Novak called and put her on the phone, I asked if she was all right, and she said she'd rather be home with me, in front of the fireplace."

"You don't have a fireplace in your house," Jim said.

"No, but we've talked about having one in the place we plan to build, out in the country on a lake somewhere. I think she was telling me she's in the country."

"Novak's estate on the Danube."

"Exactly. Then I remembered that we'd discussed hostage situations after one of her stories was aired, about a kidnaping in Libya. The victim was a German national, and in his message to his family he said his blood sugar count was low, around seventy-five. He didn't have diabetes, so he was telling them that the number of men guarding him was not that high. Sophie and I worked out a code, just in case she was ever in a hostage situation, and we made it more precise. She would give me a number and I would divide it by ten. That would be the approximate number of people she believed were guarding her. She said her sugar count was about a hundred."

For the first time in what seemed like weeks, Jim saw actual hope in his brother's eyes. "So it's the country estate, and Novak has about ten men," he said.

"That's right," Mark said. "Our odds just got better."

CHAPTER NINETEEN
VRŠAC, SERBIA

Danilo Ilić reported for work sober for the first time in a week. As he sat behind his small desk in the customs office at Vršac International Airport, he reflected on why this was so. Working the graveyard shift in one of Serbia's smallest airports was reason enough to have a few before settling in for another long and boring night, wasn't it?

But at least the reason tonight was a good one. Anja had surprised him by wanting to have sex before he left. Usually she was just too tired, what with her full-time job and the baby and all, but tonight she was almost as randy as she had been during their courtship three years ago. Ilić sat back in his chair with a satisfied smile that suddenly turned to a frown. What if she was ovulating? Was that what they called it? *Fak,* the last thing they needed now was another mouth to feed. His mood immediately soured and he wished he'd brought a flask along.

What he really needed, more than a drink, was to get another job. This one was obviously going nowhere, and going there quickly. Six months now since he'd been hired and there was still no prospect about getting a better shift, even the four-to-midnight. At least that would be tolerable. The airport was small, but got enough flights from neighboring countries to keep a customs agent busy during the day. And another thing Ilić knew about the day shift was that you could get your beak wet now and then. There were regular flights from Romania and Bulgaria whose passengers wanted to engage in business here in Serbia that might lie, it could be said, in certain gray areas. These men–and they were almost always men, he'd heard, although sometimes there were women, and good-looking ones to boot–were willing to do a little extra business with the customs office in order to avoid unnecessary paperwork and embarrassing questions.

But that never seemed to happen on the graveyard shift. Even Romanian and Bulgarian gangsters had to sleep. Well, perhaps it was time to call his cousin again. Filip had connections with some powerful people in Belgrade, or so he'd boasted. Who did he work for now, anyway? Hadn't he gotten a new job himself, just a few months ago? Maybe by now he would have enough influence to put in a good word for his country-boy cousin out here in the sticks near the border.

No, it wasn't fair that Ilić was missing out. It was time for him to get aboard the train of gravy that was lifting Serbia out of the chaos of the war. Even Zorić, who worked the evening shift just ahead of him, got some of that gray-area traffic. In fact, he'd been talking to three men out on the tarmac, just as Ilić was parking his car. Possibly the men were from that fancy jet that was sitting out there. You didn't see too many like that, even from the gangsters, who fancied themselves big shots but couldn't afford the Lears and Cessna Citations that were more common in the EU, or so he'd heard.

Zorić had clocked out after clearing the three men, and the fact that he hadn't said anything about them to Ilić meant just one thing:

they'd allowed him to wet his beak. The clock on the wall showed nearly one a.m. The mysterious visitors had departed only fifteen minutes ago, aboard a black SUV. Would Zorić have made the required entries into the customs database? Ilić logged on to the computer network–something he should've done as soon as he arrived–and searched through the entries for the previous nine hours, since the start of Zorić's shift. There had been six separate entries, involving a total of fifteen people. Three flights from Bucharest, Romania…no, nothing unusual there. Two from Bulgaria, one from Hungary. But the last one, the Hungarian flight from Kecskemét, had touched down for refueling around ten o'clock. A Hungarian Air Force Yak-52 trainer that apparently had gotten lost and wandered across the border. So much for the diligence of the Serbian air defense system.

But nothing since then. Ilić got up and went over to the window. The customs office was on the ground floor of the pyramid-shaped building that served the airport as its passenger terminal and offices, with the control tower rising from the top. From this office, he could see the airport's only runway, which ended with a sharp hundred-degree turn to the right, onto an access runway back to the terminal and the parking area. The jet was still out there, its cockpit dark but two of the passenger cabin's windows on this side were open and low light was streaming through from inside. It was an unusual place to park, wasn't it? If he didn't know better, he'd think that they were preparing for a sudden departure. Otherwise they would have taxied all the way over here to the infield in front of the terminal and the adjacent hangars.

Something was going on. Ilić stared at the jet, trying to read the tail number, but it was too dark. Closer to the terminal, there would've been better light. Perhaps that was another reason for their choice of parking space. He gave up and went back to his desk. It was probably nothing, probably some Bulgarians who were on their way to Belgrade right now. Another thought occurred to him: maybe they were Russians. They were a long way from home, but perhaps they'd come from a port on the Black Sea where he'd heard many of these oligarchs had mansions. Southern Ukraine, maybe eastern Bulgaria. The shores of the Black Sea were only what, two hours' flight time away? And these Russians would have enough money for a jet like that. They'd probably be back here and in the air by noon, maybe before. What would Russian gangsters be doing here, in the dead of night, staying dark? Whatever it was, it would be no good for somebody.

Ilić sat down and drummed his fingers on the desktop blotter. His eyes drifted over his desk and the blinking light on his phone caught his eye. Why had he not noticed it before? As was his habit, he'd taken the phone out of his jacket pocket when he arrived and set it on the desk, near the old coffee cup with the picture of Marshal Tito on it. Zorić had brought it months ago and used it to store pens and pencils. Ilić pressed the button and the screen lit up. The phone was a new Motorola Nexus, which Anja had bought him for his birthday a month ago. The first message she'd sent him had been a photo of herself in the shower. Maybe another one tonight? No, it was a text message, from Filip, of all people. *Be on the lookout for anything unusual. Call me anytime.*

The time stamp said 10:25pm. Well, now. Would Filip be

interested in these Russian gangsters that had just arrived? Excited, Ilić tried to call back, but he couldn't figure out the phone. Frustrated, he reached into his back pocket and pulled out his wallet. Was Filip's card still in there? Yes, there it was. The dragon logo caught his eye. A private security firm.

If those Russians were on some sort of secret mission, maybe on their way to Belgrade right now, might they be after someone Filip's firm was protecting? Ilić started to breathe harder. Yes, it happened in the cinema all the time, didn't it? Gangsters! Who knew what they were up to, or who they were after?

Maybe it was nothing. Maybe Filip's people would have nothing to do with these men. Ilić weighed the risk of interrupting his cousin's slumber in the middle of the night, versus the chance that it might be something, and if his tip helped Filip, why, his cousin would be grateful, wouldn't he? Might he then recommend to his superiors that they hire this sharp-eyed young man whose talents were being wasted in the graveyard shift at a country airport?

Ilić scanned the card for Filip's private cell number and picked up the handset of his desk phone. Taking a deep breath, he punched in the number.

GROCKA MUNICIPALITY, SERBIA

The buzzing phone pulled Viktor out of his doze. "Yes?" He

listened intently for sixty seconds, asked three questions, then said, "Thank you for your report, Filip. I will take it to the colonel immediately."

He signed off the call and thought about what he'd said. The phone's clock indicated twenty past one in the morning. The colonel had finally gone to bed, but not before giving Viktor and Radovan a fearsome dressing-down. What made it worse was that Novak had not flown into a rage, had not raised his voice or even used profanities. None of that. He had looked his men in their eyes and simply stated what he thought of their actions this evening, or rather their lack of certain actions, and told them what would happen to them if his guest was placed in any further danger by any of the men.

It was Novak's eyes that frightened Viktor the most. He had seen his colonel in a fury before, but this time it was different and even more unnerving. Those eyes had drilled right into him. No doubt Radovan felt the same way. They both left the colonel's study grateful that he had not shot them both on the spot.

Viktor decided that retiring to his room in the barracks would not be the smart thing to do right now. He put Radovan and the other two men to work cleaning up the mess in the woman's room. Vladimir's body was taken to the walk-in freezer and stored there. The next day it would be trucked back to Belgrade for whatever arrangements would be made. Right now that was the furthest thing from Viktor's mind. At its forefront was his desire not to screw up again.

The next thing he'd done was to put out a company-wide alert via text message. *Condition yellow. Report anything unusual. Utilize your contacts.* Filip was one of the new guys, but had come to them highly recommended and was working out well so far. He was showing initiative, thankfully. He'd reached out to his cousin and received a report that was indeed unusual. Three unknown men flying into some airport near the Romanian frontier, bribing their way through customs and disappearing. Maybe it was nothing. Men came into Serbia all the time and wanted to keep their business quiet, and it rarely had anything to do with Red Dragon's clients. The colonel had been meticulous about keeping his company clean of any involvement with the worst of the gangsters and drug runners.

But maybe this time, it was something.

Should he awaken the colonel? Viktor knew he had to make a decision, and make it quickly. If he disturbed his boss any more, he might pay for it, especially considering this was probably nothing. On the other hand, if Viktor handled it himself and it turned out to be nothing, there was no harm done. And, on the off chance it turned out to be something, Viktor would have shown initiative, proving once again that he could be trusted, that the nasty business with Vladimir had been an unfortunate error that would not happen again.

Two out of three. Viktor decided he would place two phone calls. Two teams, four men each, should be sufficient. One positioned near the safe house in Belgrade, the place where Novak had first considered stashing his hostage, and another...where? A check of a map helped him with the decision. There, on Highway 153, just west of Brestovik and the intersection with 351. A stretch of road that was bordered on both sides by farmland for two or three kilometers. A good place for a roadblock, just a checkpoint like those the police occasionally set up to catch drunk drivers. He would tell them to establish it a kilometer away from the road that led to the villa. Using the GPS app in his phone, he computed the distance between that point and Vršac, and then in the other direction to the apartment complex in Belgrade where many of the men stayed. If he roused them now, they should be on station about an hour before any vehicle from Vršac could possibly arrive.

He made the calls, emphasizing to the team leaders that speed was of the essence. Going out on a limb, he promised the men bonuses if they checked in from their stations within sixty minutes. If necessary, Viktor decided would pay them out of his own pocket. It would be worth it to show the colonel that he was on the ball.

CHAPTER TWENTY
GROCKA MUNICIPALITY, SERBIA

"I make it about three kilometers to the turn," Mark said from the front seat. The glow from his phone's GPS screen gave his face a blue-green tint. Krieger, at the wheel, gave a curt nod. Mark added, "We're passing the secondary access road."

"Are you sure about taking this route?" Jim asked from the back seat. He'd argued the point during the mission planning on the flight, saying that taking a back road would avoid coming in on what was obviously the most direct route to Novak's estate, and also the one most likely to be guarded. "We could come in on that secondary road. Might take an extra ten or fifteen minutes, but–"

"We talked about that, Jim. There are a lot of private homes along that route. More chances for us to get spotted."

Krieger swung the wheel to the right, allowing the powerful Audi Q5 to hug the curve. The road ahead straightened out into the distance, but the darkness was pierced by two pairs of headlights angling across the two-lane road in their direction. Underneath the large white beams, amber hazard lights flashed. Almost drowned out were the red tail lights of the vehicle that was about a half-kilometer ahead of their Audi. They'd encountered little traffic since leaving Vršac, but this particular car had pulled out ahead of them on the outskirts of Brestovik. Krieger had slowed enough to keep a decent distance between them.

"We might want to consider Jim's suggestion," Krieger said as he tapped the brakes. "That's a roadblock up ahead. They're facing us, so they are anticipating something coming from our direction. I don't like this."

"Police?" Jim asked.

"Doubtful," the NATO commando said. "We would see actual traffic barriers with flashing lights if it was official."

"They can get away with that here?"

Mark glanced over his shoulder at his brother. "This isn't Wisconsin."

"The other car is slowing," Krieger said as he braked the Audi almost to a stop. Jim looked through the back window. Nothing but night.

"The gap's too narrow to allow us to shoot through," Mark said, leaning forward as he stared out the windshield. "We need to turn around."

Krieger was already pulling onto the shoulder. "We'll backtrack to the secondary route." He turned the Audi across the road into a Y-turn. "Jim, get the weapons out of the back."

They'd kept their submachine guns stored in the rear cargo area of the Audi, hidden under the floorboard that covered the spare tire well. This particular Q5 had been modified to include a pair of separate storage wells designed for weapons, and the floorboard could be pulled up from the back seat as well as the rear gate side. Jim had paid close attention when they loaded the weapons at the airport. Krieger had made it clear that, on this ride, he had only two jobs: watch for any kind of pursuit, and stay close to the weapons.

They were beauties: Hechler & Koch MP7A1 models, German manufactured and firing a 4.6x30mm armor-piercing, high velocity round that could pierce twenty layers of Kevlar at two hundred meters. Jim had worked with a few light submachine guns on the OSS range, but not this model. Krieger had given him a quick tutorial on the flight, but Jim had already decided that if he had to use a gun on this mission, he'd try to stick with the Beretta M9 pistol. At least he'd trained with that one back home.

Jim passed two of the MP7s up to the front. Mark checked his over, doing it almost by feel as he kept an eye out the passenger window as Krieger shifted into reverse. "I see movement on foot down there," he said. "Looks like they're letting the car through, but I think they're mounting up."

Krieger shifted again, swung the wheel around and hit the gas as the Q5 came out of the shoulder into the east-bound lane. In seconds he ripped a tight left turn onto the secondary road, staying off the brake. The new road was narrower and unmarked. Dark houses flew silently past their windows.

They'd made it about half a kilometer when Jim saw headlights sweeping onto the road from behind. "We've got company back here," he said. He had to force himself to control his breathing.

"How many headlights?" Krieger asked.

"One pair."

"They've left one car on the main road, just in case," Mark said. "What's our play here?"

183

"We have to assume they know the road," Krieger said as he swung around a curve to the left. "They can take it faster than we can. We have to deal with them before we reach the target, otherwise we'll come under fire from two directions."

"We can assume they're hostile, then?" Jim asked, even though he knew the answer in his gut.

"Can't take the chance they're not," Mark said. "They were waiting for us. Either it was just a standard precaution Novak decided to take, or somebody at the airport tipped them off."

"Then we have to deal with them now," Krieger said, "and hope they don't call Novak before we engage."

"Something that will do the job quickly," Mark said.

Krieger nodded ahead. "We're taking that side road up there, and then I'm putting us in the ditch. Mark, you take whatever cover you can on the right. Jim and I will go to the left. When they stop to check out the vehicle, we take them. Don't open fire unless I shoot first."

"Do we try to take them alive?" Mark asked.

"If possible. Leaving a lot of bodies behind won't make it easy for us to leave the country."

"Got it." Mark looked into the back. "You ready, Jim?"

His hands were already starting to sweat, but Jim said, "Yeah."

Krieger took the turn almost at full speed, and Jim felt the Q5 sway dangerously to its right. Seconds later Krieger jammed the brakes, putting the vehicle into a controlled skid, and aimed for a shallow ditch on the right side of the road. The right front wheel went down with a splash of water. Jim was out the left side door and sprinting across the road before he remembered that this area had been drenched by a thunderstorm only an hour or so before. They'd seen the distant flashes of lightning before they'd crossed the Danube at Smederevo. He leaped the narrow ditch and four long strides brought him to a low stone wall. He balanced himself on one hand and vaulted over it, landing on soggy ground and crawling back to the wall as Krieger landed beside him.

Krieger peered over the wall, his MP7 at the ready. "Did you leave the suppressors in the vehicle?"

Jim reached into a pocket and pulled one of the sound-suppressing tubes out, handing it over to the German-American. Remembering Krieger's tutorial, Jim retrieved his own suppressor and screwed it onto the end of his weapon. There were no silencers for their pistols, however.

In the distance they heard the growl of a powerful engine. "Jim, don't fire your weapon unless we are being overrun," Krieger said. "No offense, but you haven't trained with this model."

"None taken." Jim looked behind them. A farmhouse stood about fifty meters away, its windows dark, but somewhere behind it a dog began to bark. That wasn't good. He stretched to peer over the top of the wall and saw the pursuing vehicle start to slow down. "Here they come."

The large SUV came to a stop ten yards behind the Audi, its headlights on high beam. Jim couldn't see past them to the far right side of the road. He had to trust that Mark had found cover over there.

The front doors opened and two men emerged, the driver with a pistol, the passenger carrying a submachine gun. The driver flared out to provide a good field of fire to the Audi. Jim knew

185

trained men when he saw them, and these guys were not going to go down easy. He glanced at Krieger and sensed the NATO commando had come to the same conclusion.

The driver pulled a cell phone from his jacket pocket with his left hand. Krieger raised his weapon, sighted on the driver and slid his finger inside the trigger guard, then yelled, *"Tippin Sie auf das Telefon und Sie sterben!"* Jim searched frantically through his college German, recognizing the words for "telephone" and "die." Krieger was giving them a chance, just as he'd said. Whether that would turn out to be a good idea was about to be determined.

Across the road, Mark sighted his MP7 on the head of the man who'd emerged from the passenger seat. He heard Krieger's shout in German and knew the next few seconds would be critical. He had no doubt they could drop the two Serbs and, with their weapons silenced, they could probably get away without alerting the locals. The dog was still barking from the farmhouse behind Krieger and Jim's position, though, and Mark knew they didn't have much time. If the dog's owner was roused and found two dead bodies on the road, the local police would be here in minutes.

"Ne razumem," the driver said. Mark had heard that a lot during his deployment in the Balkans. He was saying he didn't understand, but that was probably bogus. Germany was the de facto leader of the European Union and so a lot of people knew the language, or at least enough to get by. The driver was stalling.

On this side of the car, the Serb with the submachine gun brought his weapon up and crouched behind the car. Mark hoped his German would be good enough. He was only five yards away

186

from the road, using a large bush for cover. He aimed his MP7 at the man and said, *"Hande hoch!"* If this guy had ever seen any World War II movies, he'd know what that meant.

The Serb brought his own weapon around and Mark reacted immediately, moving his gunsight slightly to the man's left and upward. He squeezed the trigger and the silenced weapon produced a catlike spit. The side mirror on the SUV exploded with a loud crack. The crouching Serb cried out and slapped his hand against the side of his neck.

Mark was up from his crouch and leaped across the ditch, taking the last three yards in a stride and a half. The Serb focused on the barrel of the gun pointed between his eyes and dropped his own weapon. Mark could see blood seeping around the man's hand from the neck wound. He'd been clipped by a shard from the side mirror, and that would have to be tended to fast if the carotid artery had been nicked. Mark kicked the man's gun away. He heard footsteps and shouts from the other side of the SUV and the clatter of something falling onto the road.

"Scheiss!" Krieger leaped over the stone wall and raced to the road, Jim following and angling to the right so the Serb on this side wouldn't be able to take them both if he opened fire. The Beretta trembled in his hand as Jim fought to control it. The guys on the range had always told him it would be a different story the first time he pointed a loaded weapon at a man, and now he knew how true that was.

The Serb had reacted to the sound of the gunshot from the other side by jamming his thumb down on the phone. He brought his pistol around but Krieger was on him, swinging his MP7 around to knock the man's gun away. The German-American pivoted on his lead foot and whipped around to deliver one of the best turning sidekicks Jim had ever seen, directly into the Serb's abdomen. The phone clattered to the pavement, bounced twice and slid toward the ditch.

Krieger finished the Serb with a blow to the temple from the stock of the MP7. He looked at Jim and pointed at the phone. In two strides Jim had it. A smart phone, and on the screen was the photo of a man. The call had gone through. *"Zdravo? Jovan, šta se dešava?"*

Krieger made a slashing motion across his throat, but Jim had already punched the phone icon, ending the call. He slipped the phone into a pocket and walked quickly to the SUV, keeping his Beretta ready but pointed at the pavement. "He must've hit a speed-dial button," Jim said. "Did you hear it? What did it mean?"

"Nothing good," Krieger said. "They know we're here now. Novak will be alerted. We have only a few minutes, if that. Secure this one with your zip ties, wrists and ankles, and get his weapon as well." Jim fished the ties out of a thigh pocket of his pants and went to work on the unconscious Serb.

Mark had already zip-tied the Serb's wrists in front of him. The man was losing consciousness. Krieger came around the back of the SUV just as Mark was applying pressure to the wound, trying to stanch it with a dirty handkerchief he'd pulled from the Serb's back pocket.

"I had to fire," Mark said. "He was ready to open up on me."

"I heard the round. It punched through the car half a meter

from my left." Krieger knelt next to him and brought out his cell phone, activating the flashlight app to give Mark some light. "Carotid?" Krieger asked.

"I don't know. Maybe." He nodded to a bloody shard of glass lying on the Serb's left leg. "I wanted to take the mirror just to distract him. Thousand to one that he gets clipped right here."

"It happens. I'll see if I can find a first-aid kit. If we can patch him up, we do it and go."

"Ordinarily I'd say we should get this guy to a hospital, but we're running out of time."

Krieger opened the rear gate of the SUV and glanced to his left, toward the farmhouse. A light was on now. "We are indeed," he said.

CHAPTER TWENTY-ONE
GROCKA MUNICIPALITY, SERBIA

S ophie shivered again and pulled the blanket around her. She sat in the chair, her legs tucked uncomfortably underneath her, but it was the best way to keep them warm. The night was cool and somebody had forgotten to adjust the heat in her room. The thermostat was locked at eighteen degrees Celsius. Under the blanket, she rubbed her legs and felt the goose bumps. In spite of everything, the touch brought a smile to her lips. If she got out of here, she would be going back to her new home of Wisconsin and preparing for her first winter there, which Mark had assured her would make the English winters of her girlhood seem balmy.

She refused to get back onto the bed. Some of the dead Russian's blood was still on the quilt. The men who had dragged the body out hadn't bothered to replace the quilt, if they'd even noticed it, which she doubted. At least they'd cleaned the floor. The bra she would never wear again was still lying on the bed, and in the dim light from the bedside lamp she could see the dark spots on the fabric.

The night was chilled from something more than the falling temperatures, though. Novak had questioned her about the fight with the Russian, and she gave him just enough information to satisfy him. She'd seen his rage and did not want to provoke him any further by being uncooperative. And perhaps, she thought now, it was an even better idea to tell him what happened, because he'd looked at her with respect, and also with something else: fear.

She had seen that look before, but under vastly different circumstances. From politicians, usually, who had consented to interviews and then found themselves trapped by their own words as she expertly turned the tables on them. On two memorable occasions she'd even seen it from men who should've been much tougher, a Hezbollah commander who had made the mistake of sitting down with her in Beirut, and an Iranian general in Tehran. These were men molded by cultures that generally held women in low esteem, even contempt, and they were not pleased when a woman stood up to them.

She relished the memory of the Beirut interview, and now it came back to her again with a vivid clarity that surprised her. Two years ago, now? No, nearly three. She had cornered that fellow with his own words, hadn't she? He got angry, but she could see fear in those eyes, too. After returning home she talked about the experience with a friend of hers, a Muslim herself. "Deep down, they are afraid of us, of our power," her friend said. "They want a world where men are the unquestioned rulers. They say they are angry at Christianity, at what we in the West wear and what we read and the music we listen to, but their anger is born of fear. They fear being made equal to us."

Novak wasn't a Muslim, or at least she didn't think so. Only a small minority of Serbs practiced Islam, and in this place she'd seen no signs of religious expression anywhere. But he was a man, and definitely a man used to being in charge. She'd yet to see any women in this house. She assumed he employed women in his company, but she doubted whether he entrusted any positions of importance to them. No, men like Novak usually did not like being challenged, especially by women.

Such men sometimes relished a challenge by another man, though, and by God he would get one of those very soon. Mark was coming for her. She knew that as sure as she knew her own name. She knew...

The sound of the dog barking awakened her. The dream dissolved into nothing but vague memories, and those would soon be gone, too. She looked out the window but saw nothing in the darkness. Did the men have their pit bulls out on the grounds? Just for their evening constitutional, or perhaps making their rounds of the perimeter?

She switched off the table lamp and let her eyes become accustomed to the darkness. Not totally dark, though; there was a gibbous moon, and tonight the skies were clear, the last few clouds from the evening thunderstorm long gone. The grounds were softly lit, and somewhere in the distance she saw the twinkle of riverboat lights on the Danube. Once again she engaged herself in debate: when she escaped, should she go for the road, trying to flag down a passing car? Or the woods, in an attempt to hide and eventually get to a road? Or maybe the river? She could swim for one of the boats. She was a strong swimmer. She could make it, she...

Who was she kidding? Sophie shook her head in despair. At this time of year the water would be cold, her energy would be quickly sapped, and she would likely drown. In the woods at night she would be next to helpless. On the road Novak's men and the dogs would run her down quickly. Should she even try? There'd been nothing close to an opportunity, and it was unlikely they'd give her any in the few hours she had left.

The dog didn't bark again. Other than the sound of footsteps walking past her door once, the house was quiet. She pulled the blanket close around her legs. The quilt would feel nice right now, but it had the blood on it. The Russian's blood, the filthy cur who had meant to rape her. By God, she had shown him a thing or two, hadn't she? Yes, she had, she'd–

Tears filled her eyes. Where was God now? Sophie had never been particularly religious, and certainly many, if not most, of her journalism colleagues simply described themselves as "spiritual," whatever that meant, or were outright atheists. She and Mark had talked about it, he'd told her about his upbringing as a Lutheran, of how he'd fallen away from his faith early in his military career but had found it again over the past few years. There certainly is a God, he'd told her with complete confidence, and that God was with every one of us, each and every moment.

Was He here now? Watching her, the proud and self-confident TV journalist who'd often thought she was just fine without any sort of faith in her life, except that within herself and her ability to get the job done? She'd seen what many people thought was evil in the world, the devil at work, and she'd never really thought of it in that context. It was always about misunderstandings, grievances unanswered, prejudice and intolerance. That's how it appeared from a distance, anyway, or at least from a comfortable hotel room safely removed from the chaos she often reported on.

Mark had told her once that there were no atheists in foxholes. Maybe…maybe it was time she found some faith, in something besides herself. Yes, she'd defended herself against the Russian, but she knew that wouldn't happen again. They'd be ready for her next time, when they came to take her. There would be more than one man, there would be several, and they would…

She buried her face in the blanket and surrendered herself. "Please, God," she said through her sobs, "please deliver me. Please bring my husband."

Sophie's husband checked the map display on his phone and said, "Half a klick, then left, one more klick and a right. That's the last turn before the target."

Krieger nodded, his hands staying at ten-and-two on the steering wheel. His face was dimly illuminated by the instrument panel, enough so that Mark could see his eyes flicking every two or three seconds from the road ahead to the rearview mirror and to the instruments and then forward again. The ethnic German driver and the German-made vehicle were almost a symbiotic organism. Not for the first time tonight, Mark was grateful that Krieger had taken command of the mission.

"We won't come right up to the target, will we?" he asked.

"Negative," Mark said, scrolling ahead slightly on the map. "The last road runs parallel to the grounds of the estate, intersects with the access road about three-quarters of a klick after our final turn. We'll have to pull over and approach on foot."

From the back came the rustling sound of Jim fiddling with the weapons again. "Any sign of pursuit?" Mark asked, glancing back over his shoulder.

"Everything's dark back there," Jim said. Mark could hear the tension in his brother's voice, but he was confident Jim would perform well in what was to come. About his own performance, though, Mark wasn't completely sure. He hadn't felt like this since his very first combat operations in Desert Storm. He took that uncertainty and shoved it aside, wishing he could lock it up inside his mind somehow.

Krieger slowed the Audi just enough to take the turn safely. "We'll be coming in from the eastern edge of the grounds," Krieger said. "Remember the briefing, gentlemen. We'll still deploy as planned."

"Jim, remember your position?" Mark asked.

"Circle around to the back and cover the rear entrance," his brother said. "Prevent any escape to the river. Come into the house only if necessary."

Mark had the satellite imagery of Novak's estate committed to memory. There were two boats docked on the Danube a half-kilometer from the rear of the main house. If Novak tried to make a getaway, with or without Sophie, he would head to the river if he believed his access to vehicles was cut off. Mark knew that Novak would have contingency plans involving an escape on the water. It was about thirty kilometers downriver to the Romanian border. If Novak got out of the country, they'd never find him.

But Belgrade was even closer, less than forty kilometers to the west by car. Novak would have more men there, and in a city of over a million people he'd have no trouble evading three men who didn't know the city. No, they had to take him here, now.

Krieger would cover the three smaller buildings just to the

west of the main house. It appeared from the imagery that one was for storage and the larger one was a garage, but it was the third building that worried Mark. The satellite had caught three men outside, one of them exercising a dog on the grounds behind the main house, the other two near the front of that third building. It could've been anything, but Mark was certain it was a barracks. Novak would have people working the estate, and those who carried guns would be in the house at all times or nearby. They'd estimated the barracks could house as many as six men.

Krieger slowed to begin the final turn. "Get ready," he said. "Comms check."

Mark adjusted his tactical headset, positioning the fiber optic microphone near his lips and then turning on the transceiver attached to his belt. "Black Knight Two, check."

Jim's voice came through the headset earpiece. "Black Knight Three, check."

"Black Knight One, check," Krieger said. "Comm check complete. We stay on the net from this point."

Mark pulled his pistol from his hip holster and performed one last, needless check. For the last time, he cursed his boss's decision to recall the team from Rome. Those five men would've been handy to have right now. But, like so many times during his Army career, he'd have to make do with what he had, not what he wanted to have. They had a decent plan, and with the element of surprise it had a decent chance of success.

But for all they knew, that element was now gone. It would depend on how quickly the other team at the roadblock would react. Mark checked his watch: barely ten minutes since the ambush. Had the surviving team notified Novak right away when their comrades failed to check in? Or had they left their post to investigate first? If Mark had been in charge, he knew what orders he would've given in the event of a missed contact: report in, then check it out. But how quickly would they react?

And then there was another factor. Krieger had swiftly patched the neck wound of the Serb who'd caught the shrapnel from Mark's shot, and as they left Jim had spotted someone coming down from the farmhouse with a flashlight. No doubt the police would be called. If the men at the roadblock were monitoring the police frequency, they'd know why their comrades hadn't answered the phone. Mark gave the farmer five minutes at the outside to make the call to the Serbian version of 911, maybe another five or ten before the first police car arrived. Any way you sliced it, their original idea of spending thirty to forty-five minutes to surveil the estate was out the window. They would have only half of that now, maybe nothing at all.

If Novak knew they were coming, Mark figured their chances of success were less than fifty-fifty. They would have to adjust on the fly. He remembered a class in tactics he'd taken at the Academy. The instructor had quoted from Patton: "Good tactics can save even the worst strategy. Bad tactics will destroy even the best strategy."

The plan was as sound as three men could make it. Now it would come down to execution. They had no reserves to call in, no backup at all. They were on their own, in the dead of night in a foreign country, likely outnumbered and outgunned. Mark felt a pinprick of anxiety. He'd never operated like this before, had never gone behind the lines without any prospect of help from the rear.

He'd always admired the Special Forces guys, who did this all the time. Now he was about to find out if he had what those guys had.

Krieger started slowing the Audi. "Half a klick to the target," he said. "We're pulling into that pasture. Get ready."

As good as their plan was, it still had holes in it, plenty of them. But now Mark remembered another quote from Patton: "A good plan, violently executed now, is better than a perfect plan next week." They had no next week, only this one night. Mark checked his weapon, took a deep breath and cleared his head. He was ready.

CHAPTER TWENTY-TWO
GROCKA MUNICIPALITY, SERBIA

Krieger doused the Audi's lights as he maneuvered the SUV deftly off the road, through a gap in the fence and behind a stand of trees, reversing and then backing up before shutting down the engine. The nose of the vehicle now pointed back toward the road. Jim noted the maneuver with approval. He'd learned a lot since going to work for OSS, and now he always backed into a parking space. You never knew when you might need to make a quick exit, and he had the feeling tonight would be one of those occasions.

Mark switched off the dome light and the men got out of the Audi as quietly as possible, closing their doors slowly. Krieger kept the main set of keys but Jim knew Mark had a backup set. Each man checked his weapons.

Mark came to him and leaned close. "You ready, Jim?" he whispered.

Jim heard him loud and clear through his earpiece. "Locked and loaded."

Krieger signaled for them to move out. They began trotting along the fence line of the pasture. Jim resisted the temptation to look back toward the Audi. More than once back home he'd been reluctant to leave the relative comfort and safety of his car during a storm. He felt a twinge of that now.

It took them five minutes to get through the pasture to the edge of Novak's property. Jim had to admire how easily Krieger and his brother moved, even in the dim light of the moon. How did they avoid tripping, stepping into a hole? Jim kept up with them but feared he was almost clumsy by comparison. It was their training, he thought. They must have done this many times over the years. Not for the first time in the past couple days, Jim thought of how much he had to learn. This certainly required vastly different skills than designing marketing plans for telecoms, which had been his last job before Mark had hired him for the security firm. Not even his years of martial arts training had prepared him for something like this.

But he had to perform, and he had to do it now. This operation was too important. Lives were at stake, including his own. "Suck it up," he mumbled.

"What's that?" Mark asked.

"Nothing."

They came to the stone wall that marked the perimeter of Novak's grounds. Five feet high, about a foot thick. Krieger motioned to the top. Jim looked closely and saw the jagged glass shards implanted in the mortar. He nodded to show that he understood.

Part of their planning had been about how to deal with the perimeter. The satellite photos had showed them the wall, but not any static security measures Novak might have had in place. The wall would keep out the deer and other large wildlife, but even with the glass shards it would not stop a determined human intruder. There would likely be something more, such as cameras with infrared capability, motion sensors that would trip yard lights, maybe even remotely-controlled gun turrets. If they'd had enough time, they could've done a proper surveillance and come up with ways to defeat Novak's countermeasures.

But now they were forced to act quickly. Krieger nodded at Mark, who took a tube from his backpack. He unrolled a blast blanket, four feet square and composed of oven Kevlar ballistic fibers, and draped it over the top of the wall. After a cursory look up and down the wall, Krieger boosted himself up onto the blanket, swung his legs over and dropped to the other side like a large cat, the slight thump of his landing hardly audible. Mark motioned Jim over and then followed, rolling up the blanket as he squatted beside them.

They stayed hunkered down for thirty seconds, weapons at the ready, but there was nothing to indicate their infiltration had been spotted. Krieger pointed at Jim and then toward the back of the house. "Remember your assignments, gentlemen," he said calmly. "I will secure the barracks. When you hear the grenade go off, Mark, wait fifteen seconds before breaching the window."

"Roger that," Mark said.

"Jim, take your position near that garden in the rear right quarter of the grounds. Cover the rear exit. Prevent any escape to the boat, but be careful, if they make a break for it, they may have Sophie. Engage only if she is clear."

"Got it."

From out of the night came the sound of a siren, faint but getting closer. The Serb farmer had made the call. "Ignore it," Krieger said. "They won't be coming here." The moonlight glinted off his eyes. They were hard. "Take your position."

Mark clapped Jim on his shoulder. "Stay frosty, brother."

Jim nodded, hoping his adrenaline rush wasn't showing. "I'll see you and Sophie back here," he said, and loped off, staying low.

In the master bedroom on the top floor, Novak stared at the dark ceiling. Experience told him when it was useless to try to sleep. It had taken him years after the war to get into anything resembling a normal sleep pattern, and objectively he knew that his occasional insomnia was an impediment to functioning at the high level he demanded of himself, physically and mentally. Yet some nights, like tonight, there was just too much running through his mind. He kicked the sheet off and slid his feet out of the bed and onto the hardwood floor.

The incident between his prisoner and Vladimir troubled him. The Russian had disobeyed orders, to be sure, but in the end, would it have made any difference if he had succeeded in raping the woman? She was going to be killed anyway, right after Novak eliminated her husband.

Yes, he had to admit that it certainly did make a difference.

She had proven herself to be much tougher than he had anticipated, both emotionally and physically. Her ferocious resistance to Vladimir had stunned Novak. This was a woman with no military training? Vladimir was a thug, but he was former Spetsnaz, and Novak knew from his own military experience that a Spetsnaz soldier, even one who'd washed out as Vladimir had, did not go down easily.

And if she was that tough, how much more formidable would her husband be? Sitting here in the dark, Novak felt, for the first

202

time, a whisper of doubt about this entire endeavor. He was risking everything to bring this American to heel. His company, his future in Serbian politics, and even his own life. He scratched his chin, feeling the stubble. Perhaps...perhaps it had been a mistake to kidnap the woman. It was a decision he'd made on the spur of the moment, when the opportunity to get to Hayes presented itself. And he never made hasty decisions, did he? His entire career had been predicated on careful planning, preparing for every contingency, weighing the risks against the potential gain. He never liked to roll the dice, but this time he'd rolled them. Perhaps he'd acted in haste.

But there was his brother, calling out for him from the grave, demanding vengeance. Novak uttered a deep sigh. Dragan had been his mother's favorite. "My precious little boy," she had often said, which was why she had chosen that name. Three miscarriages after Darko, and at forty she never thought she'd have another child. Then there was Dragan. Eight years younger than his brother, Dragan had followed him around since the day he took his first steps. Followed him to school, to the gym, and finally into the Army and into war. Before she'd died, their mother had made Novak promise to watch over Dragan, and he'd sworn he would do everything he could. And he'd failed.

Dragan had died because of the American, Hayes. Novak could not ignore that, not after thirteen years, not when it was so close. No, this would have to be seen through to the end, and he realized he no longer had any choice. He could not simply release the woman. The abduction of a renowned BBC journalist would cause shock waves throughout Europe. The media would rally around one of their own and hound him mercilessly. They would dredge up the war, the Ninjas, the war crimes trials. He could not count on anyone to protect him. He had friends in Belgrade, but he had enemies, too, and they would see this kidnaping as a way to bring him down.

As he stood and stretched, there came a vigorous knocking on his door. "What is it?"

From behind he heard Viktor's voice. "Are you awake, sir?"

"Yes, dammit." He pulled a robe on and took the three quick steps to the door. He pulled it open and saw his assistant standing there, his sidearm drawn. "Report," Novak demanded.

"Sir, we must put the compound on alert. I believe the American is close."

Mark could see lights were on in the house, but only a few. He approached at a run, his MP7 up and ready, sweeping for targets. None presented themselves. He'd given Jim a five second head start to get to his position in the back, then allowed Krieger another five to start his run to the outbuilding. They would both be in place by the time he got to the house.

The question of how to enter the main building had generated more than a little debate on the flight as they prepped the mission. Based on the sat photos, there were large windows at the southeast corner of the house, on the front of the building and on the side around the corner. They concluded that this would be either a dining room or a library. Mark had argued in favor of the dining room; the house's northwest corner pointed toward the Danube, and the windows there would give a fine view of the river, a logical location for the lord of the manor to place his library and office. Where would Sophie be held? That was impossible to determine. She could be anywhere on the first floor, or the second, or even the basement, assuming she was there at all.

There was only one way to find out, and that was to get in there. They had concluded there would be no stealthy way to enter the building. The doors would certainly be locked, as would the windows. Once an entryway was breached, whoever was going in would have to move fast. Ideally, for a building of this size, Krieger would have used a team of at least six men. But there were only three of them, and two were covering other areas. Mark knew that no Special Forces officer on the planet would approve of one man going into a hostile environment, potentially with a hostage to watch out for, but they had no choice.

Krieger had suggested breaching the dining room window on the side of the house and working his way back. The NATO commando had promised to join Mark inside as soon as he could make sure Novak's reaction force, if there was one, was neutralized in the barracks. To make up for the lack of manpower, he'd brought along a few little treats to help him deal with Novak's men.

Mark reached the dining room window and hugged the wall, waited for a count of five, then sneaked a peek inside, through the one of the panes bordered by latticework. The room was dark, but a door was open on the far side, revealing a lighted interior hallway, allowing him enough illumination to see the end of a long dining table and chairs in the room. Bingo. But as he reached into his backpack for the breaching charge, he hesitated. They had no way of knowing the floor plan of this place, but he had to consider

205

what the likely layout would be. The dining room flanked the hallway, which led to the front door. Another room on the other side of the hallway, same side of the house, had to be a parlor of some sort. Nobody would have a bedroom at the front, just off the main entrance. Based on the size of the place, they'd concluded there was probably only one bedroom on the main floor. The upstairs would have more, perhaps two or three.

If Mark had a place like this and was holding a prisoner, he'd want her to be close to an exit in the event they had to make an escape, but not the front, which is where the police would come first. Novak had a boat waiting for him on the Danube, probably only two or three minutes away on foot at a quick pace. Mark was betting that Novak had a bedroom on the first floor at the rear, and that's where she'd be.

He slid along the wall, sidestepping the small bushes a conscientious groundskeeper had placed next to the house, and not too long ago, considering their small size. Eventually they would grow to the point where access to the windows would be more difficult. Fortunately, Novak hadn't thought of that a couple of years ago, or maybe he'd just bought the place recently. Mark came to the edge of the next window and peered in. Dark. He took out his penlight, cupped his gloved hand around the light as he pressed it against the glass and switched it on.

The thin beam caught a chair, then a desk, arranged to provide a good view of the river. Mark's luck was still with him. He switched off the light and peered through the glass again, noting the light bleeding through from underneath the closed door on the far side of the room. He decided to place his charge on the other side. Ducking down, he crept low and came up along the wall with the edge of the window inches away.

From within his pack he took the foot-long breaching charge, det cord wrapped in plastic, and placed it on the windowsill. He applied glue from a squeeze bottle along the vertical edge of the window, then pressed the charge into it, holding it firmly for fifteen seconds. When he was sure it would hold, he pressed the primer cord into the plug at the bottom and reeled out the wire, back under the window and toward the front of the house, until he was about seven feet away from the charge. After attaching the detonator to the cord, he unrolled the heavy blast blanket, glad to be free of its weight again. As he knelt down, movement from the rear of the grounds caught his attention. He saw a figure rush over and crouch behind a bench, next to a small flower garden.

Mark resisted the temptation to press the detonator button. Where was Krieger? He should've been at the barracks by now. He should–

From inside, Mark heard the heavy thud of footsteps coming down a staircase. He looked inside, keeping his eyes on the sliver of light underneath the door. Shadows passed, but the door remained closed. Mark put his thumb on the button.

His peripheral vision caught movement from the back grounds. The figure at the bench had risen to a crouch, and from behind the house came the snarl of a large dog.

CHAPTER TWENTY-THREE
GROCKA MUNICIPALITY, SERBIA

R adovan woke from a troubled sleep and reached for his watch to check the time, but it wasn't on the end table next to the bunk. *Govno!* Where had he left it? He'd taken a shower after returning to the barracks. Maybe it was still there. Well, he had to use the latrine anyway.

Staggering to his feet in the dark, he listened for Jakov snoring in the other bunk. Nothing. Maybe he was out with his dog. Probably couldn't sleep either. Everyone was on edge with the word that the Colonel's nemesis was arriving the next day, and then Vladimir's untimely demise had nearly pushed the rest of the men over that edge. The thick-headed Russian was literally cooling his heels in the walk-in freezer next door in the supply shed. Good riddance to him. Radovan had never liked the idiot anyway, and his attempt on the woman had nearly gotten Radovan cashiered on the spot, or worse. He'd known Vladimir would eventually cause a problem, but the woman had taken care of that, hadn't she? The Serb couldn't suppress an ironic chuckle.

With the Russian gone, that left only Radovan, Jakov and Lazar, who was in the room across the hall, the one he shared with Viktor. The other two rooms in the barracks were empty, although one of them still contained Vladimir's few belongings. As he made his way into the latrine, Radovan wondered what would become of the Russian's impressive porn collection. Well, not everything had to go back to Belgrade with the body, did it?

He searched fruitlessly for his watch, decided it must still be back in his room, and relieved himself. Pulling his briefs back up, he switched off the room's light as he opened the door. The hallway was lit by a night light, but it was darker than it should be. Was it going out? Radovan decided to check. When he took a left out of the head he saw the man standing in the hallway.

Even half-awake, Radovan knew something was very wrong. He opened his mouth to speak but the words never made it out. The man in the black fatigues moved with a speed the Serb's brain could hardly process, and then a bolt of white-hot pain lanced through him as total blackness enveloped the intruder and everything else.

Jim saw the figure loping toward him across the yard, a shadow against the gray-green of the grass, moving low and fast. When the shadow was still thirty yards away he heard the angry snarl and knew he had only seconds to get ready.

Crouching behind the cement bench, Jim brought the MP7 up, then back down as another thought moved his right hand to a special holster on his belt. He raised the canister just as the dog reached the edge of the garden, hurtled the five-foot width of the pool and launched itself at him.

The blast of pepper spray caught the dog flush in the face. The big animal yelped, crashed into the bench and tumbled to the ground, whining. Jim feared it had broken a foreleg, but the dog staggered to its feet, sniffling and sneezing, and began rubbing its massive head on the grass.

He heard a shout. *"Si provedio mog psa, kopile!"*

Still in a crouch, Jim turned and saw a man running across the yard toward him, right arm extended. The muzzle of a gun blazed and Jim ducked and rolled as the round slapped off the bench with a spray of cement chips. He didn't have enough training to use his MP7 in combat, but he did have one weapon he knew a lot about. Switching the pepper spray canister to his left hand, he reached across his body with his right and pulled the baton from the holster on his hip.

The Serb slowed to a trot as he came around the garden. Jim knew he'd have to take a chance here. He launched the canister toward the Serb and pushed off with his legs, staying low, tucking his left shoulder and head as he went into a roll. The gun barked again but the flying canister had distracted the Serb and the round missed Jim by five feet. He came up from the roll, flicked his wrist to extend the baton to its full twenty-one inch length and swept it around in an arc, right onto the man's wrist. The Serb yelled and dropped the gun.

Jim thrust the baton under the man's armpit, grabbed the far end behind the shoulder and stepped around, levering the Serb over his hip head over heels and onto the ground. A twist of the damaged wrist brought the man onto his stomach. Five seconds later the Serb's wrists were zip-tied, and another five finished the ankles.

Getting back to his feet, Jim saw that the dog had run off, whimpering. He looked down at the muttering, cursing man. Jim leaned closer. "Quiet!" A blow from the butt of the baton to the soft area under the Serb's jaw produced the desired result.

In the moonlight, Mark saw the dog attack the figure behind the garden bench. The growling turned to whimpering as the animal crashed into the bench and tumbled onto the ground. Krieger's idea to arm each of them with pepper spray was paying off. Then came the shout from the guard and the shot. Mark lowered the blast blanket to the ground, switched the detonator to his left hand and moved his right to pull his pistol from the holster as he saw Jim engage the Serb. Holy Christ, his brother was fast. He had watched the film of Jim's fight in Somalia many times, and had spent countless hours with him on the mat back home, but this was the first time he'd actually seen his brother in combat. He felt a surge of pride.

But where in the hell was Krieger? Mark checked his tactical watch again, thumbing the stud that illuminated the dial. It had been barely ten minutes since they'd left the wall at the perimeter of the estate. Had Krieger run into trouble in the barracks? Mark hadn't heard any gunfire, no shouts of alarm, nothing.

He looked back at the det cord and whispered a curse. The top of the cord had peeled away from the window frame. The damn glue wasn't holding. He set the blast blanket on the ground and crept over to that side of the window.

Well-versed in the art of dressing quickly, Novak pulled on his pants and a sweater and jammed his feet into his boots in less than ten seconds. From the nightstand he grabbed his holstered gun and clipped it to his belt. "Tell me what you know," he ordered as he passed Viktor and headed down the short hallway to the stairs.

"I had a report of an unknown aircraft landing at Vršac, with three men aboard who then disappeared. I thought it prudent to order two teams from Belgrade to put up roadblocks."

Novak turned at the top of the stairs, swinging around with one hand on the ornate wooden post of the banister. "And?"

"The team on Highway 153, between here and Brestovik, reported that a suspicious vehicle stopped short of their position and turned quickly down a side road. Two of our men went off in pursuit. They did not answer calls from the team remaining at the roadblock. They then overheard a police call about some sort of gunfight on a back road."

Novak's heart almost seized up. The American was coming! "How far from here?"

"Not sure, Colonel, but close."

Novak reached the bottom of the staircase. "Alert the men in the barracks. Release the dogs. Order the teams at the roadblocks to converge here."

"Colonel, I–"

"Just do it, damn you!" Novak resisted the urge to run, but he wasted no time in making his way to the woman's room. In the few seconds it took him, he had already calculated the odds. He was down to four men besides himself. It would take the men at the roadblocks time to get here, and he suspected that would be time he no longer had.

If those three at the airport included Hayes, then certainly he had brought two highly-trained men with him. They knew where he was, probably knew the layout of the estate, perhaps even how many men were here. Yes, they would know everything. He cursed the damned Americans and their technology. For all he knew, they could have a drone overhead right now.

The odds were suddenly no longer in Novak's favor. He made a decision. As he retrieved the bedroom key from his pocket, he saw Viktor down the side hall, speaking into the intercom at one of the four communications stations Novak had installed throughout the building.

He inserted the key into the lock, then paused. "Well?"

Viktor's face was hard as he turned away from the intercom. "No response from the barracks, sir." He pulled his pistol from his holster.

"They're here," Novak said. He turned the key and opened the door, his drawn gun in the other hand, ready for the woman to attack.

The room was dark. He flicked the wall switch that activated the table lamp and saw her sitting in the chair, a blanket wrapped around her legs. She was glaring at him.

"You might have knocked first," she said.

"We must go," Novak said.

One eyebrow went up. "Really? I was just getting comfortable."

He saw no reason to trifle with her. "Your husband is nearby," Novak said, "and he appears to have brought some friends with him."

To his surprise, she simply sat back in the chair and stretched out her legs. She smiled at him and said, "You're bloody well fucked, then."

CHAPTER TWENTY-FOUR
GROCKA MUNICIPALITY, SERBIA

M ark was applying more glue to the window frame when his headset whispered. "Black Knight Two, report." "In position," he said. "What's your situation?"

"On west side. Barracks secure. You breach in fifteen seconds, on my mark."

Mark pressed the top half of the det cord into the glue and pressed it in. "Copy."

"Black Knight Three, report."

Mark risked a glance toward the rear of the grounds and saw Jim crouching near the body of the Serb he'd taken down. "One tango down and secured," his brother said over the net.

"Be aware of squirters," Krieger whispered.

"Repeat that, One," Jim said.

"Somebody escaping through the grounds," Mark said.

A slight hesitation, then Jim said, "Roger that."

The glue was holding this time. Mark scurried back under the window to the other side. He heard more noise in the house. Was that laughter? A woman's laughter? His heart jumped.

His earpiece whispered again. "Three, two, one, mark!"

There was a crash from the far side of the house, then a loud bang. Light blazed under the closed door of the library. A dog started yapping from inside. A man shouted; a woman shrieked. Mark steadied himself, held the blast blanket up, and when his count reached fifteen he pressed the detonator button.

Jim heard the explosion from inside the house, saw the flash of light through the windows, and knew that Krieger had tossed his flash-bang grenade into the house. Seconds later, another detonation blasted a window on the near side, and Jim saw his brother throw his blast blanket over the shards of glass and climb into the dark room at the northeast corner of the house.

Crouching behind the cement bench, Jim trained his MP7 on the extension of the house that jutted into the back grounds. Large enough to house something like a mud room, he thought, and there was the back door. He counted the windows from the northeast corner. One set had to be for the room Mark had just entered, then another set, then the extension. The light in that adjacent room had gone on seconds before the first explosion, but Jim couldn't see any movement inside. He thought about running up to look, but no. He had to stay in position.

A shout, then a gunshot, and another. Jim rose from his crouch, keeping his weapon trained on that back door, and walked carefully around the garden. The unconscious Serb lay still on the grass. Where was the dog? Jim had no idea how long the effects of the pepper spray would last.

He was still twenty-five yards away from the door when it burst open. Jim immediately went to one knee and sighted his weapon, flicking the safety off. Two figures emerged, and in the moonlight he could see one was Sophie. Her wrists were bound behind her, and a man had a grip on her hair, pushing her forward. She stumbled down the three steps leading to the ground but her captor kept his grip, and in his other hand he carried a gun.

Viktor watched his boss hustle the woman toward the back room and took his position near the door of her room, hugging the wall around the corner, out of sight of the main hallway. His job now was to hold off the Americans long enough to allow Novak and the woman to escape to the boat.

"Hold them as long as you can," Novak had told him. "But do not sacrifice yourself unnecessarily. The Americans want me, not you."

Viktor had nodded and then swallowed to remove the lump from his throat. He had been with Novak for years, first distinguishing himself in battle at Glina in '91. He'd worked his way up the ranks and was a sergeant by the time of the Kosovo raid in '99 that had started all this trouble. He'd privately questioned Novak's judgment then and he had doubts about it now, but he wasn't about to surrender to the Americans. No, they would now find out again what a Serb fighting man could–

He was expecting to hear the footsteps of the intruders coming down the hardwood floor of the hallway, but what he heard instead was the clicking of a dog's toenails. The boss's little terrier came around the corner, saw Novak and stopped.

Viktor waved him back, but the mutt didn't move. It looked down the side hallway, no doubt catching his master's scent. Then it started yapping again.

"Vuk! Quiet!" Viktor had never liked the dog, ever since he'd

216

stepped in dog shit one day in the house. Normally the animal was quite good about doing its business outside, but on that occasion Novak was gone for several hours and Viktor had forgotten to let the dog outside. Well, he was a soldier, not a *prokleti* dog-sitter. The mutt took a few steps toward him, still barking. "Quiet, damn you!" he shouted. He took a step, swung his foot around and kicked the animal into the woman's vacated bedroom.

Mark's hand was almost on the door handle when he heard the shriek from the hallway. He reacted instinctively, pulling the door open and crouching along the inside wall. He saw the Serb at the corner of the hallway, pistol at the ready. The dog looked like a Yorkshire terrier and it was flopping on the floor of the bedroom, trying to crawl under the bed. The Serb had heard the door open and fired two quick shots before ducking back around the corner.

The rounds impacted the door, shoving it farther open. Cursing under his breath, Mark held his position along the inside wall, leaning forward just enough to check for any movement. He didn't hear any footsteps heading away, so the Serb was waiting for him. Mark was considering his options when Krieger's voice came through his earpiece. "Two, I'm coming into the hallway from the front end."

"Hold your position. One tango around the corner," Mark said. He plucked a flash-bang grenade from his belt.

Krieger's voice again. "Take him out and advance, Two. I'll be at your six. Black Knight Three, report."

"In the back yard. Novak and Sophie are coming through. They're heading for the boat."

217

Mark had taken one step into the hallway. "Can you take him out, Three?"

"Negative. He has a gun to her head. I don't have a shot."

"Hold your position, Three," Krieger ordered.

Mark knew that even if there was enough separation between Novak and Sophie to allow a clear shot, Jim wasn't experienced enough to take it. "Hold your fire, Jim," he said. "Do not engage unless she's free."

"They'll get away! I have to take him out!"

"Negative!" Mark shouted. "You might hit her."

From around the corner, the Serb laughed. "Hey, American," he said, "guess what? You will never see her again. Not alive, anyway. You lose again, tough guy."

Mark pulled the pin on the grenade. "We'll see about that, asshole," he said. He tossed the M84 down the hallway.

Novak saw the man in the yard as soon as they started across the grounds. Just where he would have put one of his own men. *Prokletsovo!* The accursed Americans were driving him from his own house! He blamed himself again for underestimating Hayes. He'd never dreamed the man would have the means to muster such resources. The assault team had evaded the roadblock, infiltrated his property and neutralized his guard force. They were highly trained, these Americans, not to be trifled with. He had to get to Belgrade, and the only way possible was on the water. Hayes, unfortunately, had anticipated that.

He pulled the woman's head closer. "You will do exactly as I say, or you will die," he said. He shoved the end of the pistol barrel under her ear to emphasize the point.

She had seen the man, too, turning her head as much as Novak would allow.

The moonlight glinted off Sophie's eyes, wide with fear. "Shoot him!"

Novak's hand dug itself further into her hair and pulled her closer. "He won't. No, you won't, will you, American?" He had come to a stop ten yards from the back door as Jim approached.

Jim held his MP7 just as he'd been trained, sighting on the target, but this wasn't the firing range back home. He steadied his breathing as he fought to keep his hands from trembling. "It's over, Novak. Let her go."

Novak pointed the pistol at her temple. "No, she is coming with me."

There was just enough light for Jim to get a clear view as he approached, walking carefully, slowly. Twenty yards. If he got within ten, and Novak pointed his gun away from her, Jim figured he could make the shot, unless Novak pulled her even closer. Too close for Jim to risk a shot. If they separated, even six inches…

"It's pretty simple, Novak. You let her go, you live. You hurt her, you die."

He saw Sophie's eyes shift toward him and widen. She'd recognized his voice. With the business end of the pistol still touching her temple, she didn't dare try to break loose, and Novak knew it. The Serb laughed. "Yes, American, you realize that even if you shoot me, the reflex action of my hand will pull the trigger, and her brains will be all over my back yard. I don't think you want to risk that, do you? No, I didn't think so." Novak began walking slowly, pushing Sophie ahead of him.

Jim stayed in his half-crouch, tracking the Serb, but he didn't have a shot, sure as hell not with that gun of his at his sister-in-law's head. He'd heard Krieger and Mark through his earpiece, and they'd certainly heard him talking to Novak, but had they heard what the Serb had said? Even if they hadn't, they could guess what was happening.

"Get no closer, American," Novak said as they passed him. "Take one step and I fire."

"You're signing your death warrant, Novak."

"I think not. This is my country, not yours. When we get to Belgrade, you will have a million Serbs to deal with. Not even you Americans with all your drones and satellites can find one woman in a city that large."

They were ten feet away now. Another thirty feet would take them to the edge of the grounds. The path to the river wound through a stand of woods, some four hundred yards from here to the dock where his boat was waiting. Belgrade was twenty miles upriver, no more than an hour away. If they had some way to follow him….

What had he said? Drones. "You won't get away, Novak," Jim said. "We're following you every step of the way." He could see Novak hesitate, then look back at him.

"You're lying," the Serb said. In the dim light, Jim couldn't see Novak's face, but he could see the gun still pointed directly at Sophie's head.

"Yeah? Keep thinking that, right up until that Predator puts a Hellfire up your ass. You took the wrong guy's wife, but if you let her go, we'll be on our way and you can go on doing whatever it is that you do around here." Jim could sense he was getting to this guy. It was time to push him harder. He took a cautious step forward. "Just let her go, Novak, and that's the end of it."

"You're a liar!" Novak yelled. He swung his gun hand around to aim at Jim.

Sophie dropped to the ground, yanking Novak off-balance. "Shoot him!" she screamed.

CHAPTER TWENTY-FIVE
GROCKA MUNICIPALITY, SERBIA

J im sighted and fired, but the round passed through the air Novak's head had occupied an instant before. The Serb went down on one knee, released Sophie's hair and used both hands to grip his pistol.

Even as he saw the flash from the gun's muzzle, Jim dropped to the ground and rolled right, but not quickly enough. A lance of white-hot pain hit his left bicep. He stayed with the roll and came out of it, rising to his feet and bringing his MP7 around.

Jim saw Novak struggling with Sophie on the ground and knew he couldn't risk a shot. He'd have to take him out hand-to-hand. He shucked off the sling of his MP7, let the weapon drop to the ground and charged.

The woman had bedeviled Novak for the last time. He'd gotten the one shot off before she swung a leg at him from the ground, catching him flush on the side. Now he would have to finish her before dealing with the American commando. She was a tigress, but he was not Vladimir. She managed to get in one stinging slap against his face, but he used one arm to pin hers and then brought an elbow down with a satisfying crack to her jaw.

He only had a moment to enjoy his victory. A crushing impact propelled him through the air and face first into the grass.

The grenade exploded with a loud bang, the flash of light filling every inch of the hallway. Mark dropped his hands from his ears and opened his eyes. The coughing Serb staggered through the smoke and bumped into the frame of the bedroom door. He lost his footing and crashed against the baseboard.

Mark gulped one last lungful of clean air and leaped into the hallway. The smoke was already starting to thin, enough for him to see the Serb. The MP7 could take him out easily, but he had to be taken alive. If Novak got away, this guy would likely know where he was headed.

This Serb was a tough SOB, though, fighting through the grenade's triple-whammy impact of light, sound and smoke. He steadied himself against the baseboard and brought his gun around, squeezing off two wild shots. Mark came in low and brought his shoulder up into the Serb's gut, just like he'd hit the blocking sled so many times back at West Point. The impact carried both men onto the bed.

Mark scrambled on top of the Serb into a full mount and reared back for a punch, but the Serb was quicker, whipping his gun hand against the side of Mark's head. Light blazed inside his skull, but not enough to overpower his reflexes. When the gun came around again, he blocked with his forearm and then drove the heel of his hand into the Serb's chin. The crack resounded through the room and so did the Serb's yell of pain.

Not enough pain, though. Mark felt himself bucked up and forward and then his left arm was trapped. He barely had a moment to realize he was caught up in a jujitsu mount defense as he was rolled over onto his back. The Serb was now on top and brought the gun around. This is it, Mark thought, he'd failed, Sophie would die, Novak would–

In the dim light behind the Serb, a shadow entered the room and a gun appeared, its barrel touching the back of the Serb's head. *"Frieren oder du bist tot!"* The Serb must've known enough German to understand, as he slowly raised his hands.

Mark took the gun from the Serb and said, "Took you long enough."

"I'll take care of this one," Krieger said. "Black Knight Three needs your help."

Time seemed to slow down as Jim's years of training took over. He ignored the thudding pain in his left arm and remembered what had been drilled into him for years: fight the man, not the weapon. Novak still had his gun, giving him an advantage, but not for long. Jim pinned Novak's gun arm to the ground, drove a knee into his side and then twisted the pistol from his grip. He rolled to his left, sending another bolt of pain up his arm, but managed to come up on his feet.

He never had a chance to bring Novak's pistol into play. Novak's booted foot rocketed around in a tight arc and the heel caught Jim on the wrist. The gun flew away into the darkness as another jolt of pain fired up Jim's arm. But he knew what was coming next. When Novak's other leg came in with a roundhouse kick, Jim drove a right sidekick toward the knee of the right leg, now planted on the ground.

But the pain from his arm threw him off just enough to affect his aim. The kick went inches too high, onto Novak's thigh instead of the vulnerable knee, enough to stagger him but not disable. Novak regained his balance. He came at Jim again, keeping his arms tight as he moved. He feinted with a left, then fired a right roundhouse at Jim's head.

Jim knew how to block this, left arm inside to out. He'd done it a thousand times in the dojo back home, but now his arm wouldn't respond like it always had. Novak's fist brushed Jim's arm aside and kept coming. At the last possible split second Jim ducked, just enough to alter the impact, change it to a glancing blow. He shook it off as he came back with his counter, driving a right uppercut toward Novak's solar plexus.

But this one didn't have as much on it as he wanted, and Novak was quick, far quicker than Jim anticipated, deflecting the strike so it connected with the tough pectoral muscle of Novak's chest. Novak was hardly slowed down. He came at Jim again, pulling his head down as a knee shot up.

Mark heard the pop of the gunshot from the back yard and had to force himself not to run out of the bedroom. He kept his weapon up and trained ahead of him as he advanced down the hallway and into the back room. The door leading out was still open.

From the doorway he saw the three figures in the moonlight, two of them fighting, one lying motionless on the grass. His heart seemed to leap to his throat as he recognized Sophie's prone figure.

He flipped the nearest of two switches on the wall just inside the door. Floodlights mounted on either end of the outer wall flared to life, bathing the yard with a wide swath of illumination. Mark saw Sophie move, bringing one hand up to shield her eyes, and he allowed himself to breathe. She was alive.

The fighters separated briefly, Jim's back to the house. They were a good twenty yards away. The shot that would be easy chips for Mark under any other circumstances. Now it wasn't. The angle was wrong. Jim was almost exactly in between Mark and the target. He brought his weapon up and aimed. "Freeze, Novak!"

Jim had barely been able to block Novak's knee, and now his left arm was all but useless. He felt weakness seeping in and knew he was bleeding. It was now or never. He couldn't let Novak get away, not after all they'd risked to come here. He pushed himself away just as the yard lit up from behind him. Novak brought a hand up to shield his eyes, an automatic reflex that Jim could use against him. He brought his right leg around in a roundhouse kick, aiming for Novak's exposed left side.

Mark saw his brother's kick stagger Novak. Dammit! He had to keep them apart so he could take the shot. "Jim! Break off!"

But his brother was relentless, following through with a left kick. Jim's left arm wasn't moving. Was he wounded? Mark leaped off the porch and began running toward them.

Novak barely survived the American's kick, collapsing his body at the last possible second to absorb the blow. He felt a rib crack and white-hot pain filled him. Another commando was on the back porch, yelling at the other to disengage, and now he was coming.

Govno! This American he was fighting was highly skilled, but he was also wounded and Novak knew he could defeat him. It would only take another few seconds, but with the second man coming on, Novak knew he didn't have those seconds. He closed with his opponent and pushed him back, into the path of his onrushing comrade, then turned for the forest and ran for his life, knowing that any second a bullet might find him. The trees were only twenty meters away. He could use their cover to get to the boat and make his escape to Belgrade. He leaped over the prone figure of the accursed woman and angled to his left, then to his right.

Mark knew immediately he'd made a mistake when he saw Jim being shoved backward. He'd come straight in, instead of approaching them at an angle. Now he had to compensate. He took two steps to his left. Novak was sprinting for the tree line, running a slight zigzag pattern. That wouldn't help him. Mark flipped the MP7 onto full auto, sighted on the target and squeezed the trigger. One round fired and then the weapon jammed. Mark cleared the jam, but by the time he brought the weapon up again, Novak had disappeared into the woods.

Jim knelt next to Sophie. He reached to help her up, but then hesitated. She'd taken a hell of a shot from Novak; what if her neck was broken? Relief flooded him when his sister-in-law rolled over on her side and then pushed herself up with an elbow. Jim gently pulled her to a sitting position.

She looked at him, struggling to focus. "Jin? Izzat you? Ow!" She brought a hand to her jaw, then flinched away from the touch.

"Take it easy," Jim said. "You're all right. He's gone."

"He'zh gone?" Her eyes shifted past Jim. "Mark? Oh, God…" She tried to get to her feet, failed, fell back, but Mark's strong arms caught her and pulled her close to him.

"I'm here, babe," Mark said as he cradled her. "I'm here."

"Let's get her into the house," Jim said. "She needs medical attention."

Krieger was next to them on one knee, weapon trained on the tree line. "She's not the only one," he said. "The house is secure, but we can't stay long. We need to get moving as soon as possible. Novak may have called the police for help."

"She's passed out," Mark said. "You two take her inside."

"What?" Jim asked. His arm was not completely numb, but it was getting there.

"I'm going after Novak. He'll be at the boat any minute."

"I advise against that," Krieger said. "If he's called the police, we may not get out of here. At the very least they'll be on the alert for the men who ambushed that other car."

"Don't worry about that," Mark said. "When Sophie tells her story, they won't be able to hold us. Assuming they catch us anyway."

Jim took a step toward his brother. "Mark, for God's sake, give it up! We've got her, let's get the hell out of here."

Krieger effortlessly lifted Sophie up into a fireman's carry. "I have to agree with your brother," he said. "It's over. We're getting out of here."

"Then go! If I don't finish off that bastard now he'll be back at it as soon as he's regrouped. I'll find my own way home." Mark checked his weapon, then leaned over and kissed Sophie on the cheek. "Take good care of her." Then he was off into the darkness.

CHAPTER TWENTY-SIX
GROCKA MUNICIPALITY, SERBIA

S ophie was regaining consciousness as they got back inside. Jim covered the hallway with his MP7 while Krieger carried her into the bedroom and laid her down gently. When Jim glanced back at them, he saw the bloodied bra on the quilt. What the hell had gone on in here? Had she been raped? Holy Christ, he thought, if Mark found that out, he'd hunt Novak to the ends of the earth.

"Don't try to move, just rest," Krieger told her.

"Fache hurtsh," she mumbled.

"You jaw is dislocated, maybe broken. Try moving it side to side. Gently."

Jim glanced back and saw Sophie sit up on one elbow, putting the other hand to her jaw. "Ow!"

"Can you help her?" Jim asked.

Krieger leaned over and examined her closely. "Her jaw is not out of alignment, at least as far as I can tell. Sophie, if you clench your teeth, is your bite proper?"

She hesitated, then grimaced and said, "Yesh, I think sho. Hurtsh, though."

From underneath the bed came a whimper. Jim was about to

kneel down and take a look when Krieger waved him back. "Stay focused on the hallway. I'll check it out."

Mark entered the woods at the edge of the grounds and crouched down, focusing his senses forward. In the back of his mind, his years of training were taking care of the small decisions: analyzing the terrain, the smells, the sounds, considering options, checking his own body for fatigue and injury. Those results were coming in now and they were well into the green.

Despite having little sleep in the past forty-eight hours, he was still alert and energized, but he knew that wouldn't last long. He was in great physical condition for a guy a couple years away from the half-century mark, but his last combat action had been over a year before. Hitting a bag in the gym or plinking targets on the range was one thing, being in combat was quite another. So far, the skills he'd relentlessly honed over a quarter century in uniform were holding, but he had no idea how long they could keep him going, and alive.

But as he used his tactical senses to examine the path ahead, to consider options, come up with a plan, a part of him couldn't help thinking that his brother and Krieger might have been right. They had Sophie, hurt but alive. Jim looked like he'd been winged, but not seriously. So far, they'd all come through this with only minor injuries. They could make their way back to the airport in Vršac and head for home. Worst-case scenario was to drive to Belgrade and get help at the U.S. embassy. That would lead to some potentially uncomfortable questions and even more uncomfortable answers, but if Krieger didn't come in with them, they could protect him.

Next to losing Sophie or his brother, the last thing Mark wanted now was for this operation to jeopardize his friend's career.

But that would leave Novak in the wind. As relatively little as Mark knew about him, one thing he could be sure of was that a man like Novak would not be out of the game for long. An hour from now he could be back in Belgrade. An hour or so later he'd be sitting at his desk, surrounded by his people, his resources, and from that desk he'd start planning for his next chance. Mark sensed that Novak had been flying by the seat of his pants for a lot of this. Somehow he'd been tipped off that Mark was in Italy. With assets close enough to slap something together, he'd seized the opportunity.

The next time would be different. Novak would have time to consider all of his options. He would put together a serious, well-planned operation, using all of his resources to find Mark wherever he was, and then execute his plan.

Mark had really been looking forward to building that log home on a lake. He'd been thinking about that since he was a kid, since that time his carpenter father had taken him to look at the home he was helping build for an old Army buddy who'd made it big in real estate. Well, Mark had hit it big with his six-figure job at OSS, and now that lakefront dream was within his grasp.

If Novak was still out there, though, Mark would never be able to relax out on his deck with a cold beer and the Brewers game on the radio. Sophie would never be safe. They'd started talking about having a child. How could he bring a child into the world, knowing that any minute might bring a rifle shot or a bomb that would make that baby an orphan?

No. Mark could not allow that to happen, not even the chance of it. Novak was going down, and he was going down now. His instincts and senses told him the path ahead was clear. He rose and started forward.

"How bad is the dog?" Jim asked.

"He has a broken leg," Krieger said, "maybe a couple broken ribs, but there's no sign of internal bleeding. He'll live, but he needs veterinary care. Right now he's in pain, but I don't have a medication for him."

"Give him half of an aspirin tablet, with some food, if you can find it," Jim said. "We had a Boston terrier when we were kids, a little bigger than this guy."

"I'll see what I can find," Krieger said and left the room.

Sitting up on the bed and propped up by the pillows, Sophie cradled the little dog in her lap. Jim saw that the ever-resourceful German-American had used a wooden fingernail file to splint the Yorkie's left front leg. Someone in Novak's house had been vain enough to keep some basic manicuring supplies at hand. As for Jim's own wound, Krieger had cleaned and bandaged that in record time.

"I'm taking him with ush," Sophie said.

"Who?"

"Thish little fellow," she said, petting the dog's head. "If we leave him, he'll never make it."

The trembling dog had settled down, thanks to Sophie's gentle petting and soothing, if slurred, words of comfort. "What's his name?" Jim asked.

"Dunno," she said. "They almosht killed him. One of dem tried to shoot him."

"Too small of a target," Jim said, grinning.

Sophie looked at him with eyes that were suddenly hard. "He mished becaushe I made him," she said.

"Was it the guy we have in the back room?"

She shook her head. "No, that'sh Viktor, I think. The guy I shtopped wazsh a Russian. You won't have to worry about him."

Krieger came back in with a small ball of meat in his palm. "Found some aspirin, plus raw hamburger in the refrigerator."

"I'll feed him," Sophie said. She held it to the dog's nose. After two quick sniffs, the animal snapped it out of her palm and gulped it down.

Mark had debated whether to take it slow or move quickly. He didn't know the terrain, which argued for caution, but he was also running out of time, so he decided on speed. He doubted Novak had had any time to set up a booby trap or an ambush. He had no backup, whereas Mark did. No, he'd be trying to get to his boat as quickly as possible.

The moonlight was even more restrained here in the forest, with only puddles of light here and there filtering through the canopy, but they were enough for Mark to see the well-worn path and make good time. It didn't take long before he could see the Danube through the trees and then he was in a small clearing, with a long dock leading out onto the water. A boathouse was built on the left side of the dock, its rear window dark. A speedboat floated on the right.

Mark hesitated at the edge of the woods. Now was the most dangerous part. If Novak was inside that boathouse and waiting for him to appear, he could take a clean shot through that rear window. It was twenty yards from the tree line to the dock. Mark could make it in seconds, but if Novak was waiting for him to do exactly that…

From inside the boathouse came an electronic whine, then a powerful motor roared to life. That decided the issue. Mark sprinted for the dock, his boots pounding on the boards as he raced toward the end. He was still five yards away when a large white boat shot out of the boathouse in reverse, banging into the side of the doorway.

It was a big one, maybe forty feet long, sleek and no doubt powerful. From the cockpit, a gun cracked. Mark had seen the movement and dove to the hard wood of the dock as rounds zipped overhead. He sighted his own weapon and fired a burst. The windscreen shattered from at least two rounds. Novak yawed the boat from left to right, then into a tight turn when he was about forty feet out. The inboard engine roared and foam roiled up from the stern as he shifted. The boat began to move forward, heading upriver. Mark scrambled to a kneeling position and emptied the rest of his MP7's magazine in the boat's direction, trying to lead it. He saw a few sparks from impacts, but the boat didn't slow down.

"Shit!" His frustration almost overwhelmed him, but loosing a tirade of epithets now wouldn't get him any closer to the fleeing boat. Something else would, though. He ran back to the other boat, untied the prow and stern ropes and jumped aboard.

CHAPTER TWENTY-SEVEN
ON THE DANUBE

Novak kept the throttle wide open and his bearing upriver. Habit caused him to reach for the switch for the running lights, but as his finger touched the toggle, he hesitated. No, not tonight. Just in case. If the accursed Americans did indeed have a drone overhead, they could track him even as he was running dark, but why make it any easier for them? They could very well have confederates along the river. He wouldn't put it past them.

He couldn't relax, not yet. Yes, running dark was the right move now. Traffic would be light this time of night, although the Danube was always in extensive use. Cargo vessels ruled this river, but there were also dozens of tourist liners. In fact, there was one of them, up ahead. Novak slowed slightly and turned ten degrees to starboard. The liner was lit up like a Christmas tree, heading downriver, about a kilometer away and closing. He would stay on its port side.

Ahead and to starboard was the dark expanse of Gročanska ada, a large, uninhabited island, three kilometers long and about seven hundred meters across at its widest point. To the north of the island was its smaller neighbor. Together the islands temporarily split the Danube into three channels, but this one was deepest and used by commercial traffic. It was also narrower than the central channel, and sometimes it could be crowded. Tonight, thankfully, it was just this liner and Novak's Italian-made Azimut Atlantis 43. Novak throttled the twin 400-horsepower engines back enough allow him easy navigation past the liner. He knew this island and was wary of the shoals on this side.

The rounds from the American's submachine gun had shattered part of his windscreen and stitched some holes in the Atlantis's hull, which on any other night would have thrown Novak into a rage. He had spent a lot of euros for this boat and kept it in pristine shape, fully fueled at all times, just like the smaller boat he'd left behind at the dock. But none of those bullets had found its intended target. He would live to fight another day. His throbbing ribs seemed to hurt a bit less. It was a good thing, he reflected now as he watched the oncoming liner, that he'd ordered Viktor to keep the boats prepped and ready for a quick departure, just in case. The rest of the plan had gone to *pakao*, but at least he'd done this right, and Viktor had done his job. The Atlantis was in great shape, just like its...

His stomach tightened with a sickening jerk. Had the American taken the other boat? No! He looked behind, peering back toward the dock. The moonlight, was it enough? The rumble of his own engines drowned out any other sound from back there. He couldn't see anything, and now here was the bulk of the river liner cutting off his view of the Serbian shore, but just before it did, he caught a flash of something that could've been the wake of a speeding craft. *Jebati!* He should've taken the time to disable it.

Jim heard footsteps entering the back room and leveled his weapon down the hallway. "Wisconsin!" he shouted.

The reply came back. "Badgers."

Jim aimed his MP7 back down the main hallway to cover the front door as Krieger came around the corner from the back room. "Well?"

"No sign of Mark," he said. "I found some of his shell casings at the end of the dock. Both boats are gone."

"No bodies? No blood?"

"Negative. We must go, Jim. The police could have this entire area cordoned off by now. The closer we get to daybreak the worse our chances are of returning safely to the aircraft."

Jim looked at his watch. Three-thirty-five a.m. "We have about two hours before daylight. If we leave now, we can be back in the air by then, assuming a clear shot to Vršac, and that's a big assumption."

Sophie was standing next to the bed, cradling the dog in her arms. "We can't leave without Mark," she said. Her jaw was swollen and bruised, and doubtless she was exhausted, but Jim had become very familiar with her eyes over the past several months and they were very determined now. "I have to use the loo," she said, setting the dog on the bed. "Don't let him jump off."

After she'd closed the bathroom door, Krieger came over to Jim. "You have to convince her we must leave now. We are running out of time."

"I know," Jim said. Inside, his gut was rumbling, but not from hunger. How could he possibly abandon his brother, deep inside what amounted to hostile territory? What about all this "never leave a man behind" stuff he was always hearing from military guys? Where was that now?

Krieger put a hand on Jim's shoulder. "I know what you're thinking," he said. "I feel the same way. But we have no way to pursue Mark, we can't give him any assistance. We can't call anybody else in, either. It's up to us to get Sophie to safety. If the Serbian police catch us, all bets are off."

"Your're right," Jim said. "I'll tell her."

"Mark will be all right," Krieger said. "He can take care of himself."

Jim heard the toilet flush, then the bathroom door swung open. "Give me a minute with her," he said.

The speedboat had a single 125-horse outboard engine and would be no match for Novak's boat over the long haul, but Mark didn't need it for that. When he got the boat out into the river he could see the moonlight glinting off the frothing wake from the cruiser. The bulk of an island blocked out the horizon beyond Novak. Mark headed upriver in pursuit, and when he saw the brightly-lit river liner heading toward them, a plan formed quickly. It was risky, but he had a better chance using the liner as cover than he did by coming up directly astern of the fleeing Serb, which would give Novak a clear field of fire.

The only question was whether he'd have enough time to make the geometry work. He pushed the throttle to the max and the boat leaped over the waves. The wind tore at him above the Plexiglas windscreen. On any other occasion this would be a thrill ride, but tonight different emotions were at play.

The liner came abeam of him faster than he anticipated. Novak's cruiser had just disappeared on the other side. The plan was to come around the stern of the liner and double back into Novak's path, forcing him to angle toward the island. It was hard to judge distance in the moonlight, but Mark thought there might be only two hundred feet, maybe two-fifty, between the liner and the island's shore. It would be a tight squeeze in daylight under normal conditions. And he'd only have one chance.

Bob McWilliams was leaning on the guard rail at the stern of the *Viking Aegir*, watching the moonlit Danube and wondering why in the hell he couldn't get back to sleep. His usual middle-of-the-night head call had arrived right on time, but now he couldn't drift off again. Maggie was snoring away, worn out from yet another day of power-shopping, whereas Bob and a couple of his newfound cruise buddies had found their way to the Belgrade Fortress, where the guys had wanted to know how Bob, the ex-Army guy, would have assaulted the ramparts. "I wouldn't," he'd told them. "I'd call in the B-52s and watch the show."

He chuckled at the memory but the chuckling stopped when he saw the speedboat tear-assing around the liner from portside to starboard. Or was it the other way around? Christ, where was a sailor when you needed him? But although Bob wasn't up on his nautical stuff, he was still pretty current on small arms, and the moon was bright enough for him to clearly see the guy at the wheel was getting what looked like an Uzi ready to fire. And from the way he was handling the weapon, the guy knew his business.

The boat hit the wake of the liner and leaped into the air, but the guy at the wheel didn't seem to have any trouble hanging on. The boat came down and bounced again as it hit the other wave of the wake, and as soon as the guy re-established control, he pulled her into an even tighter turn to the right.

What the hell was he doing? Bob realized the guy was turning to come back up the side of the liner. Holy Christ, was this a terrorist attack? Was he going to spray the liner with the submachine gun? But it was just one guy, that made no sense, and nobody was out in an exposed area at this time of night. Except Bob, of course, but even as he realized this, he knew he had to see, so he raced over to that side of the rail as fast as his two artificial knees could carry him and leaned over as far as he could.

No, the guy was ignoring the liner. He was maybe fifty yards behind when he finished the turn and started his run back. Bob looked down the guy's path along the liner and damn if there wasn't *another* boat, a bigger one, coming up on that side, standing off about a hundred feet from the much larger cruise liner. Bob turned back to the speedboat just in time to see the guy unlimber the Uzi over the top of his windscreen and open fire. Bob's old Vietnam-era instincts came back instantly and he dropped to the deck, hoping a stray round didn't come through their stateroom window and kill his sleeping wife.

Too late, Novak realized he'd boxed himself in. He had barely thirty meters of open water between his cruiser and the liner on the port side, maybe forty meters to the shore of the island on the starboard. He recalled that the shoreline here was rocky, giving way to a narrow beach. But he would clear the liner in just a few seconds, and then he'd be past the island with clear sailing all the way upriver to Belgrade. Just a couple dozen meters more…

As soon as he saw the speedboat roaring around the stern of the liner, he knew he was in trouble. Hayes, it could only be Hayes, damn him! And here he was, turning into a collision course, driving Novak's own boat! Was there no end to this American's devilment? Well, if he wanted to play chicken, then–

Light began winking from the speedboat, followed split seconds later by shells ripping through what remained of Novak's windscreen. Novak ducked and pulled the wheel to starboard as Plexiglas shards tattooed the side of his head and left shoulder. The cruiser yawed heavily onto its side and then shuddered with the collision of fiberglass hulls.

CHAPTER TWENTY-EIGHT
GROCKA MUNICIPALITY, SERBIA

Sophie slid into the back seat of the SUV, cradling the dog, who was now asleep. At first she'd thought the Yorkie had died, but after a moment of panic, she was reassured when his eyes opened and he looked up at her. Then he licked her hand. Tears filled her eyes and she nuzzled him, careful not to bump his splintered foreleg.

Krieger had sent Jim across the field to bring the Audi to Novak's front door. Sophie's argument with her brother-in-law about departing this wretched place was fierce but short. She just didn't have the energy to fight anymore, and her entire head was now filled with a dull ache from her swollen jaw. She hadn't given up the argument just because the mere act of speaking added to the pain; she knew Jim was right, they had to leave now. Whatever window of escape they had was closing fast. It might be shut already. She looked through the window of the SUV and down the driveway, expecting to see flashing lights any second.

Krieger was now at the wheel and Jim was about to get in the front passenger seat when he hesitated. "Wait a second," he said. "Did you hear that?"

"No," Krieger said. "What was it?"

"I don't know. Something from the back of the house. A shout, maybe."

"Probably the prisoner," Krieger said. "Get in, Jim."

"It could be Mark," Sophie said from the back, hoping desperately that it was true.

"I've got to check it out," Jim said. "I'll be right back."

Krieger tapped the wheel once, then looked at Jim.

"Two minutes."

Sophie watched Jim run back through the front door. She hoped it was indeed Mark, returning from his final confrontation with Novak. If he had the Serb's scalp with him, that would be just fine with her. On second thought–and any second thoughts weren't coming too easily because of the pain–she wanted no reminders of this house of horrors. The dog, that was different. He was as much a victim as she was, forced to live here and do the bidding of a monster. She couldn't leave the little bloke behind.

Could she leave her husband behind? She might never see him again, and that brought another sob. Her dear Mark, the warrior she'd met in Afghanistan. A natural leader, someone who'd earned the respect of British officers, no easy feat. He'd led men into battle, devoted the best years of his life to protecting his country. But there was a price, one he paid almost every night when the nightmares came. How many times had she awakened to hold him? Sometimes it was the shakes from all the close calls he'd endured, sometimes it was racking sobs for the men and women under his command whom he hadn't been able to bring home alive.

It had gotten better in the last few months, since their wedding, as they settled into their new life together. His work at OSS helped him cope with the frustrations of dealing with a civilian world that was often so very alien to the one of order and discipline he'd left behind. The nightmares had dwindled in their frequency and their intensity. It had been getting better, and then came that evening in Capua.

The dog was asleep again, stretched out in her lap, resting his head on her forearm. Sophie envied him. Even in his pain, the little guy had found some sanctuary, someone who would take care of him. Sophie wondered if she would ever feel that way herself again.

Jim had to force himself not to run through the house. The fatigue was starting to get to him. His fight with Novak had taken more out of him than he wanted to admit. What the hell was a guy in his fifties doing here, anyway? "Rescuing my sister-in-law," he muttered aloud, answering his own question. Saying the words seemed to strengthen him. He kept the MP7 at the ready as he approached the turn in the hallway.

Krieger had stashed the Serb named Viktor in the back room, and he was still there, zip-tied at the ankles and with his wrists fastened securely to a pipe next to a washing machine. He was conscious now, and he'd managed to peel some of the duct tape off his mouth, no doubt by scraping it against the washer.

He'd been trying to free his wrists, but halted as he saw Jim enter the room. "Come back to finish me, American?"

"If you don't shut up I just might," Jim said. He passed the Serb and went to the back door. The floodlights were still on. There was no sign of Mark, and there was also no sign of the Serb he'd knocked out and zip-tied before the fight with Novak. How in the hell...? Where had the guy gone? Not back to the house.

"Shit!" Jim dashed back past the Serb and into the hallway.

He heard laughter from behind him as he pounded down the hall. "You're screwed, American! You should have killed him when you had the chance!"

Sophie hadn't taken her eyes off the front of the house, hoping to see some movement through the windows, to see Jim and maybe even Mark emerge from the front door. Something was wrong, terribly wrong. Where was–

"Get down!"

Krieger's shout from the front startled her, and for a moment her only reaction was to look at him. He'd opened the door and slipped out, bringing his weapon around, squeezing off a three-round burst. Just before she ducked, Sophie saw two figures illuminated in the SUV's headlights. Gunfire ripped through the night air and three stars flared on the windshield. She fell to the seat, cradling the whimpering dog.

GROČANSKA ADA, ON THE DANUBE

The collision threw Mark against the side of the boat and he lost control of the wheel. The wake from Novak's cruiser surged against the speedboat, and Mark had to fight through the stunning cold of the water to grab the wheel. Ahead of him was darkness, but it seemed to be moving. The river liner! Mark yanked the wheel to the left and lost his balance again as the careening speedboat caromed off the side of the liner. Over the roar of the engine he heard men shouting from above.

The liner was already fifty yards behind him by the time Mark regained control of the speedboat. River water sloshed around the deck, but he didn't think it would be enough to cause a problem. What would be a problem would be any leaks caused by the collisions. He pulled back on the throttle and brought the boat around, slowing nearly to a stop. As best he could in the moonlight, he searched the inside of the hull for any cracks or punctures. It appeared to be holding, but that might not last. He had to get ashore. If he sank out here in the middle of the Danube, it would be a long swim back and he might not make it, even if he could find a life jacket.

The night was sundered by the blaring horn of the liner. Mark shoved the throttle ahead and the boat responded, leaping well clear of the liner, which had altered its course to avoid him. Would they stop? Mark figured they wouldn't. Report it, yes, they surely would. If the Serbs had a riverine police force, they'd probably deploy from Belgrade, so he had some time, although not much.

Time enough to find Novak and finish him.

The shore of the island was only thirty yards to starboard. Mark slowed his speed and stood up, looking over the windscreen. There! Novak's cruiser had beached on the rocky shore, maybe seventy-five yards ahead. Wary of the shoals, Mark stayed well offshore, closing on the cruiser. He looked for the MP7, cursed when he couldn't find it, then saw something curled around a davit on the boat's gunwale. The weapon had bounced overboard, but the sling caught the davit, thank God. Mark pulled it back inside. He was down to his last magazine, maybe ten rounds left. He'd only need one.

When Novak could see the stars above him, he knew his head was clearing. He'd been thrown from the cruiser's cockpit as the boat crashed against a large rock and flipped over on its port side. He was lying in a few centimeters of water, not enough to cushion his fall from the rocks below the surface, but enough to prevent the rocks from killing him.

He sat up, shaking his head. His pistol was gone. Looking downriver, he saw the liner in the distance, then heard the hooting of its horn. What was that, coming past the ship? God above, it was his speedboat. Hayes had survived the collision. The Danube had not claimed him. The speedboat was crawling slowly upriver, toward him.

Novak knew his only chance was to make it to the woods. It was a big island, and there might be a boat somewhere he could steal. Teenagers occasionally came over here to camp, and although that wasn't likely this time of year, it was worth a look. But having a hundred campers on the island with dozens of boats would make no difference if he couldn't evade the damnable American. Novak rolled over, ignoring the pain of his bruised body, and scrambled over the rocks onto the sandy shore.

Mark saw movement beyond the beached cruiser. It was Novak, it had to be. A dark tree line loomed ahead, about fifty yards from the shore. If the Serb made it in there, Mark might not find him till daylight, which wasn't far off. There could be police all over this place by then. He had to wrap this up quickly and get away. Not back to Novak's estate, no; Krieger would have them on their way by now.

Novak had made it to the beach, but he wasn't moving very quickly. Mark gunned the engine to get just enough momentum, then cut it off as he slid the boat onto the rocks twenty yards from the cruiser. He dared get no closer in case Novak still had a weapon. But by the way he was moving, that didn't seem likely. One leg was hobbled.

Novak knew within two steps that his left leg was nearly done for. Not a broken bone, but his knee must have twisted when he'd landed on the rocks. It hurt like a *kučka*. His chances of escape had now dwindled precipitously. But he would not surrender to this American. Not after thirteen years of waiting for his vengeance. He would go down fighting. His country might have given in to the Americans and their NATO lap dogs, given up their republics, their reputation, their national pride, but Darko Novak would not roll over like the rest of them had. With each painful step on the sand, he knew he would never be president of Serbia, never get to lead his country back to its old glory. But if he were to die here tonight, he would die like a Serbian warrior ought to die. And he would take the American with him.

The years and age seemed to slip away from Mark as he crept over the sand of the beach. The fatigue was gone. His senses were as alive as they'd ever been. All the years of training, from the Plain

248

at West Point, to Kuwait and the Balkans, Iraq and Afghanistan, and finally here. For twenty-five years he had devoted his life to protecting his country from its enemies, pursuing them into their holes, rooting them out, eliminating them. There always seemed to be more. The battle was never-ending. But with each one he took down, his friends and family back home, his countrymen, could rest a little easier.

Finally it had come down to this, the last one. The man who had ordered the assault on his sister-in-law and the kidnaping of his wife, the man who intended to kill Mark and then Sophie, was only fifty yards away now. There was enough moonlight for Mark to take the shot. He would wait till twenty yards, just to make sure. Up ahead, Novak struggled for the woods, but he'd never make it. In the moonlight he stood out like a target on the range. The Serb looked back at him, and Mark thought he could see a glint from his eyes. Was there fear behind them? Good. It was time for him to be afraid.

It was a piece of driftwood that finally did him in. Novak didn't see it, and when he brought his left foot down, the knee snapped and he fell hard onto the sand. On all fours, like an animal. Pain from the knee lanced up his leg. Behind him, he could hear the American's tread whispering through the sand. And he heard another sound, the ratcheting of a round into the chamber of a weapon.

He would not allow the American to shoot him in the back. Novak struggled to his feet and turned to face him. The American was thirty yards away, and he was aiming a submachine gun at him. Like a living thing, the crushing reality of defeat shuddered through Novak. He had truly underestimated this man. There were no drones, no platoon of commandos. Just this man and one or two comrades. They had taken on Novak and his elite guard and bested them all. What manner of man could accomplish that? A man whose wife had been taken. And when that man was well-trained, had resourceful and courageous friends and possessed a will of iron, he could accomplish much.

Novak had once thought himself to be such a man. But it had all gone to hell, and so quickly. His pained, fatigued brain could not process the thought. Forty-eight hours ago he had been slumbering in his Belgrade penthouse. There'd been a blonde next to him, hadn't there? Yes, but what was her name? He couldn't remember. Rode him like a mustang and then snored like a bulldog. Another day was about to dawn, a day of productive work at Red Dragon, and pursuit of his dream of the presidency.

All gone now.

The knee wobbled, but he would not yield to it. He would face his fate standing. When the American got within twenty yards, he stopped.

The silence was broken only by the thudding of his own heart. It was as if the entire Danube had halted, awaiting the outcome. Well, let it come, then.

"What are you waiting for, Hayes? Shoot me, and be done with it."

Mark stopped when he was twenty feet away. He lowered his MP7 from eye level but kept it pointed dead center at the target. One shot would do it, but he should fire three to make sure. Then one to the head, like he'd done to that Republican Guard asshole in Kuwait, the one who'd led the torture squad.

But that had been at the end of a firefight, and his colonel had reamed his ass about the head shot, but hadn't written him up. Mark's career might've ended back in '91 if the colonel had gone by the book.

What did the book say now? Was there even a book to begin with?

He finally said, "Why?"

Novak teetered on his bad leg, but fought to keep himself upright. He barked a bitter laugh, then said, "You killed my brother."

CHAPTER TWENTY-NINE
GROCKA MUNICIPALITY, SERBIA

J im peered around the edge of the front doorway. The Audi was still in the driveway where he'd left it. Krieger was firing from the cover of the opened driver's door. He couldn't see Sophie in the back seat, but he could see sparks as incoming rounds ricocheted off the car. He searched the distance to the car's front, back toward the barracks and other outbuildings. There! One, two guns, and now a third, opening up from the far edge of the detached garage, a few dozen feet from the edge of the house.

Jim hugged the inside wall, frantically considering his options. He had to force himself to control his breathing. That was the first thing, something the Russians had taught him years ago in his *Systema* training: breathing control. Reduces tension, allows the mind to think clearly, the body to move easily. It was for just these types of situations he'd trained for all these years. The training had brought him through the challenge of Somalia a year before, and it would bring him through now, if he just trusted it.

He could fire on the Serbs from here, but that would be fruitless. He might get lucky, but the Serbs knew these buildings, knew the grounds. They would be in good cover. He snuck another peek, and the gunman on the far left had now shifted position, moving farther left. They were trying to flank the car. That meant the man on the right would be doing the same thing. Coming this way.

252

Jim crept back down the hallway. The open doorway to his right led to what appeared to be a living room, or what they might call a parlor in these older homes. The window on the far wall was shattered, and he could smell smoke. This would've been where Krieger had come in when he and Mark assaulted the house. Now it would work the other way.

He had one leg swung through when he saw movement coming around the back of the garage. Jim quickly brought the other leg out, dropped to the ground in a crouch and took aim. The figure emerged into the moonlight and Jim recognized him as the Serb he'd taken down in the back yard.

That time, Jim had failed to subdue the man properly, and his escape had led to the firefight. This time, there would be no worrying about an escape. Jim calmly pulled the trigger. The rifle bucked slightly, and he brought it back and fired twice more. The Serb grunted and went down.

The windshield shattered as more bullets impacted. Sophie couldn't suppress a scream of terror. To get this far, and then be shot by these bastards! It was too much for her. She clutched the whining dog. The firing let up momentarily and there was suddenly another sound, in the distance: sirens.

Krieger slid back behind the wheel, slamming the door. The engine roared as the powerful Audi surged backward. Sophie almost fell onto the floor, but she grabbed the post of a headrest at the last instant, cradling the dog. "What's happening?" she shrieked.

"The police are coming," Krieger said. She looked up and saw his hand on the back of the front passenger seat, and she remembered her father doing the same thing as he backed their old Vauxhall during her childhood in England. But nobody had been shooting at them then.

The rear wheels bumped over something and brush scraped against the passenger side as the Audi rocked to the right. Krieger was driving them around the house, out of the line of fire. But surely the Serbs would pursue them? And the police would soon be blocking the road.

"Where are we going?"

"There is a helicopter." The brakes slammed and she surged back against the seat, rolling onto her side to protect the dog. She was too late letting go of the headrest post and her arm was nearly torn out of its socket. The rear door opened in front of her. Krieger was extending a hand. "Get out, quickly!"

"Can you fly it?"

"I qualified on the Eurocopter Tiger with the *Heeresfliegertruppe.* German Army Aviation. I can handle whatever this one is." He pulled her out of the car. The gunfire had stopped, but no doubt the Serbs were advancing. From beyond the grounds of the estate, the sirens were getting louder. She looked the other way and saw the helicopter pad and the dark, insect-like hulk of the machine.

"What about Jim? For God's sake, we can't leave *him* behind, too!"

He started toward the aircraft at a trot, pulling her along on unsteady legs. "When he hears the engine, he'll know to come for it. Part of our exfil plan."

"I hope he remembers."

254

"He will."

Jim didn't stop to consider the fact that he'd just killed a man. It had happened before. He'd taken two men down in Somalia before his escape. Or had it been three? The nightmares had only receded after his marriage to Gina. Maybe he'd get another round of them out of this night, but he'd deal with them if they came.

He snugged against the side of the garage and inched his way forward. Just after his shots, he'd heard the engine of the Audi roar. If Krieger was making a run for it, he wasn't doing it down the main driveway; Jim had a clear view of the small turnaround. He must've gone in reverse. But where to? Around the house, out of the line of fire. Good move.

The Serbs would pursue, though. Jim peeked around the edge of the garage. There! The one on the far left was running across the driveway, about thirty yards away. What about the guy who'd been in the middle? Jim was about to lean farther around the corner when he heard the slight slap of a boot on pavement.

He also heard the sirens, and they were getting closer. He'd worry about the police later. He had to deal with the immediate threat first. And that threat was now advancing along the driveway turnaround, ten yards away. Jim saw the silhouette clearly. The Serb didn't know he was here. Jim went to one knee, aimed and fired.

He missed. The Serb must have detected Jim's movement in his peripheral vision and reflexively ducked. Jim's round missed the top of his head by an inch.

Things seemed to slow down. The Serb went to one knee as he brought his weapon around. Jim flicked the switch to allow fully-automatic fire, but when he squeezed the trigger, it refused to move. He'd hit the safety switch instead. His training took over. He ducked and rolled to his left as rounds tore through the air above him. When he came out of the roll, he threw his weapon at the Serb.

The flying gun distracted the Serb just long enough for Jim to rush him. The collision sent both men to the ground, but Jim was on top and knew he had only seconds to use that advantage. His ground training was not as extensive as his stand-up fighting, but now it would have to do the job, or he'd be dead.

Taking a full mount position was the easy part. Putting the Serb down would be harder, and he knew he had to do it quickly. This guy's buddy could come running, and shooting, any second. Jim drove an elbow into the Serb's jaw, then again. The Serb was dazed, but not out. *Knife! Knife!* No, Jim rejected that. He had one, a very good KA-BAR, but he didn't want to kill this man. There'd been enough killing.

He must have hesitated, because the Serb roared and bucked his hips upward, shoving Jim forward, past the man's head. A punch to Jim's already sore ribs fired a lance of pain into his brain, clearing it, enabling him to focus, let his training take over. He'd brought in a Gracie Jujitsu instructor at OSS for a week. It was time to make that pay off.

The Serb was struggling underneath him. Jim brought his left knee up to pin the man's right arm, his right foot up to pin the right arm at the bicep. He used his hands to twist the Serb's head, then shot his right leg under the neck and applied the triangle. The Serb had enough strength to roll to his left, but Jim went with the roll and now both legs were around the man's neck and shoulders, and being on his own back now let Jim exert even more pressure with his legs. The Serb's face was crushed into Jim's lower abdomen. He thrashed, but couldn't make contact with his hands. His shouts were muffled. Desperate, the Serb tapped Jim's leg three times, but Jim wouldn't fall for that one. This wasn't on a mat at a dojo. This was for keeps. He squeezed as hard as he could. The Serb's body spasmed once, twice, then went limp. Jim kept up the pressure for another five seconds, then unwrapped his legs and pushed the unconscious man aside.

Jim was exhausted, the fatigue and the stress were close to shutting him down, but he couldn't stop, not yet. He got to his feet, found his weapon, scanned for the one remaining Serb. There he was, across the driveway now, but he'd stopped and was looking in Jim's direction. Beyond him, Jim saw flashing lights coming down the road toward the entrance to the grounds. He had fifteen, maybe twenty seconds before the first police car would be in the driveway. And there was another sound, from the side of the house. An engine spooling up, not the Audi's, heavier. Novak's chopper.

Jim's legs were about to give out, but he needed them for one last dash. He ran for the helicopter pad. Shots rang out, bullets shattering the glass of the front window as he ran past.

GROČANSKA ADA, ON THE DANUBE

"What are you waiting for, Hayes? Shoot me and be done with it."

Mark lowered the MP7 from eye level, but kept it pointed at Novak's center mass. One shot here would do it, but he would fire three, just in case. And the head shot, like he'd done with that Iraqi?

No, not this time. That bastard had gone down fighting. He didn't know what he'd do with Novak yet, but while he figured it out, something needed to be said. "I didn't kill your brother."

Novak teetered on his bad leg, fought to stay upright, and won. The man had guts, Mark had to give him that. No, he didn't. A man with guts wouldn't kidnap another man's wife to settle a score. He'd meet his nemesis face to face and throw down right there.

The Serb barked a bitter, pained laugh. "You may not have pulled the trigger, but you were the cause. You were his prisoner. He should have shot you and left you in the village."

"Maybe so. But he didn't. He was a soldier, he knew the risks. And besides, if you'd kept your men on your side of the border, like your government agreed to, none of this would've happened. Your brother would be alive today. So spare me–"

"You were invading our country!" Novak screamed. "It was a civil war! Did anyone from Europe intervene in your own civil war? You had no business here!"

Mark raised the MP7. "All those Kosovars you guys raped and murdered might have a different opinion, if they were still around. That's all over, Novak. I'm not here to debate politics."

"Then what are you here to do? I assume your friends have freed your wife. Yet here you are. If you mean to shoot me, then do it. Or are you too much of a coward?"

Mark put his finger on the trigger, took a breath, then

hesitated. He had always considered himself to be a warrior. He was definitely not a coward, and he refused to let himself be baited. He realized that in his own twisted way, Novak considered himself to be a warrior as well. Here he was, at the mercy of his greatest enemy, but he wasn't begging for his life, wasn't offering a bribe.

What was the honorable thing to do?

"Shoot!" Novak screamed.

Mark lowered his weapon. "I'm going to make you an offer you can't refuse, Novak."

Chest heaving, the Serb looked at him, eyes narrowed. "What are you talking about?"

"I will spare your life if you give me your word as a soldier that you will leave me and my family alone."

Novak looked perplexed, then his expression changed, to one of amusement. "That's it? That's all it will take for you to walk away?"

"That's right. What's your answer? You have ten seconds."

The Serb started to laugh. "You are joking, right?"

"Six seconds."

Novak kept laughing, so hard that he bent over. "You crazy Americans. You are stuck in 1945. The world has moved on from you. But, hey, what the hell? I accept. I will never bother you again."

"Good."

Novak kept laughing, brought his left hand up in a wave as his right went to his feet. The driftwood came up toward Mark in a cloud of sand.

CHAPTER THIRTY
OVER SOUTH BANAT DISTRICT, SERBIA

The helicopter thrummed steadily through the Serbian dawn. Below him, Jim saw quiet fields, dark stands of forest, houses where a few lights were coming on. Cars and trucks were moving on the roads as another day began.

He was glad nobody down there was shooting at them. He took his eyes away from the ground below and looked ahead, through the cockpit window. The Vršac airport was somewhere out there. "We should see the airport soon, right?" he asked into his headset mic.

"Any minute now," Krieger said. In the pilot's seat, the NATO commando handled the helicopter with almost ridiculous ease. He'd even found a pair of sunglasses. Although Vršac was only forty miles by air from Novak's estate, Krieger had flown a diversionary route, following the Danube eastward until they spotted the ruins of Ram Fortress on the right bank. The river curved around the promontory and then flowed southeastward, with Romania on the opposite bank. Krieger then changed course to due north.

"You fly this thing like you've done it all your life," Jim said.

"It is a good machine. Italian-made. Many NATO nations use the military version. Very similar to what I trained on." He flipped a switch and turned a knob on the radio. *"Feldgeister,* this is Black Knight actual, do you read, over?"

Static came through Jim's headphones, and then a voice. *"Roger that, Black Knight actual, Feldgeister responds, please give the ID code, over."*

"Identification code is Siegfried, I say again, ID code is Siegfried, please respond, over."

"ID code accepted, Black Knight actual. What is your situation? Over."

"We are inbound in a helicopter, ETA is five minutes. Prepare for takeoff as soon as possible upon our arrival, over."

"Roger that, we copy your ETA five minutes, we are initiating pre-flight. Be advised, we see no local activity, our clearance should be five-by-five, over."

"Very good, Feldgeister. See you soon. Black Knight actual, out."

Jim couldn't suppress a grin. "I recognized Siegfried, the hero of the *Nibelungenlied,*" he said. "I read it in my advanced German class in college. But the other one?"

"The Feldgeister were spirits of the corn, but also spirits of the wind. I thought it appropriate for our transportation." The German-American flashed him a tight smile. "You might say I am a student of German mythology."

Jim nodded, then looked back toward the second row of seats. Sophie was sleeping, cradling the dog. The little Yorkie was awake, looking at Jim with wide brown eyes. "First thing back in Rome, we get the dog to a vet," Jim said.

"Of course."

Jim looked out the side window again. The Danube was miles behind them now. When they'd left Novak's estate, they'd flown over the large islands just out from the Serb's dock. They'd seen one large boat run aground on the nearest island, but one swoop over the deserted beach was all Krieger said they could spare before heading downriver. There'd been no sign of life on the sand. More importantly, no bodies.

"It would've been nice to have seen Mark on that island," Jim said. They'd tried raising him on his tactical radio, but got no response.

"Yes. An outside shot. Hopefully he is safe on the river, heading to Belgrade and the embassy."

"He didn't have a cell phone with him, did he?"

"I'm afraid not," Krieger said. He fished a smartphone out of a breast pocket. "Do you need to make a call?"

"Yes," Jim said, as an idea began forming. "As soon as we land."

BELGRADE, SERBIA

Petar Petrović had many jobs around the house and at his father's shop, but this one was the one he enjoyed the most. Every October, the sixteen-year-old was responsible for preparing his family's boat for the winter. Here at the marina on the Sava River, in the shadow of the Ada Bridge, whose magnificence Petar didn't yet appreciate, he prepared the boat for its last voyage of the year, and a short one it would be, about a hundred meters or so over to the ramp where his father would soon arrive with the trailer.

Petar might not appreciate the bridge, but he certainly appreciated the boat. To him it meant a measure of freedom. His older brother was in university in Germany, and his fifteen-year-old sister had no interest in the boat except as a place to preen for the boys while wearing her bikini. It was much too cold for that today, so she'd stayed home. That was all right with Petar. He took his responsibility seriously.

It was nearly nine o'clock by his watch when he'd finished his chores. Still an hour before his father would arrive. What to do? Well, there was still some petrol in the tank, and there was no use letting it sit in there, was there? One last spin, out of the estuary into the Savo. Maybe he would take her downriver to the confluence with the Danube, about twelve kilometers. He jiggled the tank. No, not quite enough for a round trip. Okay, he would just take her down as far as the Belgrade Fair. Might be something going on there worth seeing.

The engine started right up, and Petar kept it in neutral while releasing the lines. Back behind the wheel, he eased the shift to reverse, applied enough throttle to get the boat moving, and was soon out of the slip. He'd been driving the boat since he was eleven and it was second nature now. The wind was biting and he zipped up his jacket as he drove the boat out into the estuary and made for the broad Sava beyond.

He was nearly to the Fair, three large domes and several

263

smaller exhibition halls. The biggest dome, he knew from school, was the largest in the world from the time it was opened in 1957 until the Americans built their Astrodome in 1965. He had been to the Fair a few times, usually for trade shows with his father. He was admiring the huge concrete structure so much that he almost missed the boat floating in the middle of the Sava, with the black-clad man waving at him.

Petar cut his speed and steered for the boat. When he got close enough, he shouted, *"Da li ti treba pomoć?"*

The man shook his head. "Do you speak English?" he yelled.

"Sure," Petar said. "Need help, mister?"

"Yes," the man in black said. "I'm out of gas. Can you tow me to shore?"

Mark tied the boat up at an empty slip and waved goodbye to the kid, who had a crisp new thousand-dinar note for his trouble. Another smart move by Krieger, supplying each of them with Serbian cash, twenty thousand dinar apiece, just in case. The NATO officer's resourcefulness never ceased to amaze Mark.

Cash could be used to buy silence, too, and Mark was hoping that would be the case with the kid. Finding an American clad in black tactical gear in the middle of the Savo was not an everyday occurrence, he was sure, but maybe the money would keep the kid quiet for at least a few hours. Eventually somebody would notice the abandoned boat and trace its registration number to Novak, but by then Mark planned to be safely ensconced in the American embassy, about six kilometers from here, according to the Belgrade map he purchased at a kiosk.

He had to make it to the embassy. Although he had his passport with him, he had no credit card, and not enough cash to buy a plane ticket. He couldn't call anyone to have them buy a ticket for him, either. He was on his own. Krieger had made that clear to both him and Jim on the flight to Serbia.

The map was his second purchase. His first was at a used clothing store, and all the gear he'd worn into Serbia, including the boots–too bad, they were a nice pair–went into a trash container in the alley next to the store. He still had about ten thousand dinar, worth maybe a hundred bucks U.S., but he wouldn't need all of it. He had maybe five kilometers to go.

The fatigue was almost too much to bear now. He had to rest and get something to eat. With a shock, he realized he'd hardly eaten anything in more than twenty-four hours. With his nondescript brown jacket, slouch hat and sunglasses, he felt reasonably safe from being recognized. The police presence here wasn't any more or less pervasive than in other European capitals, so even if the cops had made it to Novak's estate by now, and assuming Novak's surviving guards provided any kind of description of the assault team, Mark was reasonably sure he'd be okay for another few hours.

He stopped at a tavern, surprised it was open at this time of the morning. He ordered ćevapi, small beef sausages on flat bread, washing it down with water, although he was very tempted by the beer selection. No, he had to keep his head as clear as possible. The food and water re-energized him, but he still needed sleep.

As he munched on the last of the ćevapi, he went over the the events on the island one more time. He'd have to explain what had happened when he got to the embassy, and he decided the truth would be the best way to go. Really, he'd had every intention of letting Novak live. Yes, Paul told him back in Rome that Novak would have to die, it would be the only way to ensure the future safety of Mark and his family. Krieger said the same thing, hadn't he? Even Jim went along with that.

But he'd beaten Novak, and he was not about to shoot an unarmed, injured man, regardless of whether or not he deserved it. He was ready to walk away, back to the boat with Novak stranded on the beach, a broken man, but then came the sand and the driftwood.

His reaction was instantaneous. Even as he went over it again in his mind now, he knew every move was born of years of training and hard experience. Left hand up to swat the driftwood away, taking much of the sand with it, crouching and bringing the MP7 up, squeezing the trigger once, twice, three times. The bullets slammed into Novak's chest and pushed him backwards onto the sand. Mark saw him twitch once, twice, heard a gurgling choke from the man's throat, and then nothing.

There was no need for one more round to the head.
Mark dragged the body off the beach into the woods, then hustled back to the speedboat and headed upriver, tossing his weapons into the Danube along the way. He decided to go up the Savo when he got to the rivers' confluence, and saw the marina in the distance just as the engine sputtered and died. With no oars aboard, he had no choice but to wait for a passing boater to offer a tow. He was glad the kid had been the first one to come along. His luck was still holding.

He finished his water, dropped some dinar on the table and headed outside, got his bearings from the map and began walking. Four and a half kilometers.

There were cabs everywhere, just like any other city, but Mark didn't want to take the chance that there was an alert out for anyone trying to reach the U.S. Embassy. He stayed on foot, even as his energy was draining. Most of the way was through residential areas and parks, fortunately. Twice he saw police cars and he made sure to walk normally to the nearest alleyway or storefront to get out of sight. Neither of them stopped. Now he turned onto Kneza Aleksandra Karađorđevića Boulevard.

He hoped Sophie had gotten out. Would she be waiting for him back in Rome? Mark had enormous confidence in Krieger, and by God, his brother Jim had impressed him throughout this entire operation. For a civilian he had performed very well. He and Jim had been at arm's length for more than a few years, ever since their father died, but after Jim's experience in Somalia last year, which had led directly to Mark's own secret mission into Iran with Krieger's assault team, the brothers had buried whatever hatchet might've been there, and they'd been pretty close ever since. Mark had always tended to look on civilians, those who'd never worn the uniform, with a bit of disdain. Policemen and firemen excepted, of course, and many of them were vets as well. But even though Jim had never served, not for lack of trying, he for damn sure was a warrior. He'd proven that again here in Europe. When Mark saw him again, he'd–

When he saw the Stars and Stripes in the distance, he almost wept. He had about half a mile to go. Suddenly there was a spring in his step. He was going to make it! Soon he'd be holding Sophie again. Whatever else happened to him, he knew he'd see her again, kiss her lips, hold her close...

The black car slowed down as it approached him. Mark was on the opposite side of the street and kept walking, picking up the pace. The car sped up again, continuing past as it headed in the direction he'd come from, but he heard the honk of a horn. Someone was making a turn and someone else objected. On this side the boulevard was lined with small apartment buildings, three or four units. Mark cut through a yard and slipped between two buildings. Behind them was an access road, running parallel to the boulevard. He turned left and began jogging toward the embassy. Couldn't be more than a quarter-mile now.

He chanced a look behind him. The same car that had slowed down on the boulevard was now behind him, coming his way. No, it couldn't end like this. The freaking embassy was in sight! This street ended at the embassy grounds. He'd have to get around to the front, where the guards were stationed. If he made it to the Marines, they'd let him in. He had his passport, they'd have to let him in, even if the police were after him. Wouldn't they? That's how it happened in the movies, but this wasn't a movie, he wasn't Tom Cruise or Ben Affleck on the run from the Russians. He heard the engine roar behind him. No siren. What the hell could that mean? He began to run.

Mark had two hundred yards to go when he heard the car squeal to a stop behind him. A voice shouted, "Colonel Hayes! Wait!" English, with an American accent. He slowed, then stopped, chest heaving. If this was a trick, they could shoot him even if he was running. Screw it. He turned around. Two men had gotten out of the car, dressed casually. Neither appeared to be armed.

If they turned out to be more of Novak's men, well, he wouldn't go down easily. But he was done running from these bozos. "Who the hell are you guys?"

The driver said, "We're private contractors, Colonel. Randy Bannack from OSS sent us."

"What?"

The man from the passenger side smiled. "He said you might not believe us. Just a second." He pulled a cell phone from his pocket and punched a number. "We're near the embassy, sir. Yes, he's with us."

The man handed the phone to Mark, who was almost numb as he took it. "Hello?"

"Mark, I hope you aren't really going to quit on me," his boss said. "Your brother called and said there was still a chance I could help you out. I have a ticket to Rome waiting for you at the airport. These two friends of mine will give you a lift."

EPILOGUE
JANUARY 2013 – WISCONSIN

"**O**h, for God's sake! Can't anybody put a hit on that guy?"

"Mark, it's just a game," Sophie said. "Restrain yourself."

Outside, the Wisconsin winter was howling, driving the wind chill below zero. Inside Jim and Gina's house, though, the crackling fire in the fireplace was keeping things toasty. On the big TV screen, San Francisco's quarterback had just ripped off a long run for a touchdown, giving the 49ers a 31-24 lead over the Packers. "One solid hit and that guy goes to the sideline," Mark said. "If we'd played against a guy like that back at West Point he wouldn't last the first quarter." On the couch next to him, little Rambo looked up at his new dad with quizzical brown eyes. The green and gold sweater he'd gotten for Christmas fit the Yorkie well, although he still wouldn't bark at every Packer touchdown despite Mark's entreaties.

"Yeah, but then they came up with this thing called the forward pass." Jim handed his brother a fresh bottle of beer. "That's your limit, by the way, whether the Packers win or lose."

Shaking his head in disgust, Mark looked away from the screen and read the label on the bottle. "'Good Old Potosi.' Where'd you find this?"

"It's from a microbrewery in a small town over by Platteville, right on the Mississippi," Jim said, sitting down in an easy chair next to the couch. "Gina and I found it on a road trip a couple months ago."

Mark took a swig from the bottle. "Not bad at all. And speaking of road trips, Sophie and I took one the other day, and we may have found the spot."

Gina came in from the kitchen, the aroma of another delectable Italian dish seeming to follow her. "Dinner will be ready when the game's over," she said. "The spot for what?"

Sophie snuggled in closer to Mark. "For our cabin."

Jim sat up. "Really? Where is it?"

"On a small lake down by Wilmot," Mark said. "Five acres, about two hundred feet of lakefront. Has a small cabin on it now, but if we buy, we'll be tearing that down and building the one we want. Sophie's been looking at a few designs."

Gina sat on the arm of the chair and draped an arm around Jim's shoulders. "Just a few?" she asked, smiling.

"Well, more than a few," Sophie said. "At first I didn't think much of a log home. Outside my experience. Not too many of them in Britain, after all, but we toured a couple display models, and I was hooked."

"She'll always be a Brit, but she's slowly becoming Americanized," Mark said.

"I suppose," Sophie said. "But our child will be a natural-born American, like his dad."

Mark nodded, eyes on the TV screen. Aaron Rodgers had just completed a pass and the Packers were driving. Mark brought the beer bottle to his lips, then stopped. His eyes went wide. "What did you say?"

Sophie sat up a little straighter. "Well, he, or she, will be born here, so that means American citizenship automatically, does it not?"

Gina's hands went to her cheeks. "*Sei incinta?* You're pregnant?"

"Confirmed at the clinic just the other day," she said. Her eyes were shining. "I'm due in August."

Gina leaped from the chair and flew to the couch, squeezing her sister-in-law with a huge hug. "Praise God, I'm going to be an auntie!" she said.

Jim gave his brother a hearty handshake. "Congratulations! Evidently you still have some ammo in the magazine."

Mark swigged the last of the beer. "I'll be right back. Head call."

In the bathroom, Mark stared at the face in the mirror. He'd allowed his dark brown hair to grow out since retiring from the Army, and the gray at the temples was becoming more prominent. Sophie said it made him look more distinguished, sexier. Well, he thought, that last part certainly proved itself, at least as far as his wife was concerned.

Fatherhood. Again. His forty-eighth birthday was six weeks away. His son Eddie would turn seventeen a few weeks after that. With the boy still living with his mother in Texas, it would be another birthday Mark would miss. Hadn't there been some talk about Eddie moving up here for his senior year of high school? Yes, it had come up over the holidays. Mark was still turning that one over, and now this.

Sophie would be thirty-five when the child was born. They'd talked about kids, of course, and she'd always been in favor of having at least one, but the topic hadn't been brought up since their return from Europe. She must've stopped taking the pills. He snorted an ironic laugh. Yeah, just when she'd stopped taking hers, he'd had to start taking one himself. The hair might be looking better with a little age, but the plumbing wasn't–

A knock at the door. "Mark? Are you all right?"

He splashed some water on his face. "Yeah, babe, I'll be right out."

Sophie had that I'm-very-concerned look when he opened the door. "What's wrong?"

He smiled, trying not to force it. "Nothing. Hey, we're gonna be parents. It's all good."

"Is it?" When he didn't answer, she took his hand. "Come with me." She led him down the hall toward Jim's computer room.

"Do you think they're okay?" Jim asked.

Gina was stirring the spaghetti sauce, and the aroma was almost enough to make Jim grab the nearest piece of bread and dip it into the pot. "They're fine," she said. "It's just a shock to Mark. She didn't tell him she'd stopped her birth control."

"Oh, boy. Mark doesn't really like surprises."

"Well, he got one today. At least he doesn't care about the football game anymore."

"So…she told you she was trying to get pregnant?"

273

"I'm not sure if it was exactly for that reason. She was having a difficult time after we got back from Europe."

"That's certainly understandable," Jim said. His resistance weakening, he reached for the bread. Gina reached over to slap his hand, and he grabbed it and turned her around to face him. "And how are you doing?"

Her face had completely healed from the beating she'd suffered in Capua, and although she was as lovely as ever, something had definitely changed inside her. When it came to women, Jim considered himself somewhat more intuitive than the typical clueless male, but he was having a hard time putting his finger on this one. At home, Gina was just as, well, as Italian as ever, one of the many things he loved about her. But in the dojo she was fierce, to the point where once or twice their sensei had seen it necessary to speak to her privately about getting carried away in sparring class. A nice byproduct of that ferocity, as far as Jim was concerned, was that she'd been even more assertive than usual in the bedroom. Still, he wondered sometimes what was really going on inside his wife, and now he was glad to hear she'd been talking to her sister-in-law. Not for the first time, he told himself that he should talk to his wife more than he had been. Well, it wasn't too late for a New Year's resolution, was it?

She looked up at him, then away, gazing through the window above the sink. Outside, a deer was making its way through the snow toward their bird feeder. "I'm okay," she said. "We're both okay. The baby will be a Godsend for Sophie. For both of them."

A feeling of relief coursed through him, followed quickly by another feeling. He grasped his wife by the shoulders and rubbed

274

them, then ran his hands down along her sides to her waist. "Well, you stopped taking your pill too, didn't you?" He nuzzled her neck. "Maybe..."

"Don't even think about it," she said. "In case you forgot, I told you the baby factory succumbed to natural causes a couple years ago."

"Oh. Right."

She gave him a wicked glance as she reached for the oregano. "But if you play your cards right, mister, we can pound on the factory door later tonight, see if anybody's still there."

Mark had never really explored Jim's collection of books. There was an entire case devoted to Theodore Roosevelt. Mark had never really known his brother to be a big reader. Maybe he just hadn't been paying attention.

Sophie leaned against the roll-top desk. "I'm sorry to have surprised you, Mark."

He turned away from the bookcase. "It would've been a surprise no matter what."

Her eyes were fearful. "When we got back from Europe, I was..." She hugged herself and shivered. "I was afraid. I knew he was dead, that we were safe from him, but..."

Mark gathered her in his arms. She buried her face in his shoulder and sobbed. "I knew you would come for me," she said. "And you did. You saved me."

He nuzzled her hair, breathing in her scent. The shock and uncertainty were wearing off, replaced by his overwhelming love for her. "It wasn't just me. Jim was there, and Krieger. I couldn't have done it without them. But even if they hadn't been available, I would've come anyway." What was left unsaid was the good possibility that a solo mission would've failed, and they both would be lying in some unmarked Serbian grave right now.

Mark sensed that some sort of dam had opened up inside his wife as she continued. "And I was so afraid for so long. Not every minute of every day. When BBC said I could have medical leave for as long as I wanted, I was glad, because I wanted to stay home. I felt safe, over here in the States, in Wisconsin. If…when I go back to work, they'll send me to Europe again, to the Middle East perhaps. Mark, darling, I don't know if I can–"

He kissed her ear. "Don't worry about it. Hey, don't go back to work at all, if you don't want to. There'll be a little one coming along, and they can be a handful. I think I remember that much about it."

"And the doctor I went to see, she was so very nice, and prescribed the sedative. I stopped taking the birth control because the combination made me nauseous. But I should have told you. I don't know why I didn't. I'm sorry."

He released her just enough to hold her at arm's length. "I know why you didn't. You wanted to have a baby. You wanted to be a mother. You've always wanted it. And now it's going to happen."

Her eyes filled with tears. "Oh, Mark, I was so afraid you'd be upset with me…"

His grin threatened to split his face. His heart felt like it was about to burst. "Upset? I'm going to be a father! We're going to be parents, and she'll be the most beautiful baby on the planet."

"You want...you want a girl?"

"Yeah, I think a girl would be nice. Provided she's as good-looking as her mother, that is."

She hugged him fiercely, the tears flowing. As he held her, he looked at the photos on the shelf above Jim's desk. One was a framed reproduction of a Roman-era painting, a beautiful woman gazing outward. At the base of the painting was a sentence in Italian. Mark recognized it now: Gina had bought it in Rome while Jim and Mark were in Serbia, and gave it to him when they got home. What had he said the translation was?

Ah. He remembered. He tipped up Sophie's face to his, kissing her on the forehead. "I learned something in Italian for you," he said.

She smiled, her eyes happy again. "And what's that, o great warrior, the father of my child?"

"Non posso vivere senza te."

"And in English?"

He held her close, and whispered it in her ear. "I cannot live without you."

AUTHOR'S NOTES

One of the greatest fears any husband has is the fear of losing his wife. I know that in my own case, I certainly hope my wife Sue outlives me. The thought of living without her is almost unbearable. I get to experience this once in a while, when she travels for her business, and I spend a week or so alone at home with the dog and the cat. The first couple days, it's okay. But after that, it gets boring, and I start counting the days till she's home. (I also have to carefully plan out my housekeeping chores, to make sure they're all done when she arrives, but that's another story.)

On those occasions, I know she'll be returning home, and things will get back to normal. But suppose she wasn't coming home? I've known men who have lost their wives to an unexpected illness or accident, and the grief they go through is something I would hope never to experience. I think the only thing that could be worse is the death of a child, and we probably all know people who have been through that. The most we can do in that case is offer whatever comfort and support we can, and somewhere inside us is a voice that is saying, "It's a terrible thing, but I'm certainly glad I'm not the one going through this."

Suppose, though, that your wife, the most important person in your world, is taken from you not by disease or random accident, but by violence? Worse yet, if she is kidnaped? Abductions, even here in the United States, are a lot more prevalent than we might think. The National Center for Missing and Exploited Children says that about

800,000 Americans are reported missing every year. About five percent are under the age of 18, leaving over three-quarters of a million adults as victims of potential abduction. Certainly a significant percentage of these are people who are married.

As the owner of a travel agency, my wife frequently is on the go, and oftentimes these travels take her outside the United States. I worry about her, of course–although I don't worry as much as I used to, before she started martial arts training several years ago. It's one of those things you have to force yourself not to think about, like the times your teenage son or daughter are out of the house.

Any man whose wife or child is kidnaped is going to feel many emotions: fear, rage, sorrow, and more. Since the great majority of us don't have the training or resources to do anything about it, we have to trust in the police to do something, and quickly, to find our loved one and return her to us, hopefully unharmed. But what if you're one of those rare men who does have skills and resources that can be employed in such a crisis? Would you be content to sit next to the phone, waiting for somebody else to do something?

As I contemplated the next adventure for the Hayes brothers after introducing them in *Quest for Honor,* my wife happened to be on a trip overseas, and although the place she was visiting was considered relatively safe, there's always the chance something could happen. Most likely it would be a crime of opportunity: someone sees a chance for a quick payday and decides to take a shot at it. Suppose, though, that the criminal is not just a random hood, but someone who has skills and resources himself, and worse yet, has been waiting for such an opportunity to strike a blow against someone he considers to be his enemy? Then, you'd be in real trouble.

One of the first things I learned in martial arts training was the most important rule of self-defense: *don't be there.* But we should be able to walk safely down any street in America, shouldn't we? And in Italy, too, for that matter. I have visited Italy several times and always enjoyed it. I never once felt unsafe anywhere, whether we were in a big city like Rome or exploring the countryside of Tuscany. But we were smart about it; we didn't go very far from our hotel after dark, and we stayed away from places too far off the beaten path. It's just common sense to avoid places where the likelihood of trouble is higher than it might be somewhere else.

But you can take all the precautions that can reasonably be taken, and bad things could still happen, especially if someone has put a target on your back. That's the position Mark Hayes is in as we begin *Quest for Vengeance,* although he doesn't know it yet. Pretty soon, Mark has to make a decision no husband should ever have to make. I truly hope it's one I never have to make, either.

Some years ago, Sue and I visited Croatia. We disembarked our ship at Dubrovnik and met our guide for the day, a young Croatian who was going to lead our group on a bicycle trek south of the city. Before departing, he told us about what it had been like there during his early teenage years, when Croatia was fighting for its independence from the Serbian-led Yugoslav Federation. He pointed up toward the hills surrounding the city and said, "That's where the Serb artillery was," he said. "They would shell the city from up there. It was very bad, until the American planes came and drove them off."

Although I was proud to know that our country had been able to step up and help the Croatians gain their freedom, I wondered about the aftereffects of the conflict. The Balkan Wars ended more than a decade ago, and the Serbs were the losers. Although I have yet to visit Serbia, I have met many Serbs over here and they impressed me as being very friendly folks. But on that day outside Dubrovnik, gazing up at those hills, I wondered if there were still some Serbs out there who still held a grudge against the Croatians, and the Americans who helped them. In Mark Hayes's case, the answer was definitely a yes.

ACKNOWLEDGEMENTS

Many people had a part in the crafting of this work, most importantly my wife, Sue, who has been by my side on our trips to Italy and the rest of Europe, not to mention much of the rest of the world. Her encouragement and support have made this book possible.

Thanks also go out to the members of my writers critique group: Marjorie Swift Doering, Donna White Glaser, and Jodie Swanson. Their help in reviewing this work was invaluable. Working with Tanja G. at www.fictionbookcover.com and Amy Huntley at www.theeyeseforediting.com has been very pleasurable. I highly recommend their services to my fellow authors.

Special thanks go out to Brandon Powers, who helped me with handgun and rifle training at Fireline Shooting and Training Center in Rice Lake. Brandon now is Chief Operating Officer at Fireline's facility in Appleton, Wis. Check them out here: www.firelinestc.com. Also to my friend and fellow church choir member Ed Knutson, a former Marine and current private pilot who helped me find out more about the European air traffic control system.

COMING SOON...

It's 2015, and Mark and Sophie Hayes are enjoying their role as new parents. At Odin Security Services, though, things are not going well. The company has overextended, and cuts have to be made. One of them is the job held by Jim Hayes, and his brother has to give him the bad news.

It's not news that Jim takes well. Just a few months before, his marriage to Gina had been rocked, and now he and his wife have to try to pick up even more pieces. They decide that a getaway is in order, just the two of them, something that will challenge them both physically and emotionally, helping them repair their damaged bond. Jim finds one he thinks might fit the bill: trekking the Salkantay Trail in Peru. But as they head to South America, they don't yet know that this trek will be more challenging than they might be able to overcome.

Quest for Redemption continues the adventures of the Hayes brothers and their wives, and will be published in 2021. In the meantime, readers are invited to check out the *White Vixen* series: *The White Vixen* and *The Red Wolf* are available now, and *The Bronze Leopard* is coming in 2020. And coming in 2019, a standalone, multigenerational story of a military family facing challenges over three centuries: *The Heights of Valor*.

Made in the USA
Columbia, SC
16 September 2021